The Eagle
of
Spinalonga

For Elektra and Joshua

Also by the same author

Greek Funeral Traditions
getting to Know Thyself

This is a work of fiction, inspired by the real life achievements of Epaminondas Remoundakis, patient of Spinalonga, and of the priest who ministered to the lost souls. This book also acknowledges the heroic actions of the people of Greece during the Nazi occupation.

The Eagle of Spinalonga

Nike Azoros

Glossary

Aman	Mercy (Turkish)
Charon	Ferryman to the Underworld
Chum	Cut up chunks of meat used as fishing bait.
Dakos	Crisp Barley Rusks
Endaxi	Alright, Okay
Epitrachileon	Richly Embroidered Stole of priests of the Greek Orthodox Church
Esperinos	Vespers, Evening prayers
Hansenite	Leper, named after Gerhard Hansen the Norwegian physician who discovered leprosy was caused by a bacterium and not hereditary
Kakomiris	Ill fated
Kalé	My dear
Kali mera	Good day
Kalitsounia	Cretan Cheese pies
Kamilavkion	Tall, black, flat topped hat worn by Greek Orthodox priests
Kapetan	Captain
Kataifi	Shredded pastry
Koukla	Doll
Koulouri	Circular bread roll covered with sesame seeds
Koumbaro	Best man
Kyrie Elaison	Lord have Mercy
Loukoumathes	Fried pastry puffs like donuts but without a hole, usually

	served drizzled with honey
Loustro	Shoe shine boy
Malaka	Wanker, tosser
Meze	Snacks, Appetizers
Mirologia	Lamentations, Songs of Mourning
Panayia	The Virgin Mary
Pantokrator	Ikon of Christ the Almighty, always situated in the central dome of the church
Pater	Father
Platia	Town square
Rassos	Priests black robes
Simpethera	In laws
Tsikoudia	Clear high alcohol content spirit drink similar to Raki, Tsipouro or French Marc
Volta	Promenade, Evening Stroll
Zut	Shush

Chapter 1. The Funeral of Nikos Lambrakis

The priest placed a small bell on a table in the church, turned and motioned to Nikos to move away. He took two steps back. So did the priest - just in case. Nikos looked on as the priest opened his book of liturgical texts and began to recite the funeral service starting with the Trisagion prayer and going all the way through to the burial prayers ending as they all did with, *'you were dust and to dust you shall return.'* The priest snapped the book shut and waved the sign of the cross at Nikos.

'Am I dead now?'

'Yes, you no longer belong to the living.'

Nikos did the sign of the cross in the traditional Greek Orthodox manner, using the right hand with forefinger and middle finger pressed to the thumb. He slowly brought his hand to his forehead then to his solar plexus, to his right shoulder then to the left. He did this three times, his gaze never wavering from the priest until he began to bend to kiss the ikon of Christ.

Nikos almost had his lips upon the Savior when the priest cried out.

'No! No my child, please think of the others.'

The truth as to why the eyes of Christ in the ikon were so mournful became evident to Nikos as he straightened up. Christ was not mourning his own fate but the fate of man.

1

'Forgive me Father, I do it from habit.' Instead of turning to leave he stood firm and decided to challenge the priest, after all he had nothing left to lose.

'What about my kiss Father, don't I have a right to the kiss of peace like everybody else?' The priest pursed his lips as he rocked on the spot and looked up at the ceiling. Ah that Nikos always was sharp, he'd remembered the kiss of peace, the obligatory kissing of the body to send it on its journey in love and peace. Father Manoussos was standing directly beneath the ikon of the *Pantokrator*, The Almighty, who looked back down at him commanding him to follow the tradition, but the priest did not move.

Layman and clergyman stood in awkward silence until sounds from outside informed them it was time for Nikos to leave.

'Be well Nikos.'

'But I'm not well Father, and never will be again. Give me better last words than the useless *be well.*'

'Safe journey Nikos.' The priest clutched onto his prayer book in fear he might be moved to extend his hand out to Nikos in one final handshake. Nikos noticed the priest's knuckles turning white from the force with which he was clenching his hands.

'I'd hoped to walk out of this church one day as a bridegroom not as a living corpse,' Nikos said as he picked up the bell by its rope and placed it around his own neck. He straightened up a little as his manner became more formal.

'Please remember to tell the widow Kalliope her pension was approved and tell old Kostas we won the case, he will be recompensed for the loss of his grapes. And Father your electoral forms must be posted tomorrow, I've filled them in for you and left them on your desk.' Nikos turned to leave the church for the last time but turned around.

'Oh, I also got Thanos the goatherd accepted into school. He learnt how to read very quickly, amazing for a boy of seventeen. He is a good student. He knows all his numbers and can tell the time both ways, by the sun and with a clock. Would you please ensure the boy gets to the school, he deserves the opportunity. He could do very good things.'

Father Manoussos was still nodding. He was inwardly marveling at how the young man chose to remain professional right to the end. Even now that his own life had ended he was still considering others.

Nikos walked out of the church, he stopped to straighten the slightly askew notices on the noticeboard before he stepped out into the town square. The little bell around his neck tolled for him as he went down the steps.

The square was empty, there was no *koulouri* seller, the *loustro* was not in his usual place by the fountain and the corn roaster too was absent. The shops all had their doors closed. He knew they would reopen as soon as he left. Nikos scanned each doorway, there was not one of the shopkeepers he had not helped in some way and now not one of them was visible to repay him with the one thing he wanted to see more than anything, a smile.

A calendar was visible in the window of the Council chambers, he'd lost track of days since he had been diagnosed and declared a Hansenite. The calendar was a souvenir edition for the Olympic Games scheduled for that year; a large bold 1936 was entwined through the Olympic rings. Nikos knew the window belonged to the room where the social registry was kept. He'd gone in there seven months earlier with his sister Maria, just before her funeral service, to declare her infection.

He'd had to hold her up when her knees buckled under her as she watched the clerk locate her name on the social register. He placed his ruler across it and with his pen sliced a line right through it like an executioner's sword through a delicate neck. It had been a Friday then too, the day of crucifixions.

That day the clerk could not look at the young woman he had once considered a potential bride. He had often looked out of the window and watched her take strong steps across the square as she helped her lawyer brother with his duties. Her purposeful strides made her hips move in a mesmerising rhythm and he had often thought to himself that a woman who could walk around like that and still look like a lady would be very lively where it counts, pity.

Nikos saw movement at the window. The lace curtain parted. The clerk looked down on him and nodded three times. A Holy Trinity of meaning, one nod for greeting, one to inform that he too had been struck off the register, and one for farewell.

He knew their weary mother had to, for a second time, wail her *mirologia* not by a graveside but at a bedside. Again she had been forced to watch her pride and joy walk to church for his funeral, to be declared dead while still alive.

Back at the church Father Manoussos kissed the ikon of Christ on behalf of Nikos. It was the least he could do, but peace did not come. He had always found the funeral service to be elegant. He found comfort in soothing those left behind after sending the departed onto the next world in the natural cycle of life. There had been nothing natural in what had just happened, he had not laid anyone to rest, he had just sent a soul to hell.

The *Pantokrator's* large open eyes, designed to be portrayed that way exactly for the purpose of looking into the soul, were scorching him, burning right through his *kamilavkion*. The priest bowed in humility, and shame, and rushed outside to catch Nikos. To his relief he was still there but was about to climb onto the dray that had come for him.

'Nikos, let me help you for a change.' Father Manoussos went to lift one of his suitcases.

'*Aman*! What are taking with you, stones?'

'Books, I will need companionship, logic, and order so I take with me the greatest of the wisdoms of our ancestors. My eyes are stinging. They might be the first to go, so I will have to read fast.'

'Have courage Nikos, and faith.'

'I won't need courage there, just patience as I wait to rot. And as for faith, yes I have faith. Leprosy is very faithful, unlike people and even God, it never abandons me. We walk together every day. It has become my greatest teacher. It has made me a better philosopher than I ever thought I could be, we sit together every night and every morning there is some little surprise to remind me of how strong its faith in me is. It is the most faithful of all things. I have plenty of faith.'

Nikos looked around at his town for the last time. He took in the dressmaker's shop where his mother had worked so she could send him to Athens to become the first person in their family to go to university. He saw the normally well populated taverna where his father had invited the entire town to celebrate his son's graduation from law school. His only thoughts now were that he could not let their efforts be wasted.

'The state has declared me dead, the church has buried me, my future has been murdered, and Death is tapping his watch at me, yet I feel so alive.' Nikos shrugged in resignation.

'The Fates must have chosen me for their amusement and this pleases me much, at least I am making someone smile.'

The priest could see a copy of Plato's *The Republic* lying next to a copy of Menander's *One Verse Maxims* one of which popped into his mind immediately, '*Whom the gods love die young.*'

'Did you pack a Bible my child?'

'No Father, I am now only interested in logic. Now tell me what you want? You came running out as if you were being chased by demons.'

The driver yelled out.

'We're off!' The dray lurched and started moving away.

'I just wanted to say, go with God Nikos.'

'God doesn't go to Spinalonga. The only way God will ever go there is if you bring Him yourself.'

The priest stood watching the dray until it disappeared from sight.

Nikos lay down on the dray and his thoughts went to his mother, Theodora Lambrakis. Her anguished words upon learning her remaining child was also stricken with the curse of leprosy had never stopped haunting him.

'My son, I can't live without my family.' She kept trying to embrace him and he kept stepping back for fear of touching her, his deliberate avoidance only wounding her maternal soul even more.

'Stop trying to pull away, I do not fear the disease. Life without my children, my family, is worse than death.' Nikos relented slightly because he was wearing gloves.

He faced his mother and placed his hands on her shoulders.

'Mama, please guard your health, we need you to pray for us but I promise you that one day you will have a family again.' He did not step back as Theodora took his face in her hands and reached up to kiss his forehead. Mother and son stayed like that for a moment until Nikos gently stepped back, caressed his mother's hair, turned and left his home for ever. Theodora did not have to watch her son walk away from her for the last time because her eyes were blinded by her tears.

Nikos thought he might as well stay lying down, like a corpse on its hearse, until the dray reached the harbor. Along the way he had removed the bell from around his neck and tossed it into an olive grove where someone would eventually find it and melt it down to make nails. At least it would serve as something more useful than a siren of sorrow. He only had a few more kilometers to go before he would be where he had to be and there was no need for a bell there.

The boat was waiting. There were a few other travelers, mostly peasants going about their business. The boatman was offering help to everyone to board but Nikos did not take his hand when it was extended to him, he jumped on board instead.

The boatman greeted everyone with the usual *kali mera*, to which everyone always responded *kali mera Kapetan* as they paid their one drachma price to be ferried to their destinations. He reached Nikos and studied the well dressed, well groomed young man with the height of a Corinthian column and the face of Apollo.

'*Kali mera Charon*, here is your coin.' Nikos, with gloved hand, placed the coin into the boatman's leather pouch and seated himself at the stern, away from all. The sea breeze soothed as they sailed, sky and sea were the exact same hue of cobalt. Waves breaking into froth around them and some streaky clouds lining the air made the journey feel as if they were wrapped in the Greek flag.

As each little harbor came into view the boatman would ask if anyone needed to stop at any of them but today all were travelling to Elounda, all except one. The island had come into view some time ago and now it loomed over them. A couple of the women crossed themselves.

'God protect us,' uttered one woman.

One of the men was wearing an unusual hat for that time of year. It was made of the fur of a hare. He had been chatting away the entire time about how good the hunting was with his new carbine but he had now fallen silent.

His cousin had been sent to Spinalonga but it had been kept secret, the family had never told a soul, instead they just said that Ikaros had gone off on the ships. It was a common way to explain a sudden disappearance usually connected to a crime or to avoid an unwelcomed arranged marriage. He kept silent because relatives of lepers were often treated like lepers as well.

The boatman went to the island at least once a week to take supplies and the occasional new resident which was how he knew the meaning of the stranger's greeting. As soon as the man had called him *Charon*, the name of the ferryman of dead souls to the underworld of the ancient days, he knew he had a visit to the island coming up. He also was certain this must be the Lambrakis boy. He was the image of his late father whom he had often ferried.

The father had been full of pride for his educated son and would call Nikos his eagle. The father of Nikos would often watch the golden eagles hovering over the sea and made comment that his son was just like them, not only because he was sharp and quick but like an eagle he knew that to soar to great heights one mustn't flap around but ride the wind.

Thank the gods the man got to see his son graduate before his heart attack. Ach! Some families are just ill-fated, he reckoned to himself. The boatman stared straight ahead and asked his question with the perfect amount of nonchalance.

'Anyone for Spinalonga?'

In an equally nonchalant voice Nikos replied, 'Yes.'

The gasps were audible. One of the men tried to reduce the instant panic that gripped the passengers.

'I have a nephew in America, he says they have an island like that there too, it's called Alcatraz. They use it as a prison.'

'What do you think Spinalonga is, a playground?' snapped the man with the new carbine.

'Oh pardon my outburst but it can't be easy for those poor ill-fated ones.' The man with the new carbine grunted his appeasement. It was his guilt that had caused him to snap. He had only been able to have the new carbine because his cousin had given him everything he owned before he left for Spinalonga. The pangs of shame stung him for he hadn't sent him anything as thanks, not even a letter.

Lepers were not permitted to send letters. Somehow the authorities had come to the conclusion that the disease would find a way to seep into the ink and poison the message or maybe it would settle into the folds of the paper and spring out when opened by the innocent reader to infect them too. No, lepers did not get or send letters.

'Do we go to the island now or do I take you all to Elounda first?' the boatman asked democratically. All eyes on board turned to look at Nikos. They studied him as if he were a museum exhibit. He still looked normal, no disfigurements yet, in fact he looked better than any of them.

'I'm in no hurry.'

A woman interjected.

'Go to the island first.' She looked over at the young man.

'Forgive me stranger but you know your fate. We do not. We have children and spouses who need us, our fields must be tilled, and our animals must be fed. We have the responsibilities of life therefore we must value our own.'

Another woman leaned forward in her seat as she asked him,

'What type of work did you do?'

'Law, I had just graduated with distinctions. International law was my leaning – but.'

Everyone on board including the boatman shook their heads at the injustice. They had all taken in his dignified bearing, his city clothes, and his exquisite speech. His finesse and sophistication would now only be witnessed by the stone walls of Spinalonga.

'How old are you?' The woman asked.

'What a coincidence you should ask, I am 22, today.'

'May you reach one hundred.' Then she corrected herself.

'Oh I am sorry.'

Nikos shrugged it off. It was the polite and the most common thing to say at anybody's birthday. The woman spoke out of habitual practice. Wishing someone reached the age of one hundred was good manners and almost expected. Not to say it was often considered an insult, it meant you did not wish for them to have a long and healthy life. One of the men noticed the books peeping out of the bag on the deck.

'I can read,' he announced proudly.

'I liked Menander the best because his verses were easy to remember, the one I liked was, '*In adversity man is saved by hope.*' The woman placed the basket she had been carrying on the floor and kicked it towards him.

'I made cheese yesterday, it's good. There are olives too and fresh bread and some nice pickles, cabbage and peppers. Everyone deserves to celebrate their birthday. You will make new friends shortly, share this food with them.'

Nikos thanked her as he halted the basket slide with his foot as a goalkeeper would a lazy ball. He had been studying the island. It was, like most Greek islands, a crag of rock rising out of the sea. He spotted a couple of olive trees and a few caper bushes and nothing else. He wished he had been able to spend more time studying the island from the shore once he knew it was to be his home for the rest of his life. He might have been better prepared.

'If any more of you have food with you give it to me now.' He demanded in a firm voice.

One of the women scolded him.

'Ah you ungrateful one, this is the thanks you give us for our kindness? We are poor. We have our own battles to fight every day.'

Nikos nodded his head in understanding but the tone in his voice remained firm.

'Forgive my suddenness but take another look at this island of tears. Do you see anywhere for a sheep to graze? Look at it! Where shall I plant a lemon tree or an onion patch? Is there even anywhere on that rock for a chicken to scratch?'

There were murmurs of agreement as they stopped looking at the rock island as an intriguing mystery and looked at it from the point of view of the food producers that they were. There wasn't really anywhere to string a grapevine without a lot of work. It was possible if able bodied people tackled it but a man made weak from lack of food and a terrible disease stood no chance of making anything grow on that island, other than dread.

'You can all find an egg to boil, or stew an eggplant you have grown in your sunny courtyards but I don't even see a twig of thyme on Spinalonga.'

He looked directly at them for the first time.

'I thank you for your wishes of hope and your kind gift of food but I ask you to spare a little more so I can share your kindness with the other wretched souls already there who are probably so hungry they lick the rocks to taste a little salt.'

He then delivered his coup de grace. He coughed. Every scrap of food on board was slid over to him. *Kapetan Charon* smiled and in low tones spoke to himself as he guided his boat alongside the rocky pier.

'This one knows how to make things happen. Spinalonga will never be the same once he is there. He will make changes. Maybe he will make so many that I will be kept busy.' He was already picturing the fine new suit he would buy with the extra fares he had no doubt he would soon be making.

Nikos tilted his head slightly. He had heard a sound and was subconsciously trying to tune in so as to hear it more clearly. It was like a fast wind but it couldn't be, the breeze was gentle. The sound abated but only for a moment. Nikos stayed on alert.

Maybe it had been his imagination, or his anxiety. Life as he knew it had changed forever, it was only natural that he feel anxious - but the sound was not going away, it was becoming louder. The sound now was like a whistle, like something was plunging down at great speed. He looked at the other passengers, they didn't seem to notice anything, and they were too busy looking at the island.

The sound was coming from above them. Nikos looked up just in time to see a great eagle plummeting from the heavens and heading straight for the hare-fur hat. With its wings pulled back, its proud head aimed straight at its target, and its high speed it had all the power of one of the bullets from the hat wearer's new carbine.

Nikos' first thought was to lunge at the man to bring him down onto the deck so the eagle wouldn't break open his skull but he held himself back so as not to give the man double grief. Instead he shouted, 'Down! Get down quick!' The man ducked just in time and the eagle took a perplexed look at him before swooping up, extending its wings out and flying away.

'The eagle thought you were a hare and all this time I have been calling you an old goat,' said the boatman to much laughter from all. But the man was shaken.

'You saved me young man. Thank you.'

Nikos too, was shaken. He just waved his acknowledgment and sat in silence. The eagle incident had churned up the repressed pain of the loss of his friend Alikhan as well as the realization that he had left behind his most treasured belonging and he would never see it again. He was so dejected he had become exhausted. The negative thoughts had sapped all his strength so he just sat back and waited to reach the shores of Spinalonga.

The Mediterranean in July is like a sapphire set in diamonds, a brilliant light, vivid with intense colour. A source of life energy that has inspired and enchanted the world since before Homer, all except for the little part of it around Spinalonga. The air hung heavy, the few trees grew away from the rocks as if preparing to jump off, even the waves didn't seem to want to lap at its shores but just lay listless. It held about as much welcome as a gallows.

The base of the island was lined with thick, high stone walls revealing its origins as a fortress. Directly behind the stone jetty was a large arched entrance gate. 'Dante's Gate' the boatman said. 'Who is this Dante? Is he Greek?' asked one of the women,
'I don't know, I just know they call this Dante's Gate.'
'Dante is not a Greek name, sounds Italian.'
'Bah! Those Italians, always trying to be Greek.'

Nikos knew it must be a reference to Dante's *Inferno*, the epic poem on Hell, but right now he was trying to imagine what he would find beyond the gate. His mind was working hard to stay clear but all their noise was interfering. He wanted them to shut up so he could focus. He coughed again and everybody closed their mouths. That did the trick.

Nikos noted the architecture of the entrance, it was not of the graceful classical style but more squat and utilitarian. It was the words etched above the arch that made everyone gasp, *Abandon all hope, ye who enter here.*

A small shadow slid through the arched gate, two larger ones lumbered behind. As the boat got closer its passengers could see the shadows seemed to be wearing death masks with the mouths turned down in exaggerated manner like the ancient Greek masks of tragedy, all were draped in tattered rags. The three stood side by side and extended out their arms in ghastly welcome. When the boat bumped into the jetty Nikos was close enough to recognise the small shadow and he too extended out his arms.

'It's my sister, Maria!'

Their crucifixion poses made silhouettes against the walls that turned Spinalonga into Golgotha with three crosses, the central one bearing an innocent flanked by the two criminals, Dysmas and Gestas. The boat moored against the stone jetty and the people in the boat could see them up close. They were barely more than skeletons.

Chapter 2. Dante's Gate

Nikos could at last embrace someone. He and his sister stood on the stone jetty and held each other. Their emotions were churning yet neither could cry. Her first words to him were the same first words every new resident hears when they first arrive on Spinalonga,

'Welcome but not well come.'

Nikos could see that Maria had hardened, like her skin, but for the moment they just held each other and rocked to and fro together in time with the little waves that skipped around the jetty. They too were happy to finally see some emotion on the shores of Spinalonga.

The people on the boat were moved, not just at the sight of the siblings reunited in body and united in their fate but at the sight of the two helpers who looked like walking ancient olive trees. They were unaware of how terrible they looked as they stood by and took in the sight of healthy people.

Without mirrors to reflect their misery and because of the immunity they had developed to the sight of each other, to them it was the healthy ones who were the freaks. They were beyond caring if their appearance was disturbing, despair has no vanity.

The man with the new carbine felt his throat dry up. One of the lepers was looking straight at him. He shuffled a little closer to the edge of the jetty to bend down a little so as to get a better look. His recognition of him came out as a haunting moan. He no longer had clear speech, his trachea was on the verge of collapse, but he recognized his cousin.

The man in the boat stood up to look around him but finding nothing reached into his pockets and fumbled around to see what he had in there. He pulled out a handkerchief and a comb then reached over and placed them onto the stony jetty. The leper swayed over him like a tree about to topple over. He moaned again and pointed to his cousin's hare-fur hat.

He whisked it off and threw it to him but still the terrible phantasm did not move away. He stayed there and kept looking at him with his dead eyes. Next he pointed to his belt. The man whipped it off and cast it over onto the jetty as well. The leper soughed his thank you as he placed the fluffy, furry hat at a jaunty angle onto his grotesque head. He pocketed the rest of his bounty, picked up the bags of Nikos and lumbered away.

Nikos turned to wave at the boat. The boatman and all on the boat waved their goodbyes because they didn't know what to say. Every Greek saying of greeting and parting carried significance of health or well being so the dilemma of what to say kept them silent. But one woman did call out one word.

'Courage!'

The helper lepers walked ahead of them and Nikos and Maria followed them through Dante's gate. It led them into a long arched tunnel and for the slightest of moments he felt fresh and cooled from the protection the tunnel offered from the glaring sun. He almost felt like an athlete about to enter a stadium. The curve of the tunnel hid the end view from his sight for a while allowing him to conjure up visions of what he might find. Maybe it would be a picturesque village with houses and shops?

The image was destroyed quickly as he walked into a mass of decay. It had clearly once been a town. There were the familiar narrow cobbled streets and the high, narrow, balconied houses common to European living. They must have once been charming but everything looked as if it too had leprosy. There was a street sign hanging high on one of the buildings, The Street of Pain. Shutters were sagging from pane less windows and many of the walls had large holes in them. Piles of rags lay in all corners of the streets.

Maria led him into one of the houses, it had a dirt floor and a large crack in its ceiling so the sky was visible.

'You can share my room brother or you can find a space of your own. There are many empty houses to choose from. None of them are much good inside but there are plenty of them. I would like you stay nearby though. The men often come and take women for their own pleasure. They have not gotten to me yet and there is no one here I want so I must continue to take caution.' She spoke with pragmatism.

'Maria, what are you saying? Does the island have no law? How dare these animals do such things? Having an illness is not permission to break the law.' Nikos put his arms around her to hold her close. Maria indulged him for a while but she'd had to learn fast how to cope without having a big brother on hand and after a moment she gave him those little pats on the back that signify *'Enough.'*

'No Nikos. There is no judgment on Spinalonga because there is no law. There is just survival. We fight to eat, to sleep, and we fight each other. You can implement other laws, you will soon find out there is much need for them but do not interfere in their personal passions. It is the only pleasure left to them. You will see things you have never seen before. The Street of Pain could be renamed the Street of Porn, such are the goings on here.'

Nikos was more shocked with his sister's new wisdom of the streets attitude than he was with her terrible appearance. They had been strolling around as they spoke, as if on cue, when they turned a corner they were met with the sight of man pinning a woman against a wall and roughly pulling up her tattered skirts to reveal her nakedness. The man hooked his arm under her leg to bring it up to around his waist. He loosened his tatty trousers to free his urgency and pushed himself into the woman. The two engaged in a mutual humping for a mere moment until he groaned into her shoulder and staggered away from her. He tied up his trousers and slunk off, leaving her slumped against the wall. Maria had ignored the whole thing, immune to it, Nikos was stunned into shock.

'I am trying to remain open minded sister but to molest a woman like that on the street; is there no protection for the women?'

'Well brother first of all, no, there is no protection for us women but second, I ask you, did you see her fighting him off? No. she liked it. It is a way to forget pain.'

'Well couldn't they have gone to their own beds to meet their urges?'

'We have no beds.'

The shock of what he just saw was wearing off but the new shock of the reality that he no longer had a bed on which to sleep was worse. To take his mind off the misery of the situation Nikos focused on his reunion with his sister.

He was part pleased, part perplexed, not at the liberal lusts of lepers but with the sophisticated attitudes of his sister. When she had departed for the island she was trembling with terror. She had never spent a night away from home but his chaste little sister who couldn't look at the nude statues of the Greek gods was now blasé about public sex.

'Maria, where are we?'

'We are in hell brother. Hell is here.'

They walked back to her dwelling and went inside. She leaned in close to him and whispered,

'Did you bring any food?'

What really mattered was food, not two desperate adults uniting to indulge in something to take away their desperation, if only for a short while.

'Of course. Here in these bags. Some from Mama and some from the people on the boat.'

Maria raised her finger to her dry lips to make him keep his voice low. 'We must eat first and quickly before the others sniff the food. Once they do they will swoop down on us like the eagles you told me about, the ones with eyesight so strong they can see a fish in the boat of the fisherman and swoop down and pick it up right off the deck of the boat.'

'You remembered all those things Maria?'

'There is nothing else to do here but remember. Now eat something before they come and take it away. They will you know and before you have time to scratch yourself all the food will be gone. Oh but try not to scratch yourself, that sort of thing is discouraged here.'

He couldn't help but laugh at her macabre sense of humor and acceptance of her fate. Before his arrival, thinking about what he would find on Spinalonga made his head spin so he had decided to simply take things one day at a time. Now he realized it would be more like one minute at a time.

'Come on sister I have brought a lot of food, see these baskets are full of food. We must share.'

Maria quickly lifted up some loose floorboards and shoved one of the baskets into the space then quickly covered it up again. She grabbed one of the pies and shoved it down the front of her dress then grabbed another one and tore into it with her teeth like a wolf to a chicken. Nikos had just taken a bite of one as well when something knocked him to the ground.

The piles of rags that had been clogging up the corners had sprung to life and came running at them at high speed then launched into a lunge that toppled Nikos over. More lumps of what he had thought had been filthy rags became animated and streamed into the squalid room like a septic overflow. They screeched like the Furies as they clawed and grabbed at Nikos and his basket of food until there was nothing left, not a crumb. One of the rag wearers even grabbed Nikos' face with filthy black hands and his grimy fingers plucked the piece of cheese pie right out of Nikos' mouth. Then they were gone and a loud silence settled around them.

Nikos was shaken but stored the shock within so he could maintain the rage of the sheer inhumane conditions to which he had been sentenced. He needed the anger to keep him motivated because already he could see the danger of allowing the hopelessness to overwhelm every positive thought he had. It was Maria who acted as calm as if what just happened was a normal event. She dusted herself off and straightened her hair.

'I need to sleep now my brother. I can't walk too far anymore and tomorrow a new battle awaits. Soon it will be dark, we have no power here so everything becomes black, then at least most of them calm down and we can get some rest.' She began to spread out some old rags that were once blankets.

Nikos shook himself out of the shock and took Maria's lead in keeping calm and just getting on with life.

'Maria before you sleep, tell me about these houses?'

'They are little more than ruins now. The Turks lived here for safety when they saw we were winning the struggle for independence. They refused to leave so the government said ok you can stay but we will send the lepers there too. So the Turks left, but not before destroying as many of the residences as they could. They sent us here to these ruins and no-one has touched them since. We have no power, no furniture, no nothing. No one has any money to fix them. If we had comfortable homes at least we could feel human. This is worse than a prison, at least in prison they feed you.'

The houses were a source of hope no matter how small. In their current form they provided the most basic of shelter, barely a roof over their heads, but with a lot of effort they could become real homes. There was work to be done, lots of it.

'Okay sister, you rest.' He nestled into a corner and took a slug of water from his flask so as to rinse the tang of the leper's fingers out of his mouth. He pulled out the cheese pie he had managed to hide in his pocket and ate as the thoughts of how to improve things slowly became bigger than the thoughts of how bad things were. Sleep did not come easy. He was cold, he was uncomfortable and all through the night there was the cacophony of wretched moans and groans of suffering.

The morning was clear, crisp and most important of all, it was quiet. It was the perfect time for Nikos to take a slow walk around the town. There were many houses, all in appalling condition, there were also several buildings that had looked as if they had once been shops and other commercial outlets, there was even a large communal laundry.

Nikos absorbed it all in ever mounting outrage that this was where his country sent some of its sickest people with the most needs to a place that grew nothing, had nothing, and had barely a decent roof to shelter them.

The town had a medieval appearance and had basic infrastructure in that there were paved streets and a town square. There was no electricity but the small town square had a simple fountain with a basic hand pump that worked. At least there was a source of water.

He bent over to take a drink but someone pushed him out of the way.

'What's your rush? Do you think I am going to drink it all? Here,' Nikos stepped back.

'It's all yours sir.' He recognized him as one of the helpers that were with Maria when she met him at Dante's Gate.

'Sir, no one has called me sir for...I don't think anyone had ever called me sir. I am sorry about pushing you but here it is dog eat dog. I am Ikaros, builder, of Heraklion.'

'Nikos, lawyer, of Lasithi.' The men shook hands. Ikaros looked anywhere between twenty and fifty. His face was swollen on one side and red blotches covered his neck.

'So Ikaros tell me why is it, when we are all united in our disease, there is fighting with each other over crumbs of food?'

'When you are hungry you don't know what you are doing. But Nikos, they send criminals here, it is a cheap jail. Some of the other residents are evil, twice cursed.' Nikos nodded solemnly at Ikaros to indicate that he understood the seriousness of the situation.

'I see, well Ikaros I need to walk around to get to know the place.'

'I'll come too.'

'Not for this first time please.'

'Okay, but if you see any lizards smash their heads with a rock and bring them back with you.'

'Why would I do that?'

'Why do you think I would want a dead lizard, for an ornament in my living room? To eat of course! Once they are grilled they taste like chicken.'

Nikos only got lost once, the streets of Spinalonga were coiled like a serpent but he quickly found his bearings. He intended to know how to find his way around the place with his eyes closed anyway. His biggest fear was that he would lose his sight too soon.

Buildings tell a story. The ruins of Spinalonga town told the story that they were once functional and handsome structures but without care and attention were now sad and decaying, exactly like the inhabitants.

He heard *'Welcome but not well come,'* from everyone he encountered as he walked around. He acknowledged every single greeting and introduced himself to everyone he came across. A couple walked towards him. He, clearly a leper from the telltale signs of patches of hard skin and his downwards drooping mouth. One of his feet was wrapped in rags from which came a putrid stench that not even the crisp sea air was able to mask. She looked normal, she looked more than normal, and she was beautiful.

'Good day to you, I am Nikos.'

'Welcome but not well come, I am Kimon this is my wife Eva.'

'Kimon your foot is in a bad way, how do you disinfect it? What medicines do you have?'

'We have none Nikos, my husband suffers as do all the others here.'

'All the others? You did not include yourself?'

'I don't think I am infected yet. When Kimon got sick we had been married only forty days. He is my love, my life. I did not want to be without him and I knew he would need someone to care for him. I cut him with my knife, I made him bleed and then I cut myself and rubbed his blood into my wound so I too would become leprous, but it didn't happen. I stayed healthy.' Her eyes took on a cheeky sparkle and she burst into a conspiratorial smile.

'But the authorities don't know that and they were not going to check were they?'

'Eva, you are a saint.'

'No, I am a woman, who loves her man.' She turned to tend to Kimon who was struggling to stand and as she did she spoke to Nikos, 'The illness makes life difficult but even worse is these inhumane conditions. You are a man of the law I heard.'

'Yes, I am a lawyer.'

'We are not happy with no law and no rules. Our ancient ancestors knew that a well run city creates happy citizens. The world still learns from them, why don't we? Bring the law to Spinalonga Nikos, make the citizens of Spinalonga happy. But first of all, we need food. People with a full belly are always happy.'

He wished them farewell and walked back to find Maria, the words of Eva were echoing in his head as he tried to focus his thoughts on how to bring food and law to Spinalonga. If food and law were present health would improve too. Everything would improve.

It got dark quickly and with no power to provide light he could not read the books he had wanted to read so he used the time to think and plan. He propped himself up against a rough wall and tried to stop the shaking that had gripped him. What pleased him greatly was that he was not shaking with fear but with rage at the appalling conditions. He was pleased because he knew himself and he knew that such a rage brought action. He fell asleep trying to think of ways to get food.

When he woke a man was standing over him. Nikos had noticed most of the lepers, including his sister, had no light in their eyes. Leprosy attacked the eyes and blindness was common. The eyes of lepers were dull and glazed over as if the eyes died before the rest of the body was dead. But not this man, his eyes blazed.

'Welcome but not well come.' He hissed the traditional Spinalonga greeting. The ugly leper draped himself across the doorway of the dwelling as if he owned it. Nikos got up, went over to the great lump and extended his hand out to him.

'How do you do, Nikos Lambrakis.'

'I know who you are city boy.' He did not accept his hand but Nikos kept it held out. He stood there smiling a non threatening half smile and with his hand held out for at least a minute. Pavlos sighed and shook the man's hand just to get him out of the way. He pushed past Nikos to get into the room.

'What have you got in your bags pretty boy? Got anything nice for Pavlos?' Nikos, however, was intent on staying on a civil path.

'Kali mera Pavlos, it's good to meet you, how are you this morning?'

'Save the small town pleasantries for the newcomers who think they are here on a day trip.' He crouched down and started rummaging in Nikos's bags.

'Now let's have a look at what I can have. I know the food is all gone, that cheese pie I had last night was very tasty, haven't had one of those for years.' Nikos crouched down with him.

'I have books.' Nikos picked one up, opened it and held it out for him to see but Pavlos knocked it out of his hand.

'I can't eat books. I can't wear books. What else have you got?'

'I have nothing but books.'

'Then I'll have to help myself to something else then won't I? Maybe your sister, but maybe I already have hey pretty boy? She was a cute thing when she first came here, she'll go quickly you know. Small ones like her give up too easily.' Pavlos did a little jump to brace into fighter stance, he squared his shoulders and brought his hands up in front his face into formed fists but Nikos stood steady. He recognized such behavior, the brute was trying to provoke him into a fist fight because he knew his strengths were there, but Nikos stuck to his own strengths. He held out one of his books.

'Go on read a book, it will do you good.' Pavlos wavered and broke his stance.

'Bah! Read your own books.' He rushed out of the house.

Hmm, he left in a hurry Nikos thought to himself. From the way Pavlos ran off Nikos ascertained either the man's eyes are too weak and he doesn't want to reveal his weakness, or he can't read. He put his book back into his bag as Maria appeared with a cup of tea and a piece of bread for him, which he took gratefully.

'Thank you sister. Where did you get these from?' he asked as he greeted her with a kiss to her forehead.

'I made the bread. We get basic supplies brought over by the boatman, some flour, a little oil, maybe some onions. It is nowhere near enough but I make tea from the wild herbs that grow here and Eva helps us knead bread whenever we can get flour. Food is our biggest problem after no medical care brother. There isn't enough. We fear starvation more than we fear our illness.'

Nikos shook his head.

'It is intolerable that our country has allowed this situation. The fear of the disease is understandable but to turn Spinalonga into a scrap heap is a national disgrace.'

'There are not just Hellenes here brother. Spinalonga, the boatman says, has become the largest leper colony in Europe. Other countries send their worst cases here.'

'Then it is an international disgrace. I will commence writing letters to the government.'

'It is of no use brother.'

'Why Maria, you seem to think it is impossible?'

'It is. We are not even permitted to handle money in case it gets into the hands of someone healthy and they catch the leprosy.'

'I don't know what to say sister. I studied law not medicine but leprosy is an infectious disease. When someone has a cold do you catch it by buying your bread? I believe it cannot be caught by handling money but only by very close interaction. We must learn more. Ignorance is a bigger killer than disease. What is wrong with the world that they allow ignorance to blind them to the truth? In court it is no defense yet in this case it is used to ruin people's lives. Sister I just met a woman who virtually injected herself with her husband's leprous blood and still she did not fall ill.'

'Yes I know about Eva. She is beautiful to risk death rather than risk losing love. But, Nikos one of the others told us that before they sent him here he was in a hospital and they put everything he touched into a special oven to cook the germs away. We have nothing like that here so we can have nothing.'

Nikos knew it was time to start putting his plan into action.

'Maria, tell me, have you all ever had any meetings to discuss ways to work together?'

'No, never. Some of us talk but there are some very evil people here too, like Pavlos. But we need food first brother. If we are fed we will be stronger and will have more hope.'

The siblings stood at the edge of Spinalonga lost in their thoughts until they were distracted by a large golden eagle. They watched in studied silence as it hovered above them. It hung suspended in the air for a moment then dived down into the sea like a bullet and flew up again with a large fish dangling from its claws. Maria had turned and was already walking away but Nikos stood mesmerized. The sight of the hunting bird at work reminded him of his old friend Alikhan.

Chapter 3. The Call of Manoussos

For the second time in his life Father Manoussos was experiencing the relentless harassment of the Call. The first time had been 25 years ago when his family's next door neighbors had tried to arrange a marriage between him and their daughter. Their mothers had been very pleased with the prospect of the marriage and had even begun calling each other *Simpethera*. Other neighbors had tut-tutted when they had heard the mother of the girl call Manoussos's mother her in-law for the first time.

'Don't you know it is bad luck to pre-empt such a mystery.'

'*Zut kalé*, I saw it in the coffee cup nice and clear. Two wedding rings formed in the grounds at the bottom of the cup. It is surely a sign.' But the girl concerned knew something was not right. She would make sweet eyes at him but Manoussos would only smile nervously at her then find an excuse to either run home to help with chores or off to church for altar boy duties.

The other girls of the village would giggle their stories of how some of the boys would try to sneak a kiss or sneak a peep at their garters then try to put their hands up higher. They would walk to the ruins of the ancient town where the wall art of Priapos and his giant phallus made them all fall over laughing. They would screech with mock outrage when the boys wanted to show the girls how to show respect for the deity through phallic worship.

When Manoussos and his girl went there all he would do was instruct her that Priapos was also the god of merchant sailors, very appropriate for a land like Crete. He never tried to fondle her breasts and the only kissing that ever took place were chaste pecks on the cheek after escorting her home from church.

One day she pouted at him.

'Don't you think I'm pretty?'

'Oh yes, you are so pretty. I think you are too pretty for any life that I might be able to give you.'

'Why do you say that? We could have a good life. Between both our families we have many animals and your father has two good boats. We will live well and be able to go to Athens to hear operas and our children will go to school and learn words and numbers.'

She took his hand in hers as she spoke then placed his hand on her knee. Manoussos removed his hand from her knee and sighed as if he was giving up the ghost.

'Very well, the time has come.' He stood up before her and held out his hands for her to stand with him.

'Indeed the time has come. I can be silent no more. I must tell you what is in my heart. I can't sleep, I can't eat, I can only think of one thing.'

She jumped up so high her braids whipped her face.

'Say no more Manoussos, let us do this properly. My father is sure to be home, you can ask him now.' She grabbed his hand and started to run home.

'Wait! Ask him what? Why do I need to see your father? It is mine I need to see to explain to him that I can no longer help him with the catches.'

'We can see them both together, I'll go get them right now,' she called out as she ran ahead. The young woman knew the correct thing to do was for Manoussos to arrange for a visit to be made to the bride's home. He should attend with a mini entourage to denote he had a strong and supportive family. On his right hand side would sit the man who would stand next to him in church so the parents of the bride could see what a fine young man was the godfather of their future grandchildren but according to her there was no need to do all the standard rituals. The families knew each other so well they had been speaking of the two as a couple since they were babes, even now as she neared their houses she could see their mothers sitting on the veranda chatting over their embroidery and their fathers working on straightening the posts on their shared fence. One quipped,

'Good fences make good neighbors.'

She ran towards them.

'Manoussos wants to see us! He said there is something that he must tell us because it can wait no longer.' She was squealing so loudly with delight her mother had to drag her down to sit next to her. 'Why are you running like a wild goat? People will think you are crazy, and stop talking right now and put your head down,' her mother scolded. The girl obeyed, she was prepared to play along in the role of the reluctant bride for a few moments.

It would soon all be over and she could finally take her place with the other betrothed girls of the village and choose her embroidery patterns and start making her own trousseau not just work on those of the other girls. She lowered her gaze demurely which also served to disguise her eager smile as Manoussos walked through the front gate and approached his parents.

'*Baba*, may I speak with you and *Mama* in private?'

It didn't take long, he was direct and both his parents knew their son. They knew the countless hours he spent in prayer when the other boys were organising hunting trips. They were aware the young couples of the town would go to the ancient ruins and jest about Priapos, they knew because they had done so themselves, but their boy preferred to serve at the altar.

They knew their boy was born to be a priest. They had always known but tried at first to simply believe he was a very God loving soul who would live a quiet life.

'If you don't let me go I am sure I will die.'

His parents looked at each other in fear. They knew it was no use to try and convince him to marry the girl. They had heard stories of parents who had tried to stop their child either going to a nunnery or monastery and none of them had ended well. Once God has chosen a person it is done. To even attempt to dissuade him would be to offend God. The mother embraced her son in support while the father nodded his understanding of the situation. He leant against the doorway for a brief moment to help him accept what he must do – then went outside to tell the neighbors the news.

The girl's sobs could still be heard the next day but it was her mother who was more understanding as she sipped coffee with the mother of Manoussos.

'When a man gets the Call it is a blessing. He has heard the voice of God, be happy.'

'Your poor girl is still blubbering like the town fountain, her heart is broken.'

'She will be just fine when the son of the Mayor comes calling tomorrow. As soon as the news got out his mother came to see me to request if we would be agreeable to a family visit soon. I've seen the way that boy always looks at her during the *volta*, there might still be a betrothal in this family before the winter.'

'It's going to be quiet around here with your girl wed and my boy in the monastery.'

'Not for long. If my daughter takes after me I will have a grandchild by next Easter. At least now we have someone to pray for us.' The two women got up from their chairs. Work was waiting.

That first Call had been the easy one. Manoussos had been young and eager to begin his ecclesiastical life. This second Call was eating him alive as the leprosy would soon be doing to Nikos. Just as with the first Calling, his sleep was broken, his appetite gone and it was impossible to focus his thoughts. He became so sleep deprived he had to start using the books as prompts for the services.

Manoussos had become famous throughout the Lasithi prefecture for being the most devoted priest and for knowing all the liturgies so thoroughly he never needed even to glance at the books. He only held them in his hands out of tradition. Now he was often losing his place and even had needed to start over again. The people noticed.

He stumbled over the Nicene Creed, even the Sunday schoolers knew that one. At one baptism he almost dropped the baby during the immersion part of the ceremony. At the last wedding he performed he kept mentioning the name of the best man instead of the groom during the ceremony until the mother of the bride yelled out.

'*Pater*, wake up!'

He fasted every day instead of only Wednesdays and Fridays but his soul was not settling. He tried to do more offerings of charity to ease the inner torment. He used up all his diocese allowance to provide lunches for his parish, made with the help of the ladies auxiliary of course.

The meals were wonderful such as tender cuttlefish braised with spinach and artichokes Byzantine style. He still made yoghurt every week, so thick it could be cut with a knife, but he now gave it away to the village elders who could no longer chew. He even stopped accepting the complimentary shots of *tsikoudia* he was offered every time he went to the taverna for a chat with the townsmen.

'Why don't you drink with us *Pater*?' the council clerk asked him after Manoussos declined yet another offer of a shot of *tsikoudia*.

'The next thing you'll tell me is you prefer ouzo like a soft mainlander.'

'I don't know. I am unsettled. I just need to have this uneasiness pass. Maybe I am getting old.'

'You are younger than me Father and if you weren't a priest I could suggest some very effective ways that I use to help me feel, shall we say, settled.' The waiter brought plates of *Dakos* and *Kalitsounia* but Manoussos waved for him to take them away. Christos the clerk waved them back again.

'Now I know something is wrong, these are your very favourite foods and don't think you can fool me because you are wearing your *rassos*. I can see that under those black robes you have become half the man you were. Don't you eat anymore?'

'I can only manage to eat wild greens, some thistle root. On some Sundays I boil an egg, sometimes I can eat half of it. There is mint everywhere so I just sip tea.'

Christos bit into the *Dakos* and involuntarily sighed in delight of the flavour explosion on his tongue. Even looking at it was a joy. He let the mouthful sit on his tongue for the barley rusk base to dissolve and allow the hit of the tangle of tomato and soft salty cheese threaded with oregano and fruity olive oil.

'This has to be the best *meze*. Come on take a bite.' Christos swung back a slug of *tsikoudia* and eyed the traditional soft cheese pastries, the *Kalitsounia*.

'Ah praised be God for the hands of Cretan women, these treats belong in Paradise.' He bit into one and chewed as he spoke.

'Remember Maria Lambrakis? She made *Kalitsounia* that could make you lie down like a lamb. I had to kill her brother Nikos off too, just recently. What misfortune on one house, two children and both lepers, therefore both dead to the world. It tore my heart in two but what could I do?'

At the sound of Nikos' name the lungs of Manoussos tightened. Manoussos recalled how Nikos's sister Maria had brought trays of her melt in the mouth pastries to the Church to be served at memorial days.

'Now that I come to think of it Father that is when I noticed the change in you. It has been since her brother's funeral and departure. He was born to be great but the Fates had other ideas. You see Father no one can take anything for granted. Ach! Their poor mother worked so hard in the fields and with the needle to educate him and now she is left all alone by tragedy. *My eagle*, she used to call him'

Manoussos sat up from his slump.

'I haven't seen their mother for a while.'

'Of course not, she wouldn't dare show her face anymore. She is the mother of two lepers she would be treated like a leper herself.' Father Manoussos winced at those words. Theodora Lambrakis had been a devoted member of his congregation, always helping others, just like her son. It pained him that such a good soul was now shunned by society.

He had gone to find her a couple of weeks earlier but without success. He didn't even know how he got to be outside her house but his unease had become so intense he simply followed his soul. She wasn't home or if she was she did not come to the door.

He leaned in closer to Christos.

'This morning when I sat down to write out the weekly church program an ikon fell off its shelf. When I turned it over to check if the glass had broken I saw it was the ikon of Saint Nikolas. Is that a coincidence?'

'That is not a coincidence. Maybe Nikos or his mother Theodora is calling for you and God is making sure you listen.'

41

'*Kyrie elaison*' shouted Manoussos. 'What kind of priest am I? And I call myself a man of God. I am nothing but a fool. A buffoon like you can see it yet I walk around with my eyes closed.'

Christos the clerk was about to take another bite of the *Dakos* but the priest's words just registered.

'Buffoon?' Father Manoussos beckoned the waiter over to the table.

'Put all this food in a basket for me along with some bread, olives, some salami and I saw the cook rolling up some dolmades earlier, put some of those in there too.' Christos the clerk protested the disappearance of his lunch.

'Hey, I'm still eating.'

'Well stop, you need to lose weight.'

Father Manoussos ran straight to the house of Mrs. Theodora Lambrakis. Now he knew why there was a thorn in his heart. It had been lodged there by the last words spoken to him by Nikos Lambrakis.

The only way God will ever come to Spinalonga is if you bring him yourself.'

The house of the widow Lambrakis had all its blue shutters closed. He was relieved to see there were a few chickens strutting around within a little corral and two goats grazed under a lemon tree. He was more relieved to see she had a vegetable garden with zucchini, spinach and tomatoes growing.

He was relieved but not surprised. The Lambrakis family were productive. Even in her darkest days Theodora Lambrakis kept an immaculate house and garden. He was certain she shared her produce with anyone in need.

He called out to her in the warmest, friendliest tone he could manage.

'*Kali Mera* Mrs. Lambrakis.' He spoke out so she could hear someone was looking for her company. If he had just knocked on the door he doubted she would have opened it. She would have ignored it until the visitor gave up and went away, just as she had been doing up till now and as at the earlier time Manoussos had visited.

She appeared at her side gate. Theodora Lambrakis was still a striking woman. She wore the dull, shapeless, black garb of the Cretan woman in mourning but her firm shape showed through.

Her skin was smooth and her hair, held down as it was by her black headscarf, still shone like a glossy chestnut but her eyes had a tortured look in them. Manoussos was sure she never even looked in the mirror anymore.

'What do you want here Father?' Her voice was no longer soft. He extended out his hand to offer the basket to her. He held his hand out just long enough to allow her to decide if she wanted to bow and kiss it to receive the blessing and to show that he did not fear being near her. She did not kiss it but stood upright and unfathomable like a sphinx.

'I've brought you some food.'

She was brusque and grabbed the basket out of his hands without even looking in it.

'I accept this food and you can bring more if you want. The people here are all hungry but why have you brought it and why now?' He could see where Nikos got his sharpness from.

'I have enough food to eat Father, just, but I don't need much. What appetite do you think I have with both my children dead but walking, buried but above ground? I can never hold them again. I will never see them again. I will never know grandchildren.' Manoussos reached out to touch her shoulder to offer comfort but she pulled away.

'If you have come to persuade me to come to church again by handing me a basket of food you are wasting your time. Any God that won't watch over my children at Spinalonga can't do anything for me either.'

She looked in the basket and nodded her approval. She pulled out a few olives and some bread. Father Manoussos knew this was a neighborhood in need but in order to keep the majority of his parishioners at ease he had avoided any visitations – until now.

The neighborhood was now considered the breeding ground of lepers. No one knew how it happened and no one bothered to try to find out the source of infection. They were too scared to come close. Theodora Lambrakis brought him up to date.

'There is wretchedness everywhere. Over there is the house of a man whose wife was sent to Spinalonga, she left behind three little ones and a strong husband. He could no longer take his boat out to go catch fish because of his little ones so I offered to watch them while he tries to make enough money to keep them in shoes. Then no one would buy his fish for fear they would get the disease too.

They are clean and they have had the tests to prove it but people treat us all like lepers too. No school will take his children so I teach them what I know. At least they will be able to write their names and know how to count how many drachmas they have, not that they have many. I can teach the girl to cook and sew and the boys will learn how to shoot and fish so they will survive. The others have no one. Society has failed us. The church has failed us.'

The priest bowed before her and kissed her hand as the laymen should do whenever they meet a priest. He fell to his knees.

'Forgive me. Forgive my blindness to all the suffering. I was consumed with thoughts of protecting the community.'

'The only thing my children and the other poor souls did wrong was to get sick.' Manoussos ached for them as she spoke.

'Theodora the day your son Nikos left here he said something to me and it hasn't given me any peace since. Now I know what I have to do. I must help these people and let them know we have not forgotten them.'

She softened slightly.

'Very well and just how are you going to do that?'

'Theodora the last words of your son are still ringing in my ears. I hear nothing but them over and over. He said to me, *God does not go to Spinalonga.* I will take Him there. God goes to everyone.'

'You have been called?'

'Yes, I have been called.'

'When do you go?'

'As soon as I can but I will need a few days to arrange the ecclesiastical matters. I came here to bring you this food and to ask your forgiveness for my having abandoned you and the others here. I will atone by serving those who have true need.'

He left, but returned a few days later. Theodora wanted to learn more of his plans.

'What about the people of this parish?'

'A new priest has already arrived. I sent a letter to the bishop of Crete to request a transfer and for assistance with food programs and charity drives.'

Manoussos and Theodora both knew it would be difficult work because Greece was already trying to recover from the hardships caused by the Balkan wars. It seemed wars were unceasing. As soon as one was over a new battle would commence. To other nations Greeks seemed so inexplicably passionate. Patriotism is a way of life for a Greek. For thousands of years every day had been a fight to stay alive.

The bishop of Crete got the letter and believing Manoussos needed help in his parish sent a young priest monk fresh out of Mount Athos and full of hope and charity. Manoussos knew this error was God working in one of His mysterious ways. It meant he could train him to get to know the entire parish and then it would be even easier for him to leave. Manoussos was about to leave when Theodora gripped his hand.

'Take me too.'

'No Theodora. Do not risk your own life you have so much to do for the others.'

'I want to be with my children no matter what the risk.'

'Theodora, stay here and continue the work you are doing and the work you must do with the new priest. If God wants you to be on Spinalonga it will happen when He wants it.' Her face fell but she knew he was right. Even though she needed her children they now had a new community but the community she was in needed her badly.

'Very well, I will stay here and help here and assist the new priest.' She escorted him to the door.

'Thank you Theodora.'

Father Stavros, the new priest, was learning fast and Manoussos decided to test him. They were carrying out their regular daily duties when Manoussos said to the young priest,

'I want to make confession to you.' He had to know how the priest felt about the diseased ones. Was he a true man of God who loved all equally or did he show preference to the healthy and shun the sick?

'But Father you are senior to me, it is not right.'

'Do your job Father.'

'Very well.' The young priest could not disobey the command of his superior. The two men took their positions before the great screen of the church where Manoussos knelt before the great ikon of Christ. The young priest stood and draped the *epitrachelion* over his own shoulders and began reciting prayers over the head of Manoussos. He then looked down at the kneeling senior priest and asked,

'What troubles your soul?'

'Disease has struck some of our people but instead of us showing them love and sympathy we treat them worse than demons. We claim to be in health but in truth we carry the worst ailment of all. We are the diseased ones, we are spiritually diseased.' The young priest struggled to find a response of guidance for the troubled man and allowed his discipline to guide his speech.

'Father we are guided to do so by our Bible. We are told in Leviticus 13: 46 *He shall remain unclean all the days during which he has the infection; he is unclean. He shall live alone; his dwelling shall be outside the camp.*'

'I know very well what the Old Testament says, but we are Christians, we follow the teachings of Christ. You recalled the verse in Leviticus well. Do you not then recall?

Luke17:12-14

'Then as He entered a certain village, there met Him ten men who were lepers, who stood afar off. And they lifted up their voices and said, 'Jesus, Master, have mercy on us!' So when He saw them, He said to them, 'Go, show yourselves to the priests.' And so it was that as they went, they were cleansed.'

'Our Savior gave the lepers hope and their faith cured them. It was His command that they come to see us, the priests. He sent them to the temples, yet we not only drive them away, we also kill them off while they still breathe.'

The young priest hung his head, he was humbled and moved. He removed the *epitrachelion* from around his neck and draped the embroidered cloth over the head of his confessant as the tradition dictated, then recited the prayer of forgiveness over Manoussos.

Afterwards the two priests embraced and gave each other kisses on each cheek. Manoussos could feel the relief pumping in his veins. His choice to leave had been the answer to the burning ache within his viscera that nothing had been able to ease, nothing that is until he had made his decision.

The bishop of Crete was visiting the Lasithi prefecture and had invited all of the local priests to meet for a council. Manoussos would have attended anyway but this was the perfect opportunity to speak personally with the bishop about why he had not received any word about the transfer he requested.

After the general council meeting Manoussos took his place in the line up to receive a personal blessing from the bishop. It did not take long for his name to be called. The two Holy men greeted each other with the traditional embrace and kiss on both cheeks as well as each other's hand.

'Tell me your news of Lasithi my brother Manoussos. I have received many glowing reports of your love and dedication to the people of your parish.'

'Thank you Your Grace and I thank you for sending me Father Stavros, he is well received and well liked.' The bishop could sense Manoussos was not his usual calm self in spite of the polite words he spoke.

'Any other news for me?'

'Yes your Grace, a request actually.'

The bishop nodded for Manoussos to keep talking.

'I requested a transfer away but have not yet heard your decision. Father Stavros has been made familiar with all of the parochial matters and I feel confident he will do well.'

'A transfer? Yes I did receive your letter but I thought you were suggesting you were tired and were in need of assistance, so I sent Father Stavros. So tell me where is it you wish to go Manoussos?'

'Your Grace, it is not my wish but that of the Almighty. I have been Called. I seek advice from you if you know if there are any churches where I seek to go and if not, would the Patriarch see fit to send me to build one?'

The bishop had already asked his question and would not repeat it, to him wasted words were as bad as wasted food, a sin. He arched an eyebrow, looked at the priest and drummed his fingers on the arms of the bishop's throne. Manoussos gulped and then blurted out the words he had been aching to speak for so long.

'I have been called to Spinalonga, the fallen there have great need, they believe God has abandoned them, this must not be permitted to continue, no soul should feel unwanted by God.'

The Bishop stopped drumming. He leaned forward sharply.

'Manoussos do you know what you ask? It is a complete slum there for the most wretched of humanity.' The bishop rubbed his forehead and shook his head.

'And as for any church, I do know well that there is one there but it has fallen into ruin. We almost sent a cleric to deconsecrate it but then we decided we would not take the risk.'

Manoussos spoke quietly.

'I do not consider the residents to be wretched humanity. They are souls in need, and as for the church being in ruins, I will rebuild it. The souls there will need a place to pray. Please your Grace, give your approval to my request for a transfer to Spinalonga?'

The bishop waved a damask enclosed arm at him in dismissal.

'I must decline your request Manoussos. The residents of Spinalonga have been pronounced dead by the state and church. You know full well the mysteries cannot be given to the dead, it is a sin. They have no further need of any ecclesiastical services.'

'Your Grace, The Church was mistaken to do so and the practice must cease immediately. These people are ill not dead. How is it possible to carry out a burial service on a person who is standing, then walks out of the church of their own accord?'

'Enough!' The bishop roared.

'The answer is No! Now go back to your church Father Manoussos.'

Manoussos stayed still and calm.

'Is that how our Lord treated the lepers? Your Grace, with all due respect, I do not accept your decision. I will travel to see His All-Holiness, The Ecumenical Patriarch in Constantinople if necessary. But before I do so perhaps you might take a moment to reconsider.'

The bishop was moved by the passion and resolve pouring out of this slight man who asked for nothing for himself except to be permitted to do the work of God at the risk of a death sentence. When he spoke again it was in a quieter voice.

'Father Manoussos, please exit this space and allow me a few moments to meditate on this matter as well as to meet my other appointments.' Manoussos left the room but waited at the door.

It took four hours for the door to open again. The bishop was seated on his throne and beckoned him over. If the bishop had not taken up holy orders he might easily have become a wrestler. His presence not only filled the throne he was sitting in but the entire room. In his opulent Byzantine attire he was a splendid yet awesome sight. Even so Manoussos would not have been deterred by the decision if was still a negative one.

The bishop couldn't help noticing the slight jut of the jaw of Manoussos. It meant he was clenching his teeth, this little pit bull was ready for a fight. Some fights are not worth fighting especially when the outcome has already been determined by a greater power.

'Manoussos the name of the church on Spinalonga is Saint Panteleimon.' Manoussos smiled and clapped his hands together.

'*Kyrie Elaison.*' Saint Panteleimon was the doctor saint, the great healer, who dedicated his life to sufferers, the sick and the unfortunate. The bishop nodded at his joy.

'Yes it is appropriate isn't it? Permission is granted and God's speed.'

Sitting in the boat on the trip back to his town Manoussos felt he could have flown instead of sail, such was his elation. The first thing Manoussos did as soon as he arrived was to finalize all the details of the parish with Father Stavros. He was pleased to see all was under control so he could leave knowing all was well. Next he had to go back and see Theodora and to see if there was anything she wanted to send to Nikos and Maria.

She had become livelier since learning he was going to see her children.

'I will pack some foodstuffs Father, even better I will crate up some chickens and put one of the goats on a leash that way they can have a supply of eggs and milk and cheese.'

'No Theodora there is no need, I am glad to tell you that the council clerk told me that each resident gets a pension and a food allowance. His exact words

52

were, they have food to eat and money to buy whatever they want. No food is required but if you have a little treat or some gift to give hurry and give it now because the boat is waiting.'

Theodora had been caught unawares. She did not realize Manoussos would act so fast. She had nothing ready to send and he insisted that no food was necessary. No Greek mother would ever subscribe to that statement so she gave him the only food she had in the house, the meal she was cooking for herself, green beans and potatoes. She could eat olives and bread instead, there was zucchini in the vegetable patch and she had eggs on her table. She knew what she would be eating. Did her children?

In spite of what Manoussos told he she piled the meal into a terracotta bowl and wrapped it in a cloth. He bid her farewell and left.

'Tell them I love them.'

'They know that.'

'Tell them I am well and tell them I love them, do you hear me you crazy priest?'

'I hear you Theodora Lambrakis.'

After Manoussos had gone Theodora stood in the doorway of her son's bedroom as she often did. She would re-live conversations they'd had while he was studying at his desk. *What was that?*

Something was under his bed. Usually his suitcases resided there but they were gone now. She was a meticulous housekeeper, how could she have missed something like that? She checked herself, she had been unable to go into either of her children's rooms ever since they had gone. Theodora entered the room and bent down to see what it was that was beneath the bed.

Once she had pulled it out from the dark she recognized the unusual bag. It had belonged to Alikhan, the best friend of Nikos during law school. Theodora felt a stab of pain in her soul and needed to sit on the floor. Alikhan too had met with a tragic fate and Theodora was powerless to fight off the wave of frustrated rage that engulfed her so totally it was exhausting. She stayed seated on the floor sobbing for the magnificent young people who should have had the world at their feet but all had met with an unjust end.

She clutched the red embroidered bag close to her as she sobbed and remembered the many hours Nikos and Maria would examine the contents and be in awe of them. Nikos had treasured this reminder of his dear friend which must have been left behind in the sheer panic of the hours after his diagnosis when the authorities had announced he must leave immediately to prevent any spread of the disease.

But this would bring happiness to Nikos, he should have a reminder of his friend. It was all the impetus that Theodora needed to get up and stop crying. She grabbed the bag and ran in the hope she would make it to the harbor before Manoussos got on the boat.

Manoussos had to hurry to the harbor, the last boat of the day was leaving soon. The boatman was almost ready to depart for his usual trip along the coast to Elounda when he startled at the sight of the priest with much more baggage than usual.

'What are you doing Father, setting up a new city?'

'Possibly, a new parish at least. That much I know.'

Theodora got to the harbor just in time to see the boat with Father Manoussos onboard pulling away from the pier. She called out and he turned.

'Give this to my boy.' She tossed the package to him and for a moment both were horror struck as Manoussos fumbled with the package and it threatened to fall into the sea to be lost forever. The only way to save it was to drop the bowl of food Theodora had sent for her children. The food fell into the sea and the bag of Alikhan threatened to follow.

Theodora's hand shot to her mouth but with his hands now free Manoussos managed to flip the package, he caught it and held it high to show Theodora it was safe before he tucked it into his *rassos*.

'Be well Theodora.'

'Courage Father Manoussos.'

The boatman had developed a new habit ever since the trip where he had met Nikos Lambrakis. Every time the boat approached the island of tears he would ask, sometimes out of curiosity and sometimes just to shock,

'Anyone for Spinalonga?' As yet no one had answered but this time he heard,

'Yes,' spoken by the priest sitting in the stern.

Nikos had also developed a new habit of reading the classics every night after standing at the water's edge of Spinalonga to watch the eagles. He wandered around with Plato tucked under one arm and the other arm up to shield his eyes from the sun as he scanned the skies. He had been so absorbed in his eagle watching he had not noticed the arrival of the boat and the loud bumping sound it made when it hit against the stone pier startled him,

'Oh my God!'

'Yes indeed, right here on Spinalonga.' The voice came from the water and there standing upright with one hand extended out to touch his, like the hand of God to Adam's, was Father Manoussos.

Chapter 4. Alikhan

'Meet your roommate,' said the landlord. The Parthenon was in better condition than the rooming house Nikos had found in Athens but it was cheap and within a short walk to the University of Athens where he needed to be to finish his law degree. He'd agreed to have a roommate because it made the rent even cheaper.

From behind the landlord stepped out a young man who looked like a bear, broad of chest, brown as a gypsy but with Asian eyes. The landlord left and Nikos offered his hand out for a handshake,

'Pleased to meet you, I am Nikos Lambrakis of Crete.'

'Pleased to meet you too, I am Alikhan Azamatov of Kazakhstan.'

'Your Greek is very good for a foreigner.'

'I spent a lot of time in Constantinople where I was sent to work to make money for my schooling. My best friend was a Greek whose whole family had been murdered by the Turks in the 1922 genocides in Smyrna. He had hidden from the soldiers and somehow made his way to Constantinople so I took him in. At night he spoke only Greek to me so he would not lose his language. We worked together at the port loading ships until the military found him.'

The two young men stood nodding at each other as people do when an inexplicable instant understanding is achieved. Within weeks they were more bonded than most brothers. They cooked together and every night they would study together and talked about everything.

'What shall we cook today Nikos?'

'I don't know but Alikhan did you know there is another Kazakh here at the University, also studying law.'

'Yes I know. He leaves tomorrow, he has finished his studies.' A knock on the door interrupted their conversation. Nikos got up and opened it to find the Kazakh boy standing there holding a platter on which there was a boiled sheep's head.

'Err, come in.'

Alikhan stood up as Nikos took the macabre offering from the visitor's hands and placed it on the table as the other Kazakh took Alikhan's hand in both of his and shook it heartily. Then he bowed before Alikhan, acknowledged Nikos and left.

'What on earth did you do that made him bring you a sheep's head?'

'It is a big honor to be given a sheep's head. And now we don't have to cook. When somebody brings a sheep's head you must pay attention to what part of it is offered to you. The part of the animal that you are given denotes the position you hold. It is custom to give the tongue to someone who needs to hold theirs. Mothers-in-law often give it to their new daughter-in-law.' Alikhan chuckled as he spoke.

'Yes, this is all very interesting but why did that man give the sheep's head to you, why do you deserve that honor?'

'Well my friend that is because my father is the reason he was born.'

'What! Is he your brother?'

'No.' Alikhan sliced an ear from the head of the sheep and handed it to Nikos with a smile.

'Here, we usually give the ears to the little children who must hear well what they are told to do. You have a lot of listening to do.' Nikos took the ear but put it down.

'Is your family some sort of chiefs of your tribe?'

'Sort of. We are Berkutchi.' Nikos sat back and waited for his friend to explain further.

'The Berkutchi are the most mysterious people of our country, we are the most respected and are thought of almost as miracle workers. We are the eagle hunters.'

'So how did your father help that boy to be born?'

'When a woman has trouble making a baby she comes to the Berkutchi to ask for their blessings. The people believe that if we can master the eagles then we can master all aspects of nature. They believe we have divine powers that will help them. Nine months after the boy's parents visited my father, the boy was born.'

After the unusual visit Nikos asked every possible question to Alikhan about how to catch an eagle. He asked so many he would frustrate Alikhan. 'Enough with the questions Nikos, you are never going to need to know how to catch an eagle.'

'I know it is not logical but I just can't explain it, come on tell me again about how to choose one.'

'Okay but you pay for dinner tomorrow.'

'Done.'

Yet again Alikhan explained how it was always preferable to choose an eagle that can already hunt, not a young eaglet straight from the nest.

'Choosing an eagle from the nest to become a hunter is like choosing a babe from the cradle to become a priest. You don't know its soul yet. Eagles, like children, can become restless and aggressive when they are not permitted to develop according to their natural tendencies. As a result of this no talents can be identified and no skills can be honed. This is a crime! An eagle which has already developed its own hunting skills, and loves the hunt, is the best hunter of all, and this, as in humans, is often an inborn trait.'

Nikos leaned forward to pour more coffee into Alikhan's cup and keep him talking.

'I remember being with my father when he was helping another Berkutchi choose an eagle. We were up high in the rocks watching a nice kantubit stalk her prey. It was amazing.'

'What is a kantubit?'

'Eagles have different names for certain years of their life. A one year old is a balapan, a two year old is a kantubit, and a three year old is a turnekl, and so on. This particular kantubit was very clever. We stayed up in the caves for two weeks, barely sleeping just so we could watch her. I'll never forget the way she was watching a herd of goats.

Instead of swooping in to pick one up she waited until one had separated a little from the herd to go to nibble at some grass growing right on the edge of the cliff. She swooped down and knocked it off the edge, the goat fell, died on impact, and the kantubit just picked it up without having to deal any struggle. She took it to her nest and had herself a fuss free feast. It was like watching an assassin commit the perfect hit.'

'So how did you actually catch her?'

'Some secrets we Berkutchi can never tell. Our ways are steeped in mystery and they will stay there. But what I will tell you is that your eagle and you must suit each other. So before you ask what kind of eagle shall I look for, ask yourself, what kind of man am I?'

Nikos leaned in further to listen carefully.

'My father, may he rest in peace, always called me his eagle. He said I act like one, I study, I shadow then I strike.'

Alikhan smiled his approval and reached into the suitcase under his bed and brought out a strange red bag, it was completely covered with embroidery.

'But you are a lawyer now Alikhan, you have no need of catching eagles.'

'Are you a Greek?'

'Of course.'

'Can you stop being a Greek?'

'Never.'

'Well I am a Berkutchi, even if I become King of Astana I will always be a Berkutchi.'

Alikhan sipped his coffee then continued. 'You don't just wake up one day and decide to catch an eagle. It takes weeks even months of watching the birds to see if she has what it takes.'

'Why do you always say she?'

'The best hunters are the females, just as in life hey my friend. I know they say man is the hunter but it is the woman who is more ruthless, more cunning, and anyway if a man is without a woman to tell him what is needed he would just sit around all day and scratch his balls. Men hunt to please women. So we Berkutchi men use women eagles to hunt, besides they are almost twice as big as the males so they are much stronger and can pick up bigger prey. We once had an eagle so big she could pick up a wolf.'

He began to unfurl the unusual red bag.

'You must be very prepared, you need a hood readymade so you can slip it over their head and keep them in darkness. You need a thick leather glove or their talons will shred your arm to pieces. You need a *bardak*, the wrist support, a stand for the eagle to sit on. An eagle can weigh up to eight kilos, you try carrying that on your wrist. And you need the cuff for the leg on which to attach the chain.'

As he spoke he had pulled out of the bag every piece of equipment he had described and had laid them out on the bed.

'My grandfather presented me with his eagle equipment before I left for Athens. He said he wanted me to have them before he died. If Allah blesses me with a son these will become his.'

'I hope God does bless you with a son, he would be proud to be born a Berkutchi and proud to own this fine equipment.'

Alikhan became solemn as he stood before Nikos.

'My dear friend, we have become each other's brother and I tell you now my brother that if anything happens to me and I die without a son, these items of the Bekutchi will become yours. I know you would honor them and protect them.' Nikos was startled by the request.

'Why wouldn't you pass them on to your family?'

'Each male in my family has their own and they have heirs to whom they can pass them on. This is my equipment to do with whatever I like and I choose to pass them on to you should anything happen to me.'

Nikos smiled. 'Yes we are better than brothers, and nothing will happen to you. But just to make you feel at ease, I promise should anything ever happen to you and you are still without heirs, I will honor them.'

Alikhan added, 'You will also need a very fast horse to run with it once you see it swooping down to get its prey. Without a fast horse it is more difficult but you can teach your eagle to bring the prey to you.'

Nikos laughed, 'Forget the horse you still haven't told me how you actually catch an eagle?'

Alikhan was engrossed in his own heritage and was enjoying the fact that for the first time in his life he was speaking of eagle hunting with someone other than another Berkutchi.

'Once you have decided upon the bird you want you must leave bait for it. Use something irresistible like a freshly slaughtered lamb or goat or rabbit. You must take on the traits of the eagle, cunning, stealth and speed. Do not waste one movement. Have you ever noticed that eagles do not flap around? They use Nature and work with her. They ride on the thermal breezes like a man skis down a mountain, using minimal energy but going far.

You must become like an eagle yourself. Do not take your eyes off her as she comes in for the bait. As your eagle is approaching the bait you must be fast, faster than you have ever been before in your life. Choose the exact moment, the one where she is right at the bait and all her attention is on grabbing the bait, not on flying away. She will be off guard only for that one second. That is when you must strike. Throw a net over her or she will fly away. Then cover her with a thick blanket. She must be kept covered, the dark will confuse her.

There will be a struggle to get the shackle and chain on so it doesn't fly away, and to put the hood on without getting your heart ripped out, but that is part of the skill of the Berkutchi. If you can build her trust in you she will allow you to get close. But keep her in the dark and always remember to feed her only from your own hand. She will reward your efforts by learning very fast, so fast you will think she is part human. I do not think it is a mistake that the eagle is the symbol of the gods. You will come to trust her and she will come to trust you.'

After that Alikhan said no more about eagles and as soon as they licked clean the bones of the sheep's head the topic of eagles got put away like the red bag.

'Do you see yourself ever getting married Nikos?' Alikhan asked one afternoon.

'Well I certainly hope so, one day. The only reason I am not chasing women is because of my studies. I will go back to Crete soon and then I will be only too happy to start taking a good look at the girls of my town. What about you?'

'Yes I want that very, very much.' Nikos had noticed Alikhan had been very preoccupied lately and they hadn't been sharing every meal together as they usually did but Nikos had not questioned his friend's whereabouts. A man has a right to go off on his own when he so feels the need but Nikos knew the time was right to ask,

'Alikhan, have you met someone here in Athens?'

Alikhan was beaming as if the sun itself was resting in his mouth.

'Yes Nikos, I have met the most beautiful woman in the world, right here in Athens and I want to be with her, will you stand by me?' He sniffed.

'I must be catching a cold, my beloved has not been feeling too well lately, I probably caught it from her.' He winked at Nikos who smiled at his friend's happiness,

'Alikhan of course I will stand by you but who is this girl? I am surprised you have not told me of her sooner.'

'Forgive me Nikos but we have had to keep things very quiet for a while because she has a brother who is like a wild man. He does not believe women should be outside of the home and he wants to choose her husband.'

Alikhan stood up and pulled a letter out of his pocket.

'There is something else I have not told you. I have made an application to be accepted into the diplomatic corps and have been accepted, by Turkey. That is where I met the girl, at the embassy. She is Turkish.' He said the last sentence slowly.

Nikos stayed silent. It was hard for any Greek to get excited about his best friend going to the Turks. He knew that both countries had to work hard to put their history behind them but still Nikos sighed.

'You have made a difficult but brave decision my friend. Are you certain of how you feel and have you met her brother?'

'I am certain of how I feel. I love her. And I have not met her brother as yet, but if he is too unreasonable and refuses to bless our marriage I could always elope with her and take her back to Kazakhstan with me.'

'That is hardly a diplomatic thing to do.'

The brother of the beloved of Alikhan was not a diplomatic man and the lovers knew it. He would bring other equally fanatical family members with him to carry out a swift termination of the relationship. Alikhan didn't care what they would do to him, as long as they did not hurt his beloved. She had told him they would show no mercy to her should she bring dishonor to the family by becoming involved with anyone other than someone they had chosen. Thank goodness her father was an understanding and diplomatic man.

She was fortunate to be born of a father who was one of the team that worked with the late former prime minister of Greece, Eleftherios Venizelos, and the President of Turkey, Kemal Ataturk, in forging the treaty of friendship between the two countries. Her father had been one of the original Young Turks, to further prove he was a progressive thinker he insisted his daughter have a place in the modern world.

He trained her himself in diplomatic matters and believed he should set an example for the equality of women in his society. He sent her to help the poverty and disease stricken unfortunate ones. She assisted with bringing food supplies to a leper colony and helped set up a school in a remote village in the Trebizond. He was the one who then placed her as a cultural attaché in the Athens embassy.

But the old man should have given equal focus to his son who had become influenced by the radical old guard who considered the progressive thinkers like his father to be traitors, they were westernizing too much, and were too tolerant. The young radicals like his son showed their protest to change by being as anti-west and anti-Christian as possible.

The liberal thinkers, like his father, were a danger to Islam.

Nikos and Alikhan sat together in the Zappeion gardens, the Greek sat on a bench in thinker pose and the Kazakh stood in philosopher stance as he related the entire background of his beloved. He ended his speech with a big sneeze.

'Alikhan, you have been sniffing and sneezing for days now, let's go and get you a cup of tea.'

'Yes, I know but also my beloved is still not feeling well, she too has been ill for days.' Nikos still had their earlier conversation ringing in his head and chilled at those words.

'Alikhan, think for a moment will you. You said she worked in leper colonies.'

'Relax, the uneducated believe you can catch it just by being close but only a small minority actually catches it.'

But Nikos did not relax,

'What if you are in that minority? Anyway, apart from the fact her brother might kill you, how would your family feel? You are from a strong culture, your parents must be so proud to have a lawyer son. They must have plans for you to marry a girl of your own people.'

'My family will love her because I love her and I am hoping because I am a Sunni Muslim like most Turks her brother will not be too upset.'

'I hope you are right my friend.'

Alikhan hoped he was right too even though in his heart he knew the over exaggerated sense of moral code of the extreme radicals. They believed women should never be seen and here was his beloved working in a Christian country and wearing Western dress, not even covering her hair. As long as her father was alive she was safe. He had to marry her and take her away before anything happened to the old man.

Nikos made his friend a cup of tea back in their tiny shared room. Alikhan was sneezing and coughing the entire time, spreading the leprous molecules into the air for his friend to breathe in, just as he had breathed them in from his beloved.

'Thank you for the tea Nikos but I must go and see her now, we have much to plan and discuss. She was a little anxious yesterday because her brother said he was coming to Athens to see her.'

The eyes of Alikhan betrayed his concern even if he tried to make his voice sound light and carefree.

'But I am sure everything went well. I will bring her back here to meet you. Be well my friend.'

'Be well, and be careful.'

Alikhan walked quickly, he wanted to get to his love as soon as possible. She lived in a room in a lovely old villa in the *Monastiraki* section of old Athens not too far from their rooms. He entered the courtyard of the house and slowed down instead of rushing to the door as he normally did. The sign they had devised to indicate that the coast was clear wasn't there.

They had agreed on a lit lantern in the window as in the ancient legend of Io and Leander but the lantern was not in its place in the window, yet the door to her room was open. He pushed the door so it opened wider and saw the lantern lying broken on the floor. Her precious carpet, a gift from her father, was all bunched up against the wall.

Then he saw the back of her, she was sitting on a chair but when he looked closer he saw she was tied to it, her hands were tied behind her back and her feet were bound. He tried to move fast but couldn't. He slowly walked around to face her but her brother stopped him.

He was as terrifying as the descriptions she had given of him. He was a full head taller than the stocky Eurasian Alikhan and had the massive chest and broad shoulders of the famous Turkish strongmen. The vicious look on his face made clear his violent intent. He looked just like how the ruthless Mehmet 11 must have looked when he declared he would bring down the walls of Constantinople, no matter what it would take.

'Stop there you Kazakh dog.'

'What have you done to her? Have you no respect for your father?' He tried to step past him to see her but the brother grabbed his arm in a wrestlers hold that forced Alikhan to twist around in pain. Her brother rasped into his ear.

'The old man is dead, now my word rules in this family. She has paid the price for dishonoring the family.' As he spoke he turned Alikhan around until he was facing his beloved.

Her beautiful almond shaped eyes were now frozen open wide in terror, her soft, luscious mouth that he had kissed so lovingly was stretched taut in a grimace of shock. The beautiful white linen shirt he had watched her painstakingly pin tuck during the evenings when they had sat together was now stained red with the blood that had poured out of her and lay in a viscous puddle in her lap and the gold chain with the heart shaped pendant he had bought her was wedged in the great gash across her throat.

Alikhan fell to his knees before his beloved. He barely felt his hair being grasped. He was in so much shock he did not even notice his head being pulled back and he barely had time to gasp when the Turk drew the knife, still dripping with the blood of his beloved, across his throat to give him the same fate.

It was the knock on the door that woke Nikos. He was still dressed from trying to stay awake waiting up for Alikhan to bring his beloved to meet him. He became concerned as night fell and still no word, hopefully there had been no complications with her brother. When he opened the door and saw two solemn faced policemen standing there he understood that he was going to hear something bad but was not in any way prepared for how bad. The policemen delivered the terrible news with a merciful swiftness. They were also ordered to pick up all of Alikhan's belongings to send back to his family along with his body.

It was all over so quickly it was like a cyclone had whisked through the place, within hours all traces of his dear friend were gone. Nikos found the way to honor Alikhan and to try to soothe his own sense of loss and pain was to follow the traditions with which he was familiar. Nikos felt he had to mourn his friend correctly, Muslim or not, he would follow the Greek funeral traditions for him.

He asked one of the women from the staff at the university to make the traditional offering of *kolliva*, he took the decorated dish of boiled wheat to the church to be blessed and to light a candle for the safe journey to the other world for Alikhan. There was nothing left now but to return home.

Nikos had to hurry to Piraeus to catch the boat back home, he wished he had something of Alikhan's as a memento of their friendship but the police had taken everything. He threw his few belongings into his suitcase, his law degree went in first, and took a final look around. Something was poking out from beneath the divan Alikhan used as a bed. Nikos bent down to see what it was. In the dim dustiness beneath the bed he made out the joyful red embroidery of the eagle hunting equipment of Alikhan.

He picked up the richly embroidered bag and clutched the bag close to him so he could feel he was embracing his friend. *How did the police overlook it, should I get it to them so Alikhan's family can have it? No! The contents were bequeathed to me by Alikhan personally. It was his wish that I have it.* His thoughts consoled him, any initial guilt was gone. He put the bag into his suitcase and left for Crete.

Chapter 5. The Hand of God

When sunlight breaks through a mass of clouds to form rays of light fanning out, Nikos would call them the fingers of God. A giant divine hand was caressing the world. Nikos couldn't help noticing with some irony that Manoussos was standing right in the centre of the fingers of God phenomena that was in the skies that day. It was almost as if God was personally hand delivering him to Spinalonga. It made his initial statement of, 'Oh my God!' have double meaning.

'Well you did tell me that the only way God will come to Spinalonga is if I bring Him.' But Nikos wasn't feeling joyful. He was hungry and angry and before him was the priest for whom he had done so much work yet he had agreed to read the prayers of death over both him and his sister.

'What else did you bring with you apart from God?' Manoussos could hear the disdain in his voice which showed that Nikos did not share his feelings of joy at their reunion.

'I bring the love of the bishop and the Holy Texts and other ecclesiastical items of course.'

'The people here are not monks on a path of denial. These are sick people in need. Didn't you even bring a loaf of bread or a roll of bandages?' Manoussos looked bewildered.

'No I did not. Naturally it was my first instinct to do so and began to organize such things but I was told that you had no need of anything because you all receive a good pension and ample food rations.'

'Who told you that?' It was the first time Manoussos had ever heard Nikos roar and it was terrifying.

'The council clerk, Christos. He told me. I didn't tell him I was coming here but I just asked him if he were going to Spinalonga what would he take. He said he would save the space for his own items and not load up the bags with too many other things because you all have more than enough here.'

'Oh I am sure he did. You should have trusted your first instincts.' Nikos kicked the stones in front of him so they sprayed up like a little wave breaking.

'What pensions? What ample food rations? Now I know how that fat clerk got so fat.' Nikos spat at the ground and kicked again. Two helpers had since arrived and they too were taken aback that the new arrival was a priest. Nikos went and stood with them.

'Do we look like have money and food? Take a look around you!'

Manoussos finally noticed how thin Nikos had become and the two helpers looked repugnant and smelled foul. Manoussos suddenly felt like a total fool. He had been too obsessed with his own ego, his Call, to think logically about where he was headed and their needs. He had blindly trusted the greediest man he knew.

'Please Nikos, God will provide.'

'God came empty handed!' Again Nikos roared at him as he turned around to leave. The two helpers shrugged at each other and picked up the priests belongings. They moaned in haunted whispers.

'We will take these to the church. Whenever you are ready, go there.' They disappeared through Dante's gate and Nikos was about to follow them. It was then that Manoussos remembered the bag he had tucked inside his *rassos*.

'Nikos, wait.' But Nikos did not even slow down. Manoussos knew he had to say something that would make him stop.

'Nikos, your mother sent you something. Of course she wanted to send food – and did. It is my fault it didn't make the journey. But she sent you something else.'

Nikos stopped and stood still for quite a while before turning around to see what it was Manoussos had. By the time he had turned around the look of rage was gone and the anxious look of a young boy had taken over his face.

As Manoussos pulled the package out from his *rassos* he had the privilege of watching the anxious look on the face of Nikos Lambrakis morph into a gaze of sheer rapture as if he had seen an angel. Theodora had wrapped the bag of Alikhan in a woolen cardigan she had knitted for Maria. The knit had stretched like a lacy veil around the bag allowing the red embroidery peep through. Nikos had to blink to check if he really was seeing what he thought he was seeing. Manoussos stepped forward and handed the bag over with both his hands as if it were a sacred ceremonial sword.

Nikos received it with equal ceremony and stood holding the parcel as if it were the Holy Grail itself. He stroked it with tenderness. His best friend and his adored mother had both touched this bag.

Manoussos could see the effect it was having on Nikos and how tightly he was clutching onto it, he also noticed the volume of Plato he had under his arm.

'Nikos, please remember that *'Good actions give strength to ourselves and inspire good actions in others.'*

Nikos snapped out of his reverie of his mother and of Alikhan and faced the priest who came to a starving colony with almost nothing but books in his bags.

'Just because you remember one quote by Plato don't think that you can impress me Manoussos? Here is one of my favorite quotes, *'Man will never be free until the last king is strangled with the entrails of the last priest.'*

No sooner had he gotten out the words of the French writer, Denis Diderot he stopped in regret. He believed in them but he had regretted saying them. Nikos then remembered his own arrival. He too had filled his bags with almost nothing but books. But Nikos was moved and Manoussos knew it. He knew the man well enough to read his body language. He might still be incensed by the injustice of his situation but he was undeniably moved by the priest's presence. Nikos was looking at the ground, trying to reign in his emotions. To stay in the logical, he asked a logical question.

'So Manoussos why have you come here?'

'To rebuild the church so you and all the others can attend services and know that God did not abandon you, and neither did I.'

'But you personally read the Trisagion prayers over me. We here are all dead and buried in the eyes of the church. To invite us to attend service and then offer us communion means you go against the canons of the church. A sacrament cannot be offered to a dead person. It means you defile the body of Christ.'

'I have received sanction to do so from the Patriarch.'

'Well from a legal point of view that means the Church has identified its error by the very fact that it sent you here.'

'They didn't send me here, I asked to come.'

'Really! Nikos raised his guard again. He wanted to work on controlling his temper but he also needed his inner fury to spur on the actions he needed to take. The thought that Manoussos came out of curiosity so his own soul could feel eased further stoked that fury.

'Come with me. Come and see something.'

He guided the priest down to a stretch of land along the high wall. It looked like a cemetery but there were no markers or crosses on the walls. A fresh grave had been dug and some men were carrying a body wrapped in rags. They threw it into the grave and started to cover it by shoveling over dirt. Nikos watched as the priest instinctively went over and started reciting the Burial prayers over the body.

'Stop!' said one of the men.

'Don't you understand Father? A man cannot be buried twice. We have already received our funerals, this is just a place to dump our bones.'

'Every man deserves a prayer, especially now the illness has taken him.'

'No the illness didn't take him,' said Nikos. 'He drowned. We are so hungry and weak that we try to catch a few fish to eat but in our battle to fight off our hunger sometimes the sea wins. More of us die from hunger or from attacks from each other than from the disease.'

'Holy Christ.' Manoussos closed his eyes and crossed himself. He composed himself after a moment then continued reciting the Burial prayer. The others all stood by and for the first time since they were stricken by their disease enjoyed taking part in a traditional ceremony again even it was for a funeral other than their own.

'Come to church tomorrow my children, bring the others,' he said hopefully but everyone walked away. Nikos, with his book under his arm, walked away too.

The books of Nikos had been responsible for a new ritual developing on Spinalonga. Every evening after the siesta Nikos would sit on his front step and read from one of his books on philosophy. Every night the other lepers would gather around as if they happened to be in the neighborhood. Nikos would look up from his reading as if surprised to see them and he would read a quotation or share a thought with them.

Sometimes he staged it in order to teach them something or to get their opinions on a matter. He liked to involve the crowd. Once he asked,

'How many types of happiness do you think there are? Or is happiness all the same'

'There is more than one type of happiness I think,' said a woman.

'The first one is when we indulge in something that feels very good but does not last long, so we want more of it. It gives us a short lived burst of pleasure, like a piece of baklava or a good glass of wine, or a new garment.'

'Or when you have a woman,' added a man from the back of the group. The men laughed their agreement. She ignored them and continued.

'The second type of happiness must be when you have everything you need. There is enough to eat and you are warm and sheltered. You have a family and you feel comfortable and content.'

Nikos stayed silent while his former neighbor spoke. He knew his own mother was now helping raise her three little children while her husband tried to sell his catches of fish. He knew she knew of these things because they had often sat on the front veranda and discussed them.

'Keep going Ariadne, you are doing very well.'

'Then the third type is when we have an inner drive to complete something on our own, to achieve a goal that only we can accomplish and we can only do it by a great push of courage. When we achieve that we are truly happy. We feel worthy and capable of anything.'

Nikos seized the moment to reel them into his plan.

'Can a sick person be a happy person?' Nikos asked of them. There was a small silence as everybody concentrated on the question then the response came as one voice.

'Yes!'

'We were sent here to die yet here we all stand, breathing and alive. We are living citizens entitled by our noble birthright to the exact same rights of any other living citizen of Hellas and I intend to see to it that I bring all these rights to you all. We are citizens of the city state of Spinalonga and we will be treated as such.'

From within the crown someone said,

'You are going to need a miracle to do that. You are going to need God's help and God doesn't come to Spinalonga.'

Nikos smiled a small ironic smile.

'I said those words myself once but for now I will just keep my mind open. Anything can happen.'

Chapter 6. The Fourth Divine Good

When Nikos strode away from Manoussos the priest ran after him. Nikos ignored him as he tucked the bag of Alikhan into his trousers and buttoned up his jacket. It had become much looser on him now so it easily concealed the extra bulk of the bag.

He walked through Dante's gate, now oblivious to his surroundings but Manoussos was having a whole new experience. The first thing to hit him was the stench. It was the smell of putrid flesh. The next thing was the decay of the houses. They were ruins that offered little shelter. Decay was all around him even when he closed his eyes the stench saw to it that he could not escape the truth. Manoussos bowed his head in shame at the church's abandonment of these blameless souls.

Nikos had walked ahead to sit in his usual place on his front door step to calm down. Plato's *Laws* fell open to a page in chapter one and the first sentence he read told him exactly how to begin the task he had set himself; that of making Spinalonga run like an efficient city state.

He was trained in applying laws but here the population was either fragile or hostile or both but he had to make a start and Plato always provided some sort of answer.

The Cretan laws are with reason famous among the Hellenes; for they fulfil the object of laws; which is to make those who use them happy; and they confer every sort of good.

Nikos marveled yet again at how the clear and logical thinking of Plato was as accurate and fresh today as it was when it was the norm so long ago. None of his words had lost their power over the centuries. They were just as exceptional and enlightening as they must have been when first written. Logic and truth never fade.

When he looked up to observe what was happening around him, there had to be fifty people just sitting, staring at the ground or at him. Yet again a crowd had gathered. He had a forum.

'What are you reading lawyer?' Ikaros asked him.

'I am reading Plato.'

'What does Plato have to say?'

'He says there are two types of good.'

'How can there be two types of good. Good is good, bad is bad,' one of them commented.

'Well according to Plato there are two types of good. There is the divine and the human. Each of the two types of good has four elements; and Plato says that the human hang upon the divine.' Manoussos stayed well behind but was able to witness the gathering. Nikos kept speaking.

'Guess which one of the four human good is first?'

'Health,' said Pavlos.

'Yes it is Health.'

The crowd murmured their agreement with irony. 'After Health the second was Beauty, third was Strength and fourth was Wealth.'

82

'Well then Plato is no use to us, all of the human goods are absent on Spinalonga, and if the human goods are absent there is no point even knowing what the divine goods are,' came a voice from the crowd.

Nikos looked at the book again.

'No, Plato says the human goods hang upon the divine.'

'What does that mean?'

'It means the more of the divine type of good we develop, the more of the human type of good manifests in our lives.'

'Alright then lawyer read on and tell us the four divine goods.'

'Of the divine good things Wisdom was placed first, followed by Temperance, Justice and Courage.' Nikos saw the irony again and laughed to himself.

'It appears I have more divine good within me than human good.'

'Wisdom, Temperance, Justice and Courage' Eva repeated.

'I think Courage is the one to start with.'

'Why do you say that Eva?'

'Because when someone sets out for a task or when something difficult arises that is the first thing people say to each other, *have courage*. It must be a tradition from our ancient times that has stuck.'

Nikos remembered how he and Father Manoussos had often discussed such things and how they shared in the study of the great texts and then they would have a vigorous debate about which books serve humanity better; the religious texts or the philosophical ones. The population had yet to learn there was now a priest on Spinalonga and he wondered how they would react when they would find out.

'Wealth.' Nikos uttered.

'I know wealth could fix a lot of problems but we have none.'

'Ah, your ego is so human, recall all the divine goods again,' commanded Manoussos.

All turned towards him. Manoussos, with his beard and robes, looked like a dark version of Plato himself. Nikos had to admit if there was one thing about Manoussos it was his use of words. He didn't speak much but when he did it was direct and meaningful. Manoussos believed words were like water, an overflow was destructive, none at all at the wrong time was just as destructive, just a trickle was often not enough but a few well placed ones had the power to spring forth life.

Nikos re-read the list of the four divine goods and he looked to number four, Courage. Manoussos sat on the rock across from Nikos while everyone around was whispering.

'When did a priest arrive?'

'Is he sick too?'

Manoussos nodded at the faces all around him then addressed Nikos,

'What is Courage?' That sounded simple enough, Nikos was sure he could answer that one.

'Courage is being brave, it is having no fear.'

'Is that what you think Courage is, having no fear? A child has no fear when they run ahead of their mother to paddle in the sea does that mean they act from courage?'

'No, that is the innocence of a child.'

'Then what is innocence?'

'It is the lack of knowledge that something might be harmful or very difficult but having the faith that it is not.' Nikos thought he answered that one well.

'What then if we do have the knowledge that something is harmful to us?'

'That is fear and fear does not let us proceed.'

The crowd was enthralled in the repartee between the two learned men. Manoussos continued.

'When would one proceed in the face of fear plus the knowledge that something may harm?'

The words poured out of Nikos.

'When we have the knowledge that the thing that must be done is difficult and might be harmful but we proceed regardless of the fear, it is either for a greater good or for love.'

Manoussos leaned forward, 'That is Courage.' Manoussos got up and walked away to stand by the wall. The words that had been required had been said. There was no need for more.

Nikos remembered when he had read Aristotle's *Politics* and read in the opening paragraph, *the ultimate object of the state is the good life*. Nikos looked up at the sky so the words of Manoussos and Aristotle could settle into his brain. Happiness and a good life were not just created by the individual, the state had to provide for them as well and that would take some courage.

'What would make you happy right now?' He asked it as an open question to them all.

'Food!' said one, 'and a nice glass of wine.'

'A bed' said another.

'To walk without pain,' came from one woman.

'Death,' said a voice from under a pile of rags.

'An egg, soft boiled with some good bread to dunk into the yolk. I have the courage to swim to Elounda to get a fresh egg.' said Ikaros.

All the lepers laughed, and then groaned in hungry agreement.

Nikos laughed too, mostly with joy, he had found where to start. The simple pleasures were the basis of happiness. All it would take to begin to bring them to Spinalonga was a little courage. The street philosophy was invigorating them all. He continued talking to the crowd.

'We need to work out our sources of food. What do we have that could provide food?' The gathered crowd provided answers.

'The sea! If we had a boat we could fish.'

'They will never provide us with a boat in case we try to escape,' someone bitterly responded.

'The sky!' Ikaros said. 'If we had a carbine we could shoot birds. I used to go hunting for ducks and geese.'

'Sure, they can deliver the carbine along with the new boat,' came back a sarcastic comment.
'But a carbine would be good. We could have rabbits and wild goats all the time if we were on the mainland.

Nikos shared their frustration, there was food everywhere around them but there was no way for it to be gotten. All the philosophy in the world was not going to help their stomachs get full. Food, they needed food. People could work wonders with a good meal in their stomachs. The health authorities sent over a supply package every week. It contained bread, some dried pulses, a few onions and sometimes there was coffee or a few bananas. The inhabitants of Spinalonga needed a lot more food than the meager weekly rations provided.

Manoussos did a gentle cough to remind them he was still there. The crowd had gone silent at the sight of a priest but then gasped when Maria came charging through the crowd and almost bowled several people over. She had heard from the helpers that there was a priest on the island and that Nikos knew him. Once she saw it really was Manoussos himself standing before her she greeted him.

'Father, welcome and not well come. How sad that you too are stricken with the terrible curse. How is Mama?' She began to bend so as to follow the tradition of kissing the hand of the priest. Before she touched his hand Manoussos spoke.

'I do not have the disease my child, and your mother is well.' Maria froze midway through her bow when she realized she was about to touch a healthy person. Manoussos looked around at his new parishioners and extended out his hand for her to kiss. He even helped her by bringing his hand up closer to her face. Maria hovered over it for a second then with a slow and graceful action put her lips onto the back of the hand of Father Manoussos then stood back upright in another slow and graceful motion. The young woman smiled at the priest whose eyes were now rimmed with tears. He blinked them away and made a point of not wiping his hand on his *rassos*, not even discreetly.

'Your mother sends you her love. She is continuing your work Nikos, she is teaching the underprivileged to read and write and she is running the assistance programs at the church.'

Nikos and Maria looked at each other but then quickly looked away. Their eyes too had begun to fill with tears, but now was not the time to shed them. Nikos saw the hypocrisy of speaking before the crowd on matters of civility and social structure when he had been anti-social himself to Manoussos, who had done no wrong other than carry out the canons of the church.

Nikos's voice crackled when he did speak.

'Father, tell us what is it that made you come here and put your own life in danger? You could barely be in the same space as me and yet now, well, here you are.'

'Yes here I am. I had to come. Since the day you left it was your voice ringing in my ears so loud I couldn't sleep. So I thought it best if I come here myself and check on you.'

'The boat must be leaving now Father, you should hurry to make it,' said Maria.

'The boat has gone. I am staying here.'

The rest had gathered around to hear what the priest was saying.

'He says he is staying here,' Ikaros called out to the others. Haunted voices began to jeer him from within the crowd and he answered each one with as much sass as they gave him.

'Go back priest and if you come back again bring some chickens next time.'

'I will but next time I will bring a goat too.'

'There is no church for you here priest.'

'Yes there is.'

'It is in ruins, like us.'

'As we will rebuild it so you will heal.'

'There is no saint for lepers.'

'Yes there is, Lazarus raised from the dead, like you.'

'He has an answer for everything this one, maybe he can survive here?' Someone said.

Eva came forward, bent and kissed his hand.

'Welcome Father. You have brought a little light into a very dark place but I am not sure that you will be able to get anyone to come to church again. There has been so much suffering that the people have lost all faith.'

'But I have not my child.' Nikos could see the crackles of excitement within the crowd. He knew that it was not about going to church again.

'Tell me, you are all saying words of defiance yet I can see some of you are smiling. What is it that has made you all so more enthusiastic?'

It was Kimon who answered.

'There is a priest standing here discussing church services. Just a few minutes earlier we were all sitting together as in the old days of the Agora and we were discussing philosophy. This population was in total despair just this morning. Today we are feeling like we live in a normal town where good things can happen. Maybe tonight we will go to sleep and look forward to waking up for the first time since we became ill, if we only had some proper food.'

Nikos touched the shoulder of Kimon in empathy but kept his back turned to Manoussos. The priest knew there was no more to be said to Nikos today and turned to leave.

'Nikos, I am here to serve. I will do whatever it is you require, all you need do is ask.'

Nikos slammed his book shut and walked away to the refuge of his hut, furious with himself all the way. He knew he was acting like a child but at that moment he did not care. He felt he was entitled to a bad mood and he was frustrated so he let his rage churn him up within.

If Nikos wanted to see Spinalonga run along the lines of an orderly ancient city state then he needed to source food or find a way to have the fish lifted out of the water, the birds to fall from the sky and get the rabbits and goats to fly across from the mainland. He reached his dwelling and was sweating from his anxiety and the fast walk home. He unbuttoned his jacket and almost went to throw the book across the floor but checked himself. In his entire lifetime he had never thrown a book, to him that was as bad as burning them.

The package that Manoussos had handed him from his mother fell to the floor and the bag of Alikhan fell out from under his jacket, cheering up the dark place with its red embroidery. Nikos knew enough of the Cyrillic script to be able to read the little tag that was poking out from the bag, he could read the name easily, Alikhan Azamatov, Berkutchi.

Father Manoussos walked into the ruined church, his reunion with Nikos had not gone quite as he had hoped but he had time to work on that. He rested his hands on his hips and looked around him as he tried to work out how and where to make a start on rebuilding the utter ruin that was once the church when Nikos burst through the doorway panting as if he had run a marathon.

'Manoussos, you said if I needed anything to just come and ask.'

'Of course Nikos, what is it?'
'I need you to help me catch an eagle.'

Chapter 7. Pavlos

The Greek prison system of the nineteen thirties was not clogged. Petty crime, spousal abuse and fraud were not even investigated. Even some killings were not classed as murders because they were often reported as accidents and also not investigated. For someone to be imprisoned during such times usually meant they were a pretty nasty character, like Pavlos Damnatakis.

Once, not too long ago, a pretty young woman named Irena Venetis was out walking to the bakery so as to bring bread to her mother. She was dressed in her best blue dress and her skirts swished around her ankles as she walked. Young Miss Venetis looked charming. She had begged to be allowed to wear her mother's dangling earrings with the matching necklace and bracelet of golden florins even though it was not the done thing.

Someone might see her so bedecked with gold and think she was already betrothed. Her mother didn't want to risk her daughter's chances of making a good match.

'Please Mama, I will only wear them to the bakery and back. Let me feel what it is like to wear such fine things and pretend I am already a married woman.' Her mother permitted her to adorn with the gold, what was the harm in it after all?

Pavlos was standing on the street corner looking out for a victim whose pocket to pick when he caught sight of the glint of gold coming towards him. He also noticed the lovely creature the gold was adorning. He nestled himself back against a doorway and waited for her to come closer. The sun was in her eyes so she didn't see him leaning back into the doorway until he reached out a filthy paw to attempt to snatch the bracelet from the girl's wrist. She screamed and bolted away but Pavlos leapt back into the shadows. He liked what he saw so why rush? He watched her rush into the bakery and rush out again laden with breads.

He had seen where she had gone and followed her to her house and watched through the windows as she dumped the bread on the kitchen table and sat and sobbed in the aftershock of the attack that almost happened. He ducked his head so she wouldn't see him when she left the kitchen to go into another room. Pavlos stepped quietly to the back door and then walked into the house as casually as if he owned it. Within a few strides he had located her bedroom and found her removing the jewelry. She did not have time to scream. He covered her mouth with his hand and with the other reached out to grab the gold but found the sensation of a young woman's smooth skin too irresistible to walk away from.

He pushed her onto her pretty brass bed with its sheets of embroidered pink roses, ripped open her dress, pinned her tiny frame down and thrust himself into her. Her whimpers of agony only made him feel more powerful and he was grinning as he pounded into the tiny girl so hard that if she had lived she would never had been able to bear children.

When her whimpers turned into screams he placed his huge rough hands over her delicate face and pressed hard until the screaming stopped and she stopped struggling. He was surprised he had killed her, it had not been his intent but it was a convenience. He now had what he wanted and she would not be around to lay any blame. He was walking out of her room when her little brother ran in from playing outside, as soon as the boy saw the wild looking man he ran out again.

The rapist chased him, caught him, picked him up and smashed him against the stone wall of the house crushing the little boy's head.

'Bah, I hate these complications.'

Pavlos exhaled a deep breath and wandered through the house stuffing his pockets with anything of value. He stopped in the kitchen, picked up a big knife and sliced a fat slice of the freshly baked bread that Irena Venetis had brought as her final chore. Screams from outside interrupted his thievery. The mother had returned from church to find her young son brains splattered on the back veranda. The evil intruder quickly snuck up to her from behind and clapped his ugly, bloodied hands over her mouth to stop her screaming. He dragged her into the house and stabbed her into silence.

He was still in the house when the father of the Venetis family returned home from his chores. He had rushed home to prepare for his name day celebrations, his sister was coming to visit and he knew his wife needed help with setting up the lamb to be put onto the spit to roast.

He did not get to see the sight of his young son's smashed body like the little son of Hector and Andromache thrown onto the city walls of Troy nor did he see the face of his angel daughter now turned a mottled purple, and he was blessed not to see the love of his life, whose body he pressed against each evening, now lying on the kitchen floor with her intestines lying next to her. What he did see was that the long iron skewer for the spit that had been standing to attention in the courtyard was not in its place. He had put it there this morning in preparation for passing it through the whole lamb he had over his shoulders.

He slumped the lamb carcass onto the outdoor table and looked around to find the skewer but didn't have time to fully turn around before the devil himself rushed at him and pushed the skewer into him, straight into his heart which would have broken had he seen what had happened to his family. He slumped onto the outdoor table too, right next to the carcass of lamb he was going to feed to his guests that night.

The killer had taken more than lives and some trinkets, he had also contracted the leprosy they themselves did not know they were carrying. Pavlos was only caught because he was not smart enough to go to a jeweler in another district to try to sell his booty. The jeweler recognized the gold jewelry. He personally had sold it to the victims. Pavlos was imprisoned that very day. His victims were of the percentage of the population that were carriers but had yet to manifest any symptoms but in the murderer the symptoms showed up quickly.

'Transfer the prisoner to Spinalonga,' came the demand from the prison doctor. Pavlos was furious. He had quickly established himself as one of the top dogs in jail and was enjoying himself along with the three meals a day and the decent bed that he did not have to scrounge for every night.

'If you come close I will spit on you,' was the response of Pavlos to the interruption in his routine when the guards came to take him away. But the guards were not that easily deterred. They merely aimed their guns at him.

'You are leaving here Damnatakis, you can leave on a boat or you can leave in a box, you decide.'

Pavlos didn't want to leave but also was not ready to die. He put his hands up over his head to signify acquiescence.

'Turn around and put your hands behind your back.' They cuffed him and led him out of the prison on a chain.

'Is there a jail on the island?' One guard asked the other.

'No his disease is his sentence, he is both isolated from society and on a death row of sorts.'

'Isn't why I am asking occurring to you? What about the other sick people, don't they have enough to worry about without a murdering rapist among them?'

'Just fill in your forms and get on with your work. These people are already dead. We have the living to think about.'

'Well shouldn't we be informing the medical authorities or communicating directly with Spinalonga? These people have a right to know they will soon have a demon among them.'

'You can't do that.' The senior guard offered.

'You might write to them but we discourage it. They might write back to us and drool all over the paper in an attempt to be evil and share their misery.'

The guard looked heavenward and stretched out his arms in an imploring gesture and the senior guard realized his exaggeration.

'Okay we have spoken enough, let's go.'

The action that needed to be taken was simple, lepers go to leper colonies. But the guard with a conscience did write a letter to the Department of Health outlining his concerns about placing such a vicious criminal into the leper colony. His letter was opened by a nurse on temporary office duty after a distinguished service in the hospital tents of the battlefields. She read the letter, folded it and put in into her pocket. Her name was Angela Venetis.

Back on Spinalonga Pavlos had beckoned his little team of thugs to follow him and to leave the others who were still crowded around Nikos.

'But Pavlos he talks of things that are of benefit to us. I want to feel useful again, before I got this curse I was a stonemason, I helped build houses, now I help you battle the sick for scraps.'

'So Ikaros, this is how you repay my friendship, by listening to the slick speak of a city boy?'

'He talks sense Pavlos, you talk fear, and I've had enough fear.'

'*Ela* Ikaros, if you've had enough fear go light a candle at church but you can't can you, it's in as much ruin as we are.'

'Can you believe the priest came empty handed?' said one of the others.

'That is the charity of the church for you. I say we show him how we worship, Spinalonga style.'

Chapter 8. Artemis, Goddess of the Hunt

Layman and priest stood on the highest point of Spinalonga and examined the empty sky.

'Nikos, how are we going to do this? We need to be high up near where they keep their nests don't we?' Nikos raised his head and closed his eyes as if in a trance and tried to recall every eagle conversation he had ever had with Alikhan. His response to Manoussos was the same one with which his friend would always start his conversations.

'It is the most difficult thing to train an eagle. You must become like the eagle yourself. An eagle is wise, strong and patient.'

'What if you are not like an eagle, what if you are a goat or a monkey?' Nikos laughed at Manoussos.

'Don't laugh Nikos, I see people all the time, they believe they are lions but really they are sheep.'

'That was another thing that Alikhan used to say.

'Ask yourself first who you are? Do you know who you are?'

They fell silent at the sight of an eagle soaring above them. Nikos smiled to himself. Every day he had watched an eagle soaring over Spinalonga, he was sure it was the same one by the white band across the tail feathers. As if it knew it was being observed it gave a command performance for the two of them. The eagle circled over the sea in graceful curves then did an elegant swerve, swooped down to the surface and plucked a fish right out of the water. The eagle then soared up and away with the large salmon still struggling in its claws.

'Wasn't he magnificent Nikos?'

'Yes, she certainly was.' Nikos smiled in satisfaction.

'That is my eagle, she scouts here every day. This must be her territory. The best hunters are the females Manoussos, they grow bigger, stronger, smarter and wiser than the males.'

'Oh I knew that a long time ago,' chuckled Manoussos. Nikos was still marveling at the sight they had just seen.

'Did you notice how completely in control she was? Her wingspan must have been almost two meters wide! And her glide has so much power.' Manoussos nodded in awe.

'She was like a goddess descending from Mount Olympus.'

'Yes, like Artemis, the goddess of the hunt. That is our eagle Manoussos, our goddess Artemis.'

Nikos had been thinking all night about how to lay the bait to try to entice Artemis to come in close. Getting any bait was difficult. Even if they both sacrificed a full month's allowance to order a fresh chicken through the boatman the entire population of Spinalonga would lynch them for it as soon as the boat left. He still had to find a way to deal with the crooked clerk but first the best thing to do was stick to the plan of sourcing more food on their own.

Nikos had decided to keep his eagle hunting a secret from everyone for two reasons. He did not want to get their expectations up in case he failed. The task he had set himself was a big challenge he might not be able to carry out. It would not be fair to give the promise of fresh fish and meat every day and then not be able to deliver the promise. He knew nothing about catching eagles or hunting and here he was trying to do both.

The other reason was until he had succeeded in his mission he had to keep the bag of Alikhan safe and out of the hands of Pavlos. He would not care what it was for or what it meant to Nikos. Pavlos would just take it because he wanted to.

Nikos had been watching Artemis the eagle every day for weeks. He had come to recognize her by the white band across her tail feathers. He also liked her style. She operated in the way he did. She was a brilliant tactician. She would first check the terrain, scouting out the best conditions and the best catch then strike hard and fast, and leave.

Watching her helped alleviate his hunger. There was simply not enough food. Already he had to do his belt up a further two notches and he had only been on Spinalonga for three weeks. Finding food for himself was challenge enough, where was he going to find a suitable enough bait to tempt an eagle? Manoussos patted Nikos on the shoulder as he walked away. Anyone else would have said something obvious like, 'I am going to the church to try to do some cleaning so I will see you tomorrow.' Not Manoussos, he said it with a gesture and a look his eyes.

Nikos went to sit on the walls of the old fortress to watch his eagle. He had been getting to know her better and better each day. Today's watching was different. Artemis was circling closer to Spinalonga than he had ever seen her do before. It was exciting to think that she was right above him now. Her wingspan was greater than the height of a man. He took an inward breath of admiration just as he had done when a truly beautiful woman had walked past him. It was a surprisingly similar attraction which produced a surprisingly similar effect. Not of sexual attraction, it was more like a feeling that he wanted to be near her, close to her, and for her to know that he was worth knowing, but she would always be a magnificent mystery. Just as he had admired curves then, he did now. And just like a woman, she was captivating.

But what was she hunting on Spinalonga? He went to the edge of the fort walls and looked over to see what was below. There stood Ikaros, wearing his cousin's hat of hare-fur. He was scouting the coastline. It was a common thing for the residents of Spinalonga to do. Sometimes interesting or useful things washed up on the shore of the tiny beach. Ikaros was walking up and down to search every centimeter.

It was the hat that was interesting. The hat was of the fur of the hare but the design and coloring of the hat also made it look like a hare, but it was only obvious if one viewed it from above. From where Nikos was standing it appeared as if Ikaros was wearing an animal on his head. Artemis too, thought she was looking at a real hare. He watched in fascination as she swooped down to begin her dive at her prey but Ikaros heard Pavlos yelling for him. He uttered a curse at having been interrupted and ducked through Dante's gate.

Artemis was clearly surprised by the sudden disappearance of her target. Nikos watched her jerk her majestic head in momentary surprise but she smoothly eased up and floated off to scan other parts of the area for a prey that would not dart away. He kept watching as the magnificent she-raptor turned her regal head back towards the island as if to say,

'I'll be back.'

Nikos had found his bait. The only problem was how to get the hat from Ikaros without arousing any suspicion in Pavlos.

'Nice hat *malaka*.'

Ikaros was startled. '*Malaka* yourself, are you hiding in every corner? Don't you have a regular place to sit? Do you have to go around scaring the souls out of people?'

'I like surprises. Now give me the hat.'

'Do us all a favor and go jump off the cliffs of Spinalonga.' Ikaros said as he kept walking along.

Pavlos didn't like being brushed off so he reached out to grab the hat off Ikaros's head but Ikaros ducked down just in time making Pavlos lose his footing and tumble over. He bellowed in frustration and lunged at Ikaros and the two men fell together and rolled on the ground gouging and gripping at each other.

This was the scene Nikos walked into when he descended from the top of the island to try to find Ikaros and to try to find a way to allow him to borrow the hat without giving away the secret of what he was doing. The hat had fallen from Ikaros' head when they began fighting and was lying right in front of Nikos's feet like a little rug.

In the meantime a whole group had collected around the two fighters watching the battle. No-one bothered to pull them apart, they would eventually but for now they were enjoying the excitement too much.

Nikos looked around him, no one had noticed the hat. If he acted fast he could grab it and be out of sight before either of the combatants would see him.

There was another lunge at each other and the crowd roared but they all sensed things were going too far so they all began to get between the men. It was the perfect moment, everybody was turned away from him. He grabbed the hat, tucked it into his shirt and ran to hide it under the floorboards along with Alikhan's bag. It was almost a relief when nobody could find the hat, that way there would be no more fighting. Nikos promised himself that if he did succeed in catching Artemis he would leave the hat in a place where Ikaros would easily find it again but for now he had to sit and keep watching Artemis until the time was right.

Nikos initially felt like an imposter, a pale imitation of the true Berkutchi like Alikhan but the logic of Plato set him straight. Every night when he read Plato he thought to himself how the entire world had read his works and not only learned from them but applied them to their own laws. Did that make them imposters? No. Nikos too would apply the knowledge he had learned from Alikhan as best he could now he finally had some bait.

Watching Artemis in flight was mesmeric. She commanded the sky. Even among other eagles she stood out. Both men were awe struck just by watching her. Nikos had no option but to enlist Manoussos but he did not regret his decision. Manoussos was a man of few words and those he did speak had weight. Most importantly of all, the men enjoyed each other's company even if they had nothing to say. They were just as happy to sit in silence together, a true sign of friendship.

After just a few weeks on the island Nikos already had to move his belt so much further in he had to make another hole with a stone and a nail he managed to pull out of an old piece of timber. He was worried about how much he had weakened physically and he could see how the island and its lack of decent living conditions had sapped the psychological strength out of everyone else. That was something he also had to do something about but the first was getting some food. Manoussos would supply the extra strength he knew he would need to catch Artemis.

'Well Nikos, you still haven't told me how we are going to go about catching this eagle?'

'Haven't you noticed anything after all the days we have spent up here watching her?' Manoussos lifted his head and made the 'tsk' sound in the way Greeks say no.

'You haven't noticed how she does not waste a single movement? She understands her own body. Look how she is scanning the seas now for a fish. This is the right time to lay the bait Manoussos. She is out for the hunt. Let's go!'

They went to the very highest point on Spinalonga, the flat stretch above the fortress walls, and laid the hare-fur hat on the ground on the most open part of the space. Nikos had tied two strings to it and handed them to Manoussos.

'Here, be the puppet master and jiggle these now and again to make it look like the hare is moving around.' Nikos made sure everything else was laid out and ready. Satisfied they were prepared for what he hoped would come he then sat back out of view behind the rocks and waited.

The items in Alikhan's bag were all laid out in a neat row on the ground. They had unfolded the net, the blanket lay in wait and the hood was in Nikos's pocket as was the short leash, the strong piece of leather they would use to tie to its leg. The well padded leather glove and wrist support were off to the side on standby.

'Nikos, once we throw the net over it we must secure it down. Such a powerful bird could just fly away.'

'I have already got the stones ready to place all around. We must be quick in doing so.'

'Then we also cover her with the blanket?'

'Yes, she must be kept in the dark.'

Nikos looked up.

'There she is. She has seen it. Look she is circling.'

Nikos knew exactly what she would do. He had spent so much time watching her he was now familiar with her methods. He whispered to Manoussos.

'If she stops circling and just hovers for a moment it means she is about to strike. Once she begins her dive she will tuck her wings in around her till she looks like a big teardrop. She will become like a merciless big bullet shooting down her target.'

They sat back in their shadowed hiding places and watched her.

Nikos had placed the bait well, in a place of good visibility and the hat was stuffed underneath with rags so it looked like a plump and juicy treat. With Manoussos maneuvering the strings it looked as if it was a hare having a lazy graze on the grass. It was only a matter of seconds before the great raptor saw the bait. Both men saw the very moment the eagle spotted the bait and they both reached for the net at the same time. She tilted forward slightly and formed into a great droplet, like the sky was shedding a tear.

From the ground the men could hear a sound like a great gust of wind getting louder and louder as the bird plummeted to the ground in a controlled and targeted trajectory. Just before she reached the ground she pulled up and extended out her feet to expose her talons which were spread out as deadly daggers ready to pierce the flesh of the bait.

Nikos could feel his heart pounding in his chest. Manoussos did the sign of the cross and both men tried to steady their breathing like athletes before sprinting out at the start of a race. She was about to impale the bait upon her claws when the men struck. They had each taken two corners of the net and then sprung forth to throw the net over her the minute they had seen her approach the ground.

In her surprise at the unexpected event she had let go of the bait in the split second before the net draped over her and Nikos's adrenalin charged reflexes allowed him to slip his hand under to retrieve the hat. He had remembered something that Alikhan had once said.

'Keep your eagle confused in the first few days. Keep her in the dark so that when you arrive to give her food she will come to you like a love starved woman.'

'How did you manage that?' asked an impressed Manoussos as he looked at the hat in Nikos's hands.

'I don't know!' He laughed in relief.

'But for now we need to wait for a while until our Artemis calms down.' She was flapping her great wings and they had so much power in them the men were fearful she would take off and take the net with her.

They stopped speaking so as to focus on their work. In well rehearsed movements they reached for the large, heavy stones they had at the ready and placed the stones all around the edges of the net to weight it down. This gave Artemis less room to struggle and would also cause her to tire more quickly. Once the net was secure and Artemis was clearly weary, they threw the heavy cloth over the net and worked just as quickly to place several stones around that too, leaving just enough gaps to allow a little air in, but no light.

They stood back to observe their work. Their eagle trap looked like a little burial mound. Manoussos looked at Nikos then raised one eyebrow. Nikos answered his silent question.

'She will stay there for as long as it takes. We have to get her to calm down enough first to be able to put the little hood on her.' Manoussos winced. He had seen the size of her claws and beak.

'She is a big girl Nikos.'

'She sure is.' But he had not taken his gaze off the mound before them. She had stopped struggling quickly which gave him a good indication of the quality of the hunter they had caught. Just as in her natural realm and now in her captivity, she did not waste her movements. There were no energy expending useless gesticulations, Nikos sensed she was saving her strength in order to adjust to the new conditions enforced upon her and then access it again to use in maximum efficiency for an escape, exactly as he would. It was for that reason he did not attempt to lift the cloth and try to put the hood onto her just yet. She would use her reserved energy and rip him to shreds. No, now was not the time.

Night fell and Manoussos again patted his friend on the shoulder to declare he was leaving to go to his church to prepare for *Esperinos*.

'Why are you going? Stay here to keep me company. You know there will be no-one there.'

'We both have work to do. You stay here and build the trust of your Artemis and I must build trust too. They will come eventually. They will come.'

'Not tonight they won't. Stay here with me and watch over Artemis.' But Father Manoussos was already walking away.

Nikos made sure Artemis had just enough air and then settled down for the night all the while speaking to Artemis in soft tones throughout the night as if she were his paramour. Manoussos was right, it had to be just him and her. She had to learn his voice, she had to learn to come to him, and she had to learn to trust him.

Manoussos walked towards his church. The first time he had gone there he had to ask directions from Ariadne.

'I will take you there Father but it will not be of much use to you. It is barely standing and even if it was in good condition no one will attend. None of the residents of Spinalonga believe any more.'

'Then I am truly needed here.'

She led him to a small building so utterly ruined it looked more like a bomb site than a church.

'It's a real mess isn't it father?'

Manoussos smiled in wonder.

'It is a miracle it is still standing considering when it was last used, it must have been before the Turks got here for sure. We are looking at many years of neglect my child.'

'Well it looks like it too.' Ariadne said as she began to limp away but out of the corner of his eye he caught that she had turned around, hesitated then quickly did the sign of the cross. Manoussos smiled widely at the confirmation of something he already knew. Rituals gave people comfort and a sense of belonging to their past and a foundation upon which to build their future.

Manoussos struggled to get the door open even though he was well aware he could simply step through one of the gaping holes in the walls. He pushed at it hard with his shoulder until the door wrenched open and he burst through, almost toppling over. The fresh sea air swarming into the space clashed with the dormant dust and caused it to churn up in waves. Through the haze Manoussos could see the ceiling had partly caved in and over time the elements had taken their toll. He entered, initially blinded by the swirl, and walked in to the middle of the church to take a good look around. Through the haze he saw the ikons were so badly weather damaged they had become no more than dark smudges.

The dust began to clear and Manoussos noticed a patch of color glowing through the dust particles. He knew immediately from its location at the entrance to the Nave that it was the ikon of the patron saint of the church. He went to stand before it and fell to his knees to give praise to God. The ikon was pristine. It was as if were freshly painted. In the Greek Orthodox Church such an event is classed as a miracle. Manoussos gave worship to Saint Panteleimon, the doctor and healer, kissing his hands and asking for the love and courage required to heal the broken souls of Spinalonga.

Pavlos and Ikaros swayed in the doorway,

'Hey priest did you get given the funeral service too?'

'*Kali mera*. No I am healthy, thank God. I am here to serve you. Please tell the others there will be service tomorrow.'

'Are you sure you're healthy priest? Take a look around you, the church is about to fall down.'

But they did leave to tell everyone. They did not tell them not to attend service but to come and scorn the priest.

Manoussos did not allow the absolute squalor of the church to dismay him. Nor did he fret over the condition of the little house near the church he had decided to make his rectory. The thing that was eating at him was the sheer bitterness in the eyes of the people. The rejection of them by church and state had scarred them deeply. Getting them to come back to church would not be easy but he would do whatever it would take to make it happen. He would give his first service with the church as it was. He had to show that he was determined. The dust and debris were not the obstacles.

One thing that pleased him greatly was that the bell was still in the bell tower, and it worked! At 7.30am the next morning he rang the bell to tell the world of Spinalonga that church service was commencing.

And people came.

Manoussos was so overjoyed when he saw the little crowd gathered outside the church that he had to hide in the sanctuary for a few seconds while he did a little jump. He gave thanks to God and commenced the service with confidence. After ten or fifteen minutes of spirited recital and chanting Manoussos saw that no one had come in yet they were all still gathered outside. He took a deep breath and continued. When he began to recite the prayers the crowd outside drowned out his words with moans and groans terrifying enough to raise the dead.

He stopped. They stopped. He started again louder and more determined than before but the wails and moans became so loud and woeful he thought he was in the underworld itself. Manoussos continued the vocal battle right through until the time came to offer communion. He stood there with the sacred vessels in his hands waiting for anyone to come forward. He watched the door in the hope that someone might walk in, he even tried willing them to come in but only heard more moans and groans.

Just as well, he thought to himself. He'd had the suspicion that no one would attend so he had only poured a small amount of wine into the communion cup. Why waste the precious Commanderia Father Stavros had given him as a farewell gift. He stood there a little longer in the welcome silence then went back into the sanctuary.

He had to complete the communion ritual. He had offered the blood of Christ now he had to offer the flesh. He blessed the loaf of bread he had kneaded himself and baked in a pit he had dug in the hard

111

ground behind his new residence. It had taken him five hours to dig a pit twenty five centimeters deep using the lid of a saucepan. It took a further hour to get the stones with which he lined the pit to become white hot and then he baked the bread in its pan within the pit.

All throughout the process he had an audience and he knew it but it never showed. He had pretended not to notice the nosy onlookers peering over the walls. He knew he had to make an impression for being determined and meticulous.

He began to cut his specially baked loaf of bread in the traditional way a priest must. He had already first cut out the centre, the lamb, and then cut the sections devoted to the Panayia and the angels then cut up the rest of the loaf into bite size cubes and placed them in the basket. The minute he placed the basket in its place before the Royal Gate the onlookers rushed into the church screeching like the Furies, grabbed as many pieces of bread as they could then rushed out again leaving the basket spinning on the ground like a tossed coin slowly coming to rest.

Father Manoussos picked up the twirling basket and reflected to himself on his first service.

'Well, that went quite well!'

For the second service of Father Manoussos of Saint Panteleimon of Spinalonga the only attendants were the damp smudged ikons on the walls. There would have been some rats but whenever they were seen they were caught. Nikos had caught as many as possible to offer Artemis as rewards and Pavlos would also catch them then trade them, mostly to the women, for sex. One lady had found a way to grill them over hot stones and then serve them on a bed of thistles.

They tasted almost as good as the quails the tavernas served on feast days.

This silence of this service was much more eerie. At least the first time there was an interaction of sorts, macabre as it was. Today the silence was louder than the moans and groans of the hecklers. Manoussos went through the entire service with as much passion as if he was being scrutinized by the Patriarch himself but nobody came, not even for the free bread. Manoussos completed the service and went to leave to see Nikos but Pavlos was waiting outside the church with his band of followers.

'How was service Father?' he taunted.

Manoussos smiled at the group,

'Thank you for asking my child, it was very good practice for me for the time when you will all attend. Very soon this church will be full.' Pavlos rested his arm across the doorway but it also pinned Manoussos to the spot.

'So tell me Father is it still the custom for the priest to offer the communion wine to all from the communion cup?'

'Of course'

'And is it still the custom to use one gold spoon to offer it to the entire congregation?'

'Yes,' said Manoussos warily.

Pavlos's voice became very low and very calm. 'And is it still the custom for the priest to drink the remainder of the wine in the cup after communion is over?'

'Yes.' Manoussos tried to say it with confidence but he could barely get it out in a whisper. Pavlos was enjoying tyrannizing the priest. He was what he was, a torturer.

'I tell you what Father, you get this placed cleaned up and I will attend, we all will. I'll see to it,' he turned to face his retinue menacingly, 'and we will all take communion.'

He leant right in close to the slight priest who stayed as serene as a saint in martyrdom. Pavlos leant in even closer till Manoussos could smell his foul breath.

'And then we will stand back and wait for you to drink all of the leftover wine in the communion cup.'

Manoussos did not as much as blink. Pavlos was unnerved by the priest's ability to be unnerved but was even more unsettled when one of his gang, Makis, risked the ire of Pavlos in a deep but conscious need that all mankind has to assert his own self worth.

'Father, if you drink all the wine we will not only keep coming but we might even consider helping you rebuild this church.'

Ikaros couldn't help himself, emboldened by the courage of his friend he too wanted to prove his worth.

'I was a very good stonemason once Father, I can fix these walls.'

'And I can paint,' yelled another.

Pavlos clipped them both around the ears and dragged them away and the others followed. Pavlos was swearing at them all the way. Things had not gone to plan. His plan had been to intimidate but the little priest with his simple ways had foiled him without even trying and in doing so had inspired action in the others. Pavlos did not turn around to look at Manoussos. He did not need to look at him to know that the look of concern on the priest's face had been replaced by a broad smile.

Chapter 9. Flying Fish

For ten days and nights straight in a row Nikos sat by Artemis.

'You must appear in the square Nikos, people are questioning your absence.' Manoussos was right, the people had been enjoying and expecting more of the street philosophy.

'Tell them I am sick, keep everyone away. Tell them I have the flu. Lepers shun illness, they already have enough.'

It worked for a few days but the people were asking again and offering to stop by with scraps of food to aid his recovery so twice he made brief appearances to remove any suspicions of anything unusual, then he returned to Artemis.

Twice a day Manoussos came to hand over mice or lizards for Artemis and to bring some food to Nikos, usually the regular watery lentil soup that was the standard meal on Spinalonga.

'It must be difficult for you my friend. You have so much work to do of your own and how are you managing Maria's questions about my absence?' Manoussos paused just enough for Nikos to notice the cloud of concern that crossed Manoussos' face.

'What is it Manoussos? What is wrong with Maria?'

'She has fallen ill, her disease is progressing. She does ask about you and I tell her you are ill too and that when you are both feeling stronger you will see each other again but for now you both need your rest.'

Nikos busied himself chopping up the lizards and mice into chunks. Keeping busy not only got things done but helped overcome things he could do nothing about right now, like Maria's health. He had to work even faster to get a food supply going, which was the way he could best help Maria. Nikos had been speaking to Artemis almost constantly since her capture. He fed her the chopped up bits of reptile and vermin by lifting up the blanket just a touch and slipping the pieces of meat through the spaces in the net. He would fumble with the little hood in his pocket wondering every minute how he was going to place it on the head of Artemis.

Nikos had the perfect eyrie prepared for her. It was ready and waiting for her when, or if, he ever tamed her. He had moved to the furthest house of all and it had a wall of rock behind it forming a natural courtyard. In it was a dead tree, a perfect place for a perch for an eagle. But he first had to get her there. Nikos had constructed a perch for her on the top of Spinalonga as well. It was a hardy tree branch with plenty of space for her to spread out her wings. There were natural rock shelter forms up there too, almost like caves. It was up there in the cave like shelter that Nikos slept and sat with Artemis.

Nikos sat holding the little hood.

'Maybe it's time to try now?' Nikos lifted the blanket slightly to see if there would be any resistance from Artemis. Not so much as a quiver came from her. Manoussos held the blanket up so Nikos could be kneeling at the ready. Nikos tried to sneak a peek at her but could not see much in the darkness. He stood up to put on the thick leather falconry glove of Alikhan but found he was unable to use his hands freely to place the tiny hood on her.

'I want to take a look at her Manoussos, lift the blanket a little bit more.' She was revealed, sitting there like an outraged goddess kept from her palace, but dignified and solemn. He went to lift the net slowly and had enough of it lifted to be able to reach in to try to touch her.

She struck. Just one of her talons gashed Nikos through his trousers. The pain seared through him like a flame as he screamed. Manoussos dropped the blanket to re-cover Artemis and he ran to Nikos with his arms open wide not knowing what to do. Nikos screamed at him.

'Don't just stand there, piss on it!'

'What! No way, I cannot do such a thing.'

'Oh in the name of God will you just whip out your dick and piss on it. Do you want me to die of an infection? Or do you have another antiseptic lying around?'

Manoussos looked around him to check if anyone was around. No one was looking but Nikos could have cared less if he were in the middle of the town square, his pain was excruciating.

'Hurry up!' Manoussos started fumbling around under his *rassos* and stood there trying to urinate.

'I don't think I can. Maybe if you turn away'

Nikos let out a roar that would have raised the dead which was the impetus Manoussos needed to release his stream onto the bleeding ankle of Nikos. Both men sighed in relief then both men fell to the ground laughing like they had never laughed before.

'Can you imagine if anyone had seen us, what would that have looked like?' They laughed even harder till Nikos stood back up again.

'I think that was Artemis telling us she needs a little more time.' He picked up a rock and began scanning the ground. Manoussos understood what he was doing.

'Just make sure to catch one for Ikaros too. He has been doing all my catching for me. I told him you are sick and need the nourishment. '

'I just hope I can be fast enough to catch a lizard.' Manoussos smiled.

'Listen to your priest Nikos, you caught an eagle. You can do anything.'

Nikos dragged a large hollowed out rock to the blanket, filled it with water and pushed it beneath the blanket. Did eagles drink? He did not know but would soon find out if she never came to drink. He had managed to catch five good sized lizards too and had placed them by the edge of the blanket so she could smell there was food nearby. The movements he could see taking place beneath the blanket were definitely slower since her capture. He sat with Artemis, talking to her, watching the lump make minor undulations under the blanket all the time.

All through the night and most of the next day Nikos fed her as he always had done, by tossing the little pieces of meat to her under the blanket. He decided to try to get her to feed from his own hand. Each time he offered her a piece of meat, with the other hand, he lifted the blanket just a little. He cooed at Artemis.

'Come here sweet goddess, here I have something for you.' The lump in the centre of the blanket inched forward. Nikos noticed the movement and held his breath while he kept his hand steady at the opening. He moved it just a little further back so in order for Artemis to reach her food she would have to poke her head out from under the blanket.

Nikos blinked and he missed it. She'd grabbed it. Nikos could hear the crunching of lizard bones, then silence.

'My girl was hungry! I can't have my goddess unhappy. Let it not be said that Nikos Lambrakis does not look after his women. Come close, have some more.' This time he did not want to miss it so he gave all his focus to the edge of the blanket and there she appeared. She revealed her sensuous curved head and took the lizard from his hand as delicately as if she were a siren selecting a diamond ring from a tray. Throughout every night that she was beneath the blanket he stayed awake when Artemis slept, which was most of the time. Whenever she stirred he was there offering food. She woke early, with the sun, and Nikos saw to it that she ate her breakfast before he ate his.

On this morning, something told him to try again at attempting to put on the hood. Nikos pulled the hood out of his pocket and had it at the ready.

'Here is another piece of meat for you. Here, come close to me. Nice and close, yes.' He lifted up the net gently and while she was nibbling and was preoccupied. He held his breath as she angled her proud head to look directly at him with her deep set large eyes. She blinked, then went back to eating. Nikos slipped the hood over her head as easily as one would stroke the hair of a beloved child. The hood had little side extensions that kept her eyes covered. He held his breath while he monitored her movements. She did not seem disturbed in any way by the hood. He remembered Alikhan saying,

'This will keep her calm and heighten her other senses. It will make her tune in to your voice.' He exhaled his relief and decided to take the risk of lifting the blanket off one corner and take a good look at his catch. She looked a little wilted.

'Hey beauty, you deserve another one.' She could eat with the hood on so Nikos rewarded her with the other lizard. Manoussos was climbing up to check on progress and the men waved at each other. When he got closer he could see what had happened.

'That went well. I had my special ointment on standby just in case.' Manoussos patted his groin.

'Good to know.'

He had already prepared the stake days ago. Manoussos had hammered a large stake into the ground nice and deep and to it had tied one end of the long leash.

'Now the real training begins. It is time for Artemis to be flying again.'

Nikos had to plan the first flight but first he had to go and show his face around the town again and he had to check on Maria. He took a look at Artemis all tied to her leashes and sensed she would be fine there for the moment. When he returned she might be ready to start the training.

Maria was sitting on her doorstep getting some sun.

'Oh sister you are looking well.'

She smiled a weak smile at him.

'You look good too brother. I am glad you are feeling better.' He offered both his hands out to her to help her up and she linked her arm through his as they set off for a stroll. There was some activity in the square so they investigated.

There was a new arrival on Spinalonga which normally didn't cause too much fuss but this arrival was a woman from Athens, named Athena, and she was a beauty. She was holding a leash to which was attached a very appealing little dog. Athena had brought him along as he had been a loving companion in her old life and she needed him to be one for her terrifying new life.

Nikos recognized the breed, it was a King Charles Cavalier spaniel. He had often seen the society matrons of Athens strolling with them around the fashionable streets of Kolonaki. Athena had also brought along a lemon tree in a pot.

'How lovely to see a lemon tree again,' Maria had said when she and Nikos welcomed Athena.

'It is my gift to the island. I thought it might be useful. It is a lovely evergreen tree to look at so we can all feel a little better, lemons are so wonderful for so many uses and it has beautiful perfumed blossoms. I like things that are useful and beautiful.' Nikos was taken by her charming logic. As far as he knew no one had ever brought a gift to the island.

'Thank you Athena for your very thoughtful gift. Once you are settled in please come by for a coffee.'

He couldn't believe he had said it. Behind Athena's back Maria raised her eyebrows at Nikos and his unexpected invitation.

'Thank you I would like that very much.' More eyebrow raising from Maria.

'I must settle my puppy first into his new surroundings.' Maria was petting the dog.

'How nice to have such exuberance here on Spinalonga, he is adorable. What is his name?'

'This is Achilles, my little warrior.' Ariadne and Eva came and they gushed over Athena and Achilles.

'Come let us help you settle in, we will take you to one of the houses.'

Nikos had to return to Artemis. He had more enthusiasm in his steps as he rushed up to her while the others had their attention diverted by the new arrival.

That evening Pavlos got to her. He saw the pretty new arrival and headed straight for her once he saw she was alone. He raided her bags for any food and money. She had five thousand drachmas in her purse and roast lamb and fresh fruit in her basket.

Athena tolerated all his bullying, she protested at the robbery, stamped her feet at the loss of her food but turned into one of the Furies when Pavlos picked up her dog. She flew at him but he punched her away. She got up again so dazed she initially lunged at the wall instead of at him but he was ready for her. He grabbed her and spun her around then pushed her onto the floor so hard she cracked her head. He punched her hard again and spun her around to turn her face down as he got on top of her and put his ugly great face next to hers. He became excited as she sobbed hysterically.

'Please leave my doggy alone.'

His response was to moan into her ear as he released himself from his tattered trousers and roughly pushed into her. Afterwards Athena lay on the floor numb from the attack, unable to move from the pain she could only watch helplessly as Pavlos picked up the glossy, plump dog, pulled a knife out of his pocket, turned towards her and in a mocking tone said,

'I'd love to stay and chat but I have a lunch appointment.'

The last thing Athena saw before she passed out was the sight of Pavlos bringing the knife to her precious puppy's neck. Athena entered her trauma as a nun takes vows of silence to enter a convent. It was a better place to be than any other so there she would stay. She remained coiled in her fetal position until Maria and Eva found her and bathed her and fed her thin soup and bread.

Nikos came down from the peak to look for the juiciest bait he could find but was frustrated at every step. He even spoke out aloud to himself,

'Where am I possibly going to find a juicy piece of meat to reward Artemis for taking her first flight?'

Pavlos was hard at work butchering up the dog and had chosen to do so in the centre of the *platia*. He underestimated the hunger of the others. They did not see a cute dog, someone's once beloved pet and companion. They just saw meat. When Nikos entered the square he too smelt the blood, the smell of butchery. Then he saw the glistening red flesh.

'What has he done?' Manoussos said from behind Nikos.

'He has proven he is what he is, as stupid as he is cruel. The Greeks have a word for it, *koutoponeiros*, stupid and sly. His need to show his cunning and cruelty blinds him to his own failings. He makes the same mistakes over and over again, he has become predictable.'

No sooner had Nikos spoken the words the trouble he knew Pavlos would get into had begun. He readied himself to zoom in and snatch a piece of the mystery meat. Where it had come from and what it was did not bother him. The gods had provided an answer to his problem and he was not going to question it. He leant against a wall and waited. It took less time than he thought. One of Pavlos's thugs called out from across the *platia*.

'I'll get the fire ready for our feast.'

'What feast *malaka*? This is my dinner and I am not sharing.' The fight began, as usual, and as usual the crowd gathered around. Nikos had just enough time to snatch pieces of the meat and run away with the priest following him, also pocketing pieces of puppy into his *rassos*.

Artemis cocked her regal head as she sensed Nikos nearby, she could smell the meat. Nikos busied himself cutting it up into chunks. But Nikos was hurting, not from the exertion but from the pain of the memories of Alikhan. He spoke out aloud, as he often did, as if Alikhan were with him.

'*Ach!* Alikhan where are you now? Am I even anywhere near to doing any of this the right way?' He had to stop cutting up the meat and hang his head in weary grief. Doubt invaded his mind.

'I don't think I can do this my friend.'

A shadow crept across his him, blocking out the sun.

'What do you think you are feeding, a shark? Look at the size of her beak, cut it up into smaller pieces will you or you will choke your beautiful Artemis before she ever gets to fly again.' Nikos squinted into the sunlight to see who was speaking to him.

'Alikhan?'

'You chose well Nikos, she is glorious. In the past my ancestors would have paid six camels for such a bird.'

He was silhouetted against the sky, his stocky frame, his bristly hair, his ruddy cheeks.

'Good to see you are treasuring my equipment now come on, let's put it to good use. Grab the leash.'

Nikos did not need to ask again, it was Alikhan standing there giving him orders on how to train his eagle. He could question the probabilities of if this was really happening later. Nikos grabbed the leash.

'Now tie one end to your *biyalai*, your glove, there on the iron ring my grandfather himself sewed into place.' Nikos found the small metal ring on the side of the glove and tied the leash to it thanking his own late father silently for showing him how to tie secure knots for the boats.

'I heard that and I will pass on your thanks, now take the other end of the leash and attach it to Artemis.' Nikos hesitated, he turned towards Alikhan.

'Come on Nikos, use your knowledge of the knots from your father. Tie the short leash to Artemis and then tie it to the long leash.' Nikos approached Artemis.

'Don't remove her hood yet. Feed her a piece of meat, once the leash is on feed her another piece. Never let your girl go hungry Nikos. She needs to trust you will always look after her therefore she will look after you.'

Nikos stood up and looked over at Alikhan who seemed to be a lot taller than he was during life. His face was serene and his voice was firm.

'Put the *bardak* on now Nikos so we can get her to fly to you. He tied the wooden wrist support on, it felt awkward.

'Relax you will get used to it. It is more difficult without it. I would say you have about seven kilos of bird here Nikos. You are going to need the extra support. Now, give her one more piece of meat then take her *tomaga* off.'

Tomaga, that's what Alikhan always called the hood Nikos thought to himself as he slipped it off the bird by pulling on its ornate embroidered tab.

'You forgot that it was called a *tomaga* eh Nikos? Okay, now walk back till the leash is stretched out and stand there offering her a piece of meat.' Nikos stood at the end of the extended leash and waited.

First Artemis took an unsure step like the clumsy waddle of a fat woman, legs apart and wings flapping out like a crumpled dress in the wind. Nikos stood firm, holding the piece of meat with one hand up close to the wrist with the *bardak* strapped on. He waited. She took one more step then leapt up like a ballerina and landed on the *bardak*.

Nikos was put off balance by the bulk and the weight of the bird standing on his wrist. He could feel the pinch of her talons through the glove and suddenly the *bardak* did not feel so awkward. He tried to remain composed and calm. He arched his body to accommodate the space she was taking up as well as trying to keep his arm up to hold her. Alikhan's voice came from behind him.

'Quick, give her another piece of meat.' Nikos obeyed.

'And another one. Don't ever be meager with your eagle Nikos.' Nikos rewarded Artemis again.

'Now do it again. Always provide for your girl Nikos.' Alikhan seemed to be melting into the sky, his voice seemed quieter now.

Artemis was balanced comfortably on Nikos's wrist but she was a load and Nikos resigned himself to the fact he would have a sore wrist for a while until he developed some strength in his muscles. He walked over to the perch he had prepared and Artemis hopped onto it as if she had done it many times before. Nikos fed Artemis another piece of meat then walked back till the leash was stretched out and held out another piece of meat.

Did she wink? Nikos was still straining to see if she actually had when she launched into flight and sailed elegantly over to his arm, settled onto his wrist and picked up her piece of meat. Nikos did a little jump of victory and did not need to be told by Alikhan or anyone to do it immediately again but not before rewarding her with another piece of meat.

At the third attempt Artemis flew to him and nestled onto the *bardak* as if she had been doing it for ever.

'Ah Artemis, my goddess, here you deserve this.' He fed her more pieces of the ill fated puppy, grateful at least that the puppy didn't get slaughtered for nothing but that it had played a significant role in the future food supply of Spinalonga.

Nikos looked around to see if the spirit of Alikhan was still with him but he was no longer visible. Nikos angled his head, he could hear something He turned his ear towards the sound to try to tune in to Alikhan's voice. It was now a whisper but it was right in his ear.

'Your eagle is a beautiful goddess Nikos, treat her well. If she doesn't feel like learning something one day let her rest. Try again the next day. Keep feeding her well. Gain her trust. Every time she does what you want, reward her. Let her know she is special just like a woman eh Nikos. And remember that as the hunter trains the eagle so does the eagle train the hunter.'

'Alikhan, what do I do next?'

'Gain her trust. Then progress to your goal, free flight.'

'But?'

'Come on Nikos, just continue until you can sense she is ready. Then just do it. Send her off on a flight.' Nikos looked around him trying to see something but nothing was there. He looked up at the sky and asked the air,

'How will I know if I have gained her trust?'

Out of the clouds came the answer.

'If she comes back.'

Alikhan was gone but his words remained to guide Nikos. Every day, all day for the next nine days Nikos trained with Artemis. Finding rewards for her was not easy. He managed to filch another chunk of the dog meat and burdened Manoussos with more mouse and lizard catching. Through all this Nikos was surviving on lentil soup and some bread but he never left her side. He slept right next to Artemis like a dutiful husband. He whispered words of tenderness into her ear and sang her love songs and lullabies.

On the ninth day Nikos felt as if the sun kissed him awake. Artemis was sitting on her perch in full alertness. Nikos still in his semi slumber reached over and gently removed her *tomaga*.

'*Kali mera thea mou*, good morning my goddess.' Nikos did a lazy stretch and looked out into the clouds garnishing the sky over Spinalonga. The face of Alikhan peeped out from behind one and winked at him. In his surprise he looked over at Artemis and he was positive she winked at him too.

'Okay, I need a coffee.' He got busy rekindling the small fire he kept burning in the shelter of some rocks and brewed himself a double serve. He pulled a bread roll out of his bag. Coffee and a bread roll, the standard breakfast of Greeks from peasants to presidents. He noticed Manoussos had been and gone by the little pile of mice and lizards left by the stone surround of the fire.

'Here Artemis, have some breakfast,' he said as he was about to stand up and take the food over to her.

Artemis jumped off her perch and waddled over to him. She jumped right onto the *bardak*, he had fallen asleep still wearing it, and took the meat. He knew a cue when he saw one. Nikos stood up, careful not to unsettle Artemis who was still on his wrist. He slowly untied the long leash from the short one that was attached to Artemis.

With a great effort he held up his arm high then just as Alikhan had instructed him once long ago before he ever set eyes on Spinalonga, he gave a subtle flick of his wrist to give Artemis lift off. With one great flap of her wings she was airborne. His entire body chilled at the thrill of watching her soar into the blue.

'My eagle. My father always called me his eagle but I am an eagle without wings. Be my wings Artemis.'

He couldn't see her anymore, the sun had swallowed her so there was nothing to do but wait. If he had done a good enough job of making her trust him she would be back, otherwise it was more hunger and waiting to hear news from those to whom he had found a way to send letters.

Chapter 10. Clerical Correspondence

When Nikos hadn't been training an eagle, he had been writing letters.

'We can't both be here, it will be too suspicious. People will begin seeking us out and our mission with Artemis will fail,' was what he said to Manoussos when the priest first offered to sit with him.

'As you wish Nikos. I too have much to do as well as some letters to write.'

'You have paper?'

'Why yes.'

'And pen and envelopes and stamps?'

'But we can't send letters.'

You can't, but I can. I am not a leper, and I need to be able to communicate with the Church.'

'Manoussos! In the name of God!'

Manoussos understood.

'I will bring you some right away.'

'Thank you Manoussos. I have wanted to write letters from the first moment I arrived here when I saw the terrible conditions but was told that letters from lepers were not welcome anywhere. Also I had no idea things were as bad as they are.'

'There is also the problem of Pavlos.'

'Yes, there is also Pavlos.' How was he going to get his letters past Pavlos?

'I haven't thought of a plan yet for how to get the letters in and out safely without Pavlos intercepting them.'

'I have,' said Manoussos.

'I need a chanter and I choose you.'

'How will that get the letters in and out?'

'A chanter needs the texts to read from, you will require the appropriate books.'

'Oh, I see. You send letters out asking for books and the responses come inside the books.' Nikos nodded in understanding.

'But Manoussos there is one thing. Everybody knows you brought so many books to Spinalonga. You made a point of saying you brought along all the texts and a lot of us helped you carry them.'

'I know Nikos, I know. But I think God will forgive me for the terrible accident I am about to cause that will require the replacement of so many of them.'

Pavlos Damnatakis knew the exact schedule of the boatman. Unless he was busy terrorizing someone or had fallen asleep, which mercifully happened often, he was present at many of the boat landings to see who was getting what and he tried to intercept all packages in case they had any money in them. He would help himself to the money and then throw away the package so the receiver never knew if his family had sent him anything and the sender never knew if their gift had been received.

'Manoussos what letters did you say you were going to write?'

'To Father Stavros, the new young priest who took over my duties. I need a few more of the texts.'

'Perfect. Even Pavlos wouldn't bother trying to open a letter from one priest to another. I have reason to believe he can't read anyway. He only wants money.'

The first letter Nikos wrote was to the Department of Health. He demanded to know why the lepers of Spinalonga were referred to as patients yet there was no hospital. Why were there no bandages, antiseptics or walking aids? There was not so much as an aspirin. He finished off the letter stating that he will also write a letter to the League of Nations informing them of the sub human conditions of the patients. He also wrote to the Department of Power, the Department of Social Security and to Metaxas himself, the President of Greece.

'Help, help, there is a fire in the church.'

Father Manoussos was yelling from the church door. He had waited exactly for the time he knew Pavlos and the others would be heading towards the square and would be right outside the church door.

'So what,' said Pavlos as he kept on walking. Others rushed to help. Makis called out to Manoussos.

'Father I will run and bring more help. We will bring water in anything we can find to carry it in.' Ikaros and two more rushed in and began to beat at the flames with the couple of blankets Manoussos had with him. Makis and his helpers showed up quickly and splashed the water over the flames which soon died down. Pavlos leaned against the door watching and offered no help, just as Manoussos knew he would.

'Thank you so much my children. Without you I do not know how I would have managed.'

'What happened father?'

'I was filling up all the lamps with oil and lighting them so I could have a lamp burning before each of the saints as is the custom. I stumbled and knocked one over and the burning oil spread all over the pile of ecclesiastical texts I had put to one side here on the floor. Nikos has volunteered to be my chanter and once he is feeling better he will come and start reading from them. Now they are all gone or too damaged to use.' Manoussos sounded genuinely devastated.

'It will be alright father, can't you send for some new books?'

'Bravo! Thank you for reminding me there is always an answer Ikaros. I will begin writing letters to Father Stavros right away. It will take several letters because so many books were damaged it will take time to discover which ones I need. I best begin immediately.'

Pavlos finally opened his ugly mouth, 'Get your priest friends to send some money not just books.'

'Sadly dear Pavlos they have none to spare, but I also thank you for reminding me. I will ask for them to send a few seeds for herbs that we can grow in pots. We will need basil for the blessings.' Pavlos groaned and walked away muttering obscenities.

On the day the boatman was due Manoussos was standing waiting. There was no Pavlos present. The boatman looked at the white envelope which Manoussos had placed on the stone pier.

'Did you wear gloves when you wrote it?'

'Oh for goodness sake, I am not a leper and even if I were, I have done everything properly.'

The boatman sighed resignedly, put on gloves himself and picked up the letter as if it were a writhing snake.

'Please post it today, as soon as you get back.' The boatman looked at Manoussos and shrugged,

'I might forget.'

The priest pulled the few drachmas out of his pocket that Nikos had given him and placed it too on the stone pier.

'This might help you to remember.' The boatman snatched the note and sailed off to post the letter.

The letter did reach Father Stavros who obediently played along with the righteous ruse. He sent on the letter contained within the letter and did so with every letter he would receive from Manoussos.

The letter that went to the Ministry of Health was opened by the nurse who was temping in the mail room, Angela Venetis. As instructed by the supervisor she had separated out the letters for each department and then was to open the ones that were general and not addressed to any one person in particular. She read the contents and knew it had to be brought to someone's attention immediately. She went to the new junior clerk of the minister's office, his name was Thanos.

Just a few weeks earlier before Father Manoussos had left for Spinalonga he sat the young boy goatherd down to soften the blow of the news that his mentor and friend Nikos Lambrakis had gone away forever. Standing next to him was the mother of Nikos, Theodora Lambrakis.

'Thanos, Nikos has arranged for you to get an education. One of the last things he said before he left was to make sure you continue your learning, he has organized for you to take a scholarship exam to get you into a good school in Athens.'

But the boy did not take the news well. He was in shock at the news of the tragic fate of Nikos and at the challenge of leaving the safety of the lands he knew well for the wide world of Athens.

'Nikos has already educated me, because of him I know numbers, words and philosophy. He told me to read Plato every day and I do.' The boy replied almost in defiance, he was still trying to absorb the news that

Nikos gone forever. He had been father figure, big brother and best friend all at once. His leaving was too big a loss to comprehend. Theodora recognized grief when she saw it. She could see the turmoil the boy was in so she decided to help the situation along.

'Do it for Nikos.'

She said it softly but it was all that needed to be said. Thanos reached out his hand to accept the paperwork from Father Manoussos and ran home to tell his parents which did not take long. His parents were elated that their son had a chance to break out of the cycle of poverty they were stuck in. They took over the goat herding so Thanos could sit the exam the next week. He won the scholarship.

The whole town was delighted for young Thanos and for the wonderful living memorial of Nikos Lambrakis that he symbolized. But Theodora could still sense reluctance in the boy, she knew he only had the clothes he stood in and still might decline the opportunity because he was too ashamed to show up looking as he did and with no money for books or food. Mrs. Lambrakis had understood his silence and had gone to see the priest.

'Father Manoussos I am still unable to walk around freely in this town, people continue to view me as a leprophore but we need to raise some money for Thanos. If every person my son has helped gives just one drachma for each time my son did something for them we would have enough money to send this boy off wearing clothes of gold.'

Manoussos listened to Theodora's ideas, one was for a fair in the town square but to allay any fears she would have the women of the parish work together and prepare all the food. Once word had spread the local market stall keepers offered half of their profits from the big weekly market day. Extra trays were passed around in church on his behalf and even the boatman gave half of the fares he collected over three days. There was still a shortfall and Christos the council clerk somehow managed to give a generous donation from the municipality which he had always claimed had empty coffers.

The past good deeds of Nikos Lambrakis brought people to the fair the town put on in the square. Within that one weekend the total proceeds plus the donations provided Thanos with a new valise and a fine new wardrobe to put in it as well as a handsome travelling outfit with fine black brogues, a new woolen coat and more money in his pocket than his family had ever seen in their entire lifetime.

Thanos Mavrakis went to a proper school for the first time in his life at the age of seventeen. Thanks to Nikos he had no trouble adjusting to the lessons. He was as smart as any of the other students, if not smarter.

On his first day of schooling the government had sent a selector to pick out any exceptionally bright students for the entry program into the fledgling civil service. The inspector interviewed only the students who scored over eighty five percent of the exams they had set. Thanos had scored ninety seven percent. His results gained him a job with the Department of Health as a junior clerk while he continued his schooling. For Thanos this was better than winning the lottery, a paid for education and a paying job at the same time, all because of the goodness of Nikos Lambrakis.

Thanos showed up for work looking efficient and eager. On day one he was shown around and introduced to everybody then shown how to schedule some of the Minister's appointments. On day two he had to stand in for the assistant to the minister for Health who had fallen ill. The Minister liked the eager young man and by day three he was not only organizing the mail into files for him to read but even permitted to prioritize the ones he felt needed urgent attention.

The entire department was talking about the new recruit and his sharp thinking, his organizational skills and his simple yet effective manner. Nurse Angela Venetis knew he was the one who needed to see this letter first. He would ensure it would be read by the Minister and given the attention it deserved.

'It's Thanos isn't it?'

'Why yes Miss it is. What can I do for you?'

'Please take a good look at this letter and once the Minister takes action on it, that is I hope he does, please let him know that I am willing and able to be part of the medical team assigned there. It would be my honor to help these poor souls.'

Thanos wasn't sure what she was talking about but reached out to accept the letter she was holding out to him. He froze midway when he saw the handwriting. He would have recognized that writing anywhere. He scanned the letter and found out about the situation his friend was in. Thanos looked at Angela.

'Are you really prepared to go to this place?'

'They need me. Now go and see the Minister.'

Chapter 11. The Ministry of Health

Many years earlier in a small village on the mainland a man had developed an unusual rash on his arms and upper body. It was a strange rash of dry white patches and the skin beneath them was numb. The man was forty five years old and had a wife and one living child remaining from the five with which they had originally been blessed.

Their son was smart and had showed much interest in reading and history so they did everything within their power to make sure he got an education. They sent him away to get his high schooling and he was so smart the principal managed to get apprenticed him in a government department where he commenced a career path that was rewarding and prestigious. His name was Andonis Kontos.

The doctor who serviced the area was away in Italy to attend a medical symposium for two weeks so they sent the local midwife to take a look at the father of Andonis.

She declared him to be a leper. The mayor of the village was alarmed by such news and felt he could not take the risk of such a cursed illness spreading throughout the population so he called an emergency council. The council took in the nature of his misfortune and then considered all the facts of the man's life and the dangers of having him active in the community.

They tried to reach their decision with logic. The mayor outlined the facts of the man and his family.

'His only son is away working in the city and is doing well so he does not have the burden of small children left behind for us to concern ourselves with. His wife has her son to lean on for support so we are all agreed that the action we are forced to take, although cruel, is vital to ensure the health of the citizens of our village.'

They went to see him that day and found him tending to his garden which was always immaculate. He straightened with concern when he saw the entire mayoral committee standing in his front garden and not one of them was smiling.

'Gentlemen, may I offer you coffee.'

One of the said,

'We have not come for coffee Kontos. Please stop what you are doing and walk into your shed, turn, and face us.'

The mayor cleared his throat and addressed him.

'Kontos, you are a friend and neighbour of us all and in different circumstances you would be here on the council with us and I believe you would have reached the same conclusion as we have.'

'What is your conclusion?'

'We cannot allow you to spread any risk of contagion through the village.'

'So I am under some sort of house arrest until I can get taken to away to a leprosarium?'

The mayor sighed and continued.

'Kontos we are an isolated village, it is January and already the snows have blocked the roads and the heart of winter has not yet reached us. There are no carriages due to come this way until after February and no one here is prepared to have you on their carts.'

'I will wear a bell, I need to organize things.'

'Your disease is a terrible one, you will become horribly deformed and die a slow and painful death and still carry the risk of passing it on to others. We have decided on the following actions to spare you this grim fate and to safeguard our population.'

'What action?'

'Step back into your shed and stay there.'

'Stay in my shed, for how long? When do I leave?'

'You will not leave, not alive anyway.'

'What are you saying? Have you come here to execute me because I might be ill? What madness is this? We are not even certain if I have the disease. How can you sentence me to death over an assumption?'

'Your symptoms speak enough. None of us will kill you, we cannot do so but all food and water will be withheld from you until you expire. The council has decided.' They slammed shut the door on him and immediately began boarding up the window and door of the shed.

Kontos pounded on the walls and began yelling,

'Hang me instead. Don't leave me here to rot to death. My son, my son, let me see my son?'

His wife until now was speechless in disbelief but when she saw them boarding up the barn she screeched.

'Barbarians! Murderers! Let me give him a blanket, let me give him a pot of soup and jugs of water.' The mayor ignored her screams and spoke over her.

'I understand you are just being a good wife but you will only delay his suffering, he will die quicker this way.'

'Barbarians, you are worse than Turks!'

'Watch your tongue woman or we will burn down your house. Besides, do you really want to risk losing your son as well? We do this for your own good as well as ours.' Kontos screamed from within his prison. His voice now an eerie echo.

'Hang me instead of this torture. Hang me now!'

'Don't talk nonsense Kontos, that would be murder.' The men of the council agreed to take turns guarding the door to the shed to ensure no-one offered any help to him to escape. They would be armed and made it clear they would shoot first and ask questions later.

They bolted the door to the shed and walked away satisfied with a job well done. From that day on his wife was referred to as his widow while her husband was still breathing but to make things a little easier for her a telegram was dispatched to her son to leave his fancy offices and come and retrieve his mother so she could get tested and so she didn't have to listen to her husband die.

It took a week for the telegram to reach Andonis Kontos and another week for him to make his way back to the village. The village elders met him and warned him not to try to interfere with their decision as it was made for the good of the village and that he should regard the loss of his father as a noble sacrifice. His mother was half dead from the trauma of being shunned by all the villagers as a possible carrier of the disease and of the horror of hearing the frenzied beating on the door of the barn.

The snows had fallen heavily across the mountains, they were the heaviest falls that anyone could remember. The villagers said only good thing about that was that Kontos would die quicker. Andonis was trapped with no option but to listen to his father die. He held his mother each night as she sobbed herself dry and then whipped herself into a frenzy of frustration trying to get her husband out.

Andonis knew nothing about leprosy or how one contracted it. He just knew, as everyone else did, that is was a disease that defined you. If you were a leper you were a walking dead until you were truly dead. He lay on the little iron bed next to his mother's bed and all night had to listen to his beloved father moan in tortured tones. He was very weak now after two weeks without a drop of water to drink or a crumb of bread to eat and of lying in bitter cold. The moans were softer but no less heart wrenching, 'Water, water, in the name of God give me a sip of water.'

It took his father six weeks to die. The snows had just melted enough for a carriage to come and take Andonis and his mother to the train station so they could leave forever. His mother spat on everyone as they drove away and screamed at them calling them emotionless murderers and cursed them all to an agonising death. She pointed at the mayor as they drove past him and called out that she would pray every day that he die squealing like a pig.

Every member of that village went to the church that night to light a candle for protection. One month later the mayor of the village toppled over one of his bee hives and was stung so many times that his final breath was a squeal of agony. Everyone in the village would wear the *mati*, the blue eye, for the rest of their days to try to ward off the bitter curses laid upon them by the widow Kontos.

Neither she nor Andonis ever returned to the village and neither ever developed leprosy but every day for the rest of their lives they would be haunted by the hollow voice of Kontos begging for a sip of water. Nothing would ever wipe it from the memory of Andonis even when he achieved great things for his country through a lifetime of service. Eventually he would come to hold the powerful position of Minister for Health.

A knock on his door snapped him out of the focus he was in for reading the monthly reports.

'Minister Kontos.'

'Come in Thanos, what is it that I can do for you?' The minister was very fond of the young new recruit. The boy had brains and a good work ethic.

'I have your mail and I especially want you to read this one first.' The minister was startled but the boy's attitude indicated the importance of the letter.

'Thanos, the normal procedure is to check with me whether I am available to do such things.'

'Minister, I beg your pardon but you asked me not to hesitate to ask for assistance with anything. Were they empty words? The assistance I need is for you to read this letter.'

'Oh. Yes. Well give me the letter then.'

He had developed instant respect for the young man and Thanos had no way of knowing the tragic story of the father of Andonis Kontos. The minister scanned the letter initially but then leant over it to absorb every word. Thanos could see the letter had moved the Minister so deeply he was sitting and trying not to weep. The new junior clerk had recognized the writing before he even read a word. It was the steady, solid script of Nikos Lambrakis, the man who had taught him to read.

The letter of Nikos Lambrakis started off as many of the other ones did, as a request for the urgent attention of the minister. This was not just another letter outlining a case of hardship. The words of Nikos were equal to each of the moans of the dying father of Andonis. His mother safe in her comfortable room in his little villa in Phaleron was still unable to sleep at nights. By the time he finished reading it his throat was so dry he had to have a glass of water.

'Minister Kontos, what do you know about this terrible disease?'

'Nothing!' He said, and then stopped. He had blurted it out from the bitter experience of being forced to keep quiet about his suffering for people did not care about what you have endured, they only care that they are not made to endure the same. He had prayed silently for this moment for all these years to be given the opportunity to relieve other families from such unjust suffering, and now that moment had come.

'I shall leave Sir and come back at another time.'

'No. Sit here and tell me what you know, if anything, about Nikos Lambrakis.'

'Nikos Lambrakis improved my life, I have always prayed for the time to come to improve his. It is because of him I stand before you today instead of herding goats. There is so much to tell and yet so little

147

to say because simply, for me, there is no finer man in the entire world.'

'Well then Thanos, the time you have prayed for has come. I shall have to see for myself how fine a man is he. I am going to Spinalonga and you are coming too.'

Up high on Spinalonga not long after he had released Artemis to free flight Nikos had looked over the edge and watched Manoussos give the letter to the boatman. He slumped a little and put his hands in his pockets and spoke to himself.

'What if all the work I have done has been for nothing? Artemis is gone and the letter might not get posted. Ah if only the God who abandoned me was able to send me a sign.'

Nikos Lambrakis surveyed the island he had walked around so many times already. He had discovered that the derelict slums they were living in was built by the Turks and all the tunnels including the one that led from Dante's Gate were to provide for the harems of the Turks so the women could walk around and not be seen. So the imprisonment of women was now also an imprisonment for men. But other parts of the structure could be made useful again, as long as he could get people to work.

There was a great wash house with rows of large stone troughs. Nikos could see this being made operational again and having laundry facilities so they wouldn't have to walk around in filthy rags. All he would need was some soap and new clothes.

He might as well have been wishing for diamonds and pearls but he stayed true to the philosophy of Plato and applied all his focus on maintaining the application of the divine goods of Wisdom, Temperance, Justice and Courage.

To keep them in his mind, and everyone else's, he followed the example of the unknown person who had carved the inscription above Dante's Gate. He had Ikaros the stone mason pull old nails out of one of the old buildings to use to carve the four names of the divine goods into the stone lintels above the doorways of the main houses opening off the Street of Pain so they could instill some hope back into the hopeless.

Nikos learned that the island was created by man not Nature. The Venetians created it in the 1500's by digging a channel through the part of the coast that jutted out into the sea to create an island to serve as a defense garrison. It was once a part of Elounda. The locals would say they were headed to Elounda, *stin Elounda,* but the Italians couldn't say it correctly and it somehow came out as Spinalonga, long thorn. But it wasn't long. It was high.

Nikos was right in his hunch that it was once the site of an acropolis. There were no visible ruins, no graceful columns to recycle to form the chicest of benches, no imposing pediments to slice the sky and lift the eye upwards so the soul follows. Nikos couldn't see any evidence of the ancient residents of this acropolis but he could feel them. It was something Nikos would often do in spite of the hardships of war and poverty in his country and even before he became ill. He would stand at the sites of ancient cities and sit quietly in the spots where the agoras and forums were and similar places he knew the philosophers would have gathered and discussed matters of logic and wisdom. The energy permeated his mind and would give him a sense of power and calm. He sought that feeling out on Spinalonga and sitting on top of the island he found it, and so had Alikhan.

'You already have what you seek Nikos, read your books and do as they say.'

Nikos had initially been startled by the sudden apparition of Alikhan, now he was just grateful for the presence.

'How can I bring Health and Beauty, Strength and Wealth to the sickest, ugliest, weakest, poorest place on Earth?'

'Can a man have an illness and still have Health?'

'No of course not. And there are women here too.'

Alikhan tutted in annoyance.

'I do not exclude them from anything. I merely use the masculine form for ease, I can use the feminine if you wish but just know when I say *he* I mean it for all concerned.' Nikos nodded his agreement. He knew his friend had adored women, he had died for one, but he had seen so much injustice that he could no longer bear for anyone to be treated as less than anyone else.

'Let us return to my question, how can even a leper feel Healthy?' Nikos pondered for a moment.

'If good hygiene is applied there will definitely be a feeling of well being.'

'And how would one apply good hygiene?'

'It all stems from cleanliness. We need disinfectants. We would require good housing with doors that shut and windows that can close so the dust does not get in and the occupants can feel security?'

'Excellent. Is that all you would do?'

'No, we need power, there is no light. We need furniture for the houses, beds with mattresses, blankets and clean sheets, tables and chairs and good stoves. If there is good nutritious food the people feel healthy and strong, they will take pride in their appearance not just of themselves but of their homes. They will feel wise and attractive and strong.'

'You had better get to work then. Your plan is good Nikos, don't give up.'

Manoussos appeared as Alikhan melted into the sky. He had come to sit with him as he often did. Nikos wondered what Manoussos would make of his visits with Alikhan. Where they visits or were they dreams? Whatever they were it was time to share them.

'Manoussos, I had a friend called Alikhan, I told you about him, the one who was killed. Well I don't know how to tell you this but he visits me here on Spinalonga. We speak together and he advises me on many things. I know it's hard to believe.'

'I believe in everything Nikos. Nothing surprises me, yet everything is a mystery.'

'I have another mystery too. Will Artemis return?'

'What did your friend Alikhan say?'

'That my plan is good and not to give up.'

'Your friend travelled a long way to give you that advice, you must heed it.'

'I asked God for a sign you know.'

'I would call a visit from Alikhan a sign, wouldn't you? Nikos you got your sign. God delivered.'

As usual, Manoussos said it as it was then walked away to get on with his work. Nikos began to walk away too to go back to watching the skies when a large fish fell from the sky, right at his feet.

'Artemis!'

He instinctively held out his arm for her to land on but it was a touch too late, she knocked him over as she landed on the ground. Was it possible to hug an eagle? Nikos wanted to throw his arms around her and kiss her but instead he stroked her on the back of the head.

'Keep her happy,' were the words of Alikhan so Nikos crooned a sweet song to her as he pulled his knife out of his pocket and carved off pieces of fish for her to enjoy.

The fish was a salmon, at least three kilos of it. It was a good meal for a family but not enough for a starving population. Nikos knew it was too early to celebrate. It was time for more action. He fed Artemis some more pieces of the fish, complimented her again and again in the softest tones and got her to get back onto his wrist. He held his arm up and gave another flick of the wrist and sent her off again and again, each time she returned with a large fish within around thirty minutes. By sunset she had brought him six more large fish and if anyone had been looking at Spinalonga at that moment they would have seen in silhouette against the sinking sun, a man leaping around in sheer bliss.

'You must be tired my precious Artemis. You need your rest. You need your beauty sleep.' He stayed with her that night. He would take the fish down to the people tomorrow, they would last just fine in the cool air of a Spinalonga evening. Tomorrow he would send her out again in the morning and they would descend together.

During the night Nikos had dreamt of what a pleasure it would be to finally be able to introduce Artemis to everyone on Spinalonga and now the time had come. He wanted to ensure he made a good impression. He had to in order to honor Alikhan and Artemis. The fish, all eleven large glossy magnificent specimens, were plopped into the large mesh onion bag that he had taken up with him. He wanted the bounty to be on display. He slung the bag over his shoulder and began his descent to the town square where he knew around now people would be gathering to have their morning coffee together.

Kimon saw him first. Next was Ikaros who dropped his tin cup and it went bouncing down the Street of Pain but he didn't go off to chase it, he was mesmerized by the sight of Nikos Lambrakis with a huge eagle on his arm and an impressive catch of fish over his shoulder.

'I can see you have been fishing but you are coming down from the top of the island. What did you make them do, jump up into your hands?'

'Ah my friend, I did not catch them, Artemis did. The only thing I caught, with the help of Manoussos, was Artemis.'

She was wearing her hood and sat calm and godlike on the arm of her master and right at the moment where a dramatic flourish was required, she gave it. She spread her wings out to such width that half of the square fell into shade. She seemed twice the size of any human on Spinalonga. Kimon crossed himself.

'*Panayia mou*, how in the name of God did you ever master such a creature?' Nikos handed the fish over to the women to cook and they all sat together to share the feast as Nikos told the full story.

Chapter 12. The Man with the Carbine

The man with the carbine was on the boat with the boatman for the next delivery. He had seen what the boatman had loaded up as he loaded his goods on board too.

'I have to go to Spinalonga first, do you mind?'
'Oh...err, ok. But who ordered the food?'

'Nobody, it is the standard weekly supply of food that they get.' The man looked at the meager supplies. He saw a small bag of onions of maybe five kilos, and one of potatoes. A bag of lentils, a small tin of oil, a bag of flour and a box of apples completed the list.

'How many people are on there now?'
'Not sure. Maybe fifty or so.'

'Fifty people! And that is all they have to eat for a week?' The man crossed himself and then crossed himself again when he saw a priest waiting for them on the shore. Manoussos greeted them with a wave then called out to the boatman.

'Do you have a book for me?'

'No book, no nothing but the supplies today Father.' He started unloading the mere handful of bags. The man with the new carbine called out to the priest.

'Father, there is a resident on the island called Makis. He was once a fine fisherman and a very good singer. We used to serenade the girls together. He is a good man.'

'Yes I know him, he has offered to help to paint the church.'

'Eh that Makis, always helping.'

Manoussos had more to add.

'He can't sing anymore.' The man shook his head in sorrow. He whispered something to the boatman who nodded and then the man suddenly got out of the boat.

'Father I must make my soul clean.'

'Speak my son.' Manoussos invited the man to sit with him on the stones of Spinalonga for an impromptu confession.

'My name is Zafiris and I should have been the one to get the cursed disease not my beloved cousin.' He stopped speaking for a moment when he realized he was standing on Spinalonga, on the leper island. Manoussos sensed it so he got him back on his original chain of thought.

'Why do you say it should have been you?'

'I had wanted to get a message to a woman other than my wife so I asked Makis to meet her for me so she could tell him where we could meet. He told me what I was doing was wrong but I pressured him. I told him my wife was cold to me and that I was his blood and blood looks after blood. He did agree to help me, he was always helping me with anything I wanted.

The woman was waiting high up on the hill near the caves where the lepers once lived before we started sending them to Spinalonga. We didn't know it but there were some still there, living like animals. One of them, an old man, saw him coming and went to tell him to stay back but he fell and hit his head on a rock and Makis stopped to help him. He got blood all over himself. He had forgotten he had cut his hand on a fish hook the previous day. So there he was all covered with the old leper's blood that wouldn't stop pouring over him.

Makis said he told the old man, 'you shouldn't be here, you should go to the island,' but the old man got up and ran away saying it was one hundred times better in the caves of the mountains where there were pheasants and wild apples than on that piece of rock where not even weeds would grow. But the old man was blinded by his own blood and slipped backwards and fell down the ravine. Makis sent himself here to this island out of love for his family. Before he left he gave me everything he owned, everything. I was too ashamed to admit that I not only had a leper cousin but that I was the one that caused him to become one.'

The man was sobbing uncontrollably now but Manoussos knew it would pass and soon the breath of relief would come now that his terrible secret was shared and his conscience was eased. The priest knew people too well.

'Ahh!' said the man and slapped his knees with his hands. There it was, the breath of the lighter load. To give some ceremony to his impromptu confession the priest did the sign of the cross over the head of Zafiris and recited the forgiveness prayer. Zafiris got up, did the sign of the cross and went over to the boat.

'Father, I was going to *stin* Elounda with supplies from my garden for some other relatives. I give them to you and the residents. Tell Makis they are from Zafiris.'

The boatman helped him unload the items. Manoussos could see two large barrels of olive oil, a large cooking pot, a bag of onions, a bag of potatoes, jars of tomato puree, spices, melons, crates of colorful vegetables like eggplant, zucchini, peppers and a crate of six live chickens.

'Whenever you need more tell the boatman and I will send what I can.'

Nikos was strolling on the acropolis again while Artemis was resting. He was doing the mental work on how to go about implementing his plan on how to make the lepers feel healthy.

'The answer is number four,' came from a voice from behind the tree.

'Alikhan, am I dreaming again?'

'I don't know but does it matter?'

Nikos realized Alikhan had given him information.

'What is number four?'

'That is what you need to implement your plan, the problem you came here to see me about.'

Nikos looked down at the notepad he had with him, on it was listed the four goods of man. He had them in numbered order, the fourth was wealth. Alikhan was telling him to find a way for the all to have extra money.

'Alikhan, I am doing my best but nothing is happening.' Alikhan was gone.

Nikos had mentioned their need for money in every letter he had written but had yet to receive any response so he went back to his house to read for a while. He was looking down at his notes all the way, looking up occasionally to avoid tripping over anything. He knew he was close to his house so he looked up to ascend his doorstep.

Pavlos was standing in his doorway and he was holding one of the food baskets in his hands, the ones he had put in the safe keeping of Maria.

'I thought you were educated already, why do you keep reading, you must be stupid if you need to keep learning new things.'

'Hello Pavlos, and yes that is right. I do not know anywhere near enough about anything so I learn every day. What about you?' The monster that was Pavlos enjoyed hurting people so he gleefully said,

'I learned that I like the company of your sister.'

Nikos lurched forward at him.

'Relax city boy, I didn't touch her, this time.'

Nikos pushed past him to check on Maria. He found her in her house where she was comforting Aliki one of the other younger women. Maria offered the explanation before he asked the question,

'He came here and grabbed a knife and held it to the throat of Aliki. He said if I didn't clean and cook two of the chickens Makis' cousin gave us right away he would cut her throat. So he stood there watching me all the time holding the knife to the poor girl. I quickly put the chickens on the coals to grill but I couldn't make them cook any faster.' She couldn't go on talking.

Aliki stood up and went to say something but Maria put her hand out to stop her.

'Pavlos said I needed to be punished. He pushed me to the ground and went to violate me but Aliki attacked him. She jumped on his back.'

'Nikos he went to take your sister but I wouldn't let him. I know she is still innocent. I thought if I attacked him he would turn on me instead.' She looked down and gathered herself in.

'And he did.'

Brother and sister both reached out to comfort Aliki.

'Thank you for your concern but it was not as big a trauma for me as it would have been for Maria. I know she still has her innocence, I do not. My life before coming here was one of lusts, I am more accustomed to types likes Pavlos. The only difference is that in my previous life I got paid for it. Pavlos doesn't know it though, I had to put up a good fight or it wouldn't have given him what he needed to keep away from Maria. He is a man who enjoys making people suffer.'

The siblings helped Aliki to her sleeping place and sat with her while she sipped the chamomile tea they made her from the plants Zafiris had provided them. Alike was feeling better and was comfortable,

'You know my biggest dream was to have a child. I didn't care if I had a husband or not. Men come and go but you are always a mother.'

'It has always been my biggest wish too,' agreed Maria.

'Listen to me,' said Aliki, 'my dream will never come true. So if this incident results in the creation of a child, I will not allow it to be born.'

'Aliki no, babies are a blessing from God.'

'Maria, you and your innocence, just pray to your God that Pavlos did not plant a seed. Mind you there was not much there, I've seen goats with better equipment. I barely felt a thing.' The laughter was a much needed relief.

'But he did spray his seed so I will wait and see if I need to go and see the old lady Anthea. She knows of how to terminate these things, this world does not need another Pavlos.'

'Nikos' Aliki called out as he was walking away, 'there is another thing you need to organise for our great city state of Spinalonga.' He turned his head towards her to hear her suggestion. She had a worldliness he did not have and her wisdom of the street life was as valuable as his academic wisdom,

'What is that Aliki?'

'A hospital.'

Maria in the meantime was thinking about what Aliki had said. Maria understood why Aliki would feel that way about having a baby to Pavlos. The man was a monster, a rabid dog that should be destroyed. No woman would want to carry the child of such a man but if the chance to have a baby with a kind man ever presented itself then she would take it. Maria then snapped back into reality. God has decided her fate was never to know love or motherhood. She knew she would be on Spinalonga for the rest of her life.

Chapter 13. The Brotherhood of Spinalonga

Kontos acted fast.

'Draft a response to the letter immediately, and don't forget to send it to the priest first mentioned, not directly to Spinalonga, so that Nikos Lambrakis will receive the letter.'

'I already have sir. All that is missing is the date we are arriving and your signature.' The minister and his young assistant worked day and night for a week to get things organized. Phone calls started coming through from the other departments that had also received powerful letters from Nikos Lambrakis. They also received a phone call from Prime Minister Metaxas.

'Do whatever is required for these neglected souls. You have the full support of the state.'

The minister got parliamentary approval for the construction of an infirmary. In turn the people in charge of building the infirmary had to get approval from the Department of Power to provide a generator as the infirmary would need power. In the middle of all the preparations came a call from a woman.

'You are going to be building a medical centre on Spinalonga?'

'It looks that way,' said the efficient voice on the other line.

'Do they have staff for the infirmary?'

'It's a leper colony lady, there is not exactly a rush on volunteers.' He hung up. Angela shook her head at herself and went directly to Thanos as she should have in the first place.

'You are really moving fast on the Spinalonga infirmary project.'

'They have suffered enough, they need help.'

'I told you. They need me.'

Manoussos kept watching out for the boatman every day since he sent the letter. Every day Artemis was providing food for the island. Most days there were fish and plenty of them and occasionally there was hare which made a wonderful rich stew and once even a whole baby goat. Nobody could believe it when Artemis soared across the skies carrying the kid with her claws. With the extra protein in their diets the residents of Spinalonga began to feel stronger and with their physical strength improving, so did their mental strength.

Nikos would now walk around the island with Artemis on his arm. But she only trusted him. No one was permitted near her. She would hiss like Cerberus if anyone dared get too close. Everybody gazed upon them with awe. Nikos finally understood why the Berkutchi were considered to be so mysterious and powerful. They earned it. They had mastered one of nature's most incredible creatures. To catch an eagle you truly did have to become like an eagle yourself, just as Alikhan had said.

His logic had told him that even though she was trained to hunt for him Artemis was still first and foremost an opportunistic bird of prey. Such creatures are not designed to show any emotional connection. Yet she did. During their stroll down to the house after a satisfying day of hunting Nikos was murmuring to her about how wonderful she was. Artemis had her head

165

tucked in close to his as if she was trying to catch every word. One of her wings was slightly spread open and resting on his shoulder like an embrace.

Nikos too was different with her now. He was much more devoted to her than he thought he ever could be especially after what he had just experienced. The large oil barrels donated to Spinalonga by Zafiris had been put to good use. The first one had been shared out, decanted into smaller bottles for the individual to use and the other barrel was kept in reserve for communal cooking. Nikos had taken the empty oil barrel and used it as a nest for Artemis. He had cut off the top and filled the centre with sawdust and dry branches. It gave Artemis somewhere else to sit other than a perch. She seemed to enjoy it and Nikos was pleased. The day before Nikos had taken Artemis back home after a big day of hunting and there right in the middle of her nest was a large green sprig of laurel.

He removed it on a hunch and waited to see what would happen. That evening another sprig of laurel was in the nest.

'How did you bring this here my girl?' He deduced she must have made a special trip in between the hunting expeditions. He tested it one more time and removed it again. The next day, again, there was a sprig of laurel in the nest. Why she did it was a mystery but she always wanted as sprig of laurel in her nest, it was as if it was a necessity. If he ever removed it, the next day another one would be there.

'Eagles have always been a symbol of God. Even in antiquity.' Manoussos had said one day.

'It is said that when Zeus wanted to discover where the centre of the world was he released two eagles, one on each side of the world, and where they met was the centre, and that place was Delphi. Have you ever been to Delphi?'

'Sadly no.'

'Delphi, the sacred shrine found by eagles, was dedicated to Apollo and the tree sacred to Apollo was the laurel. There is still a laurel there today.'

'Why are you telling me this? You are leading up to something.'

'We do not have a laurel tree on Spinalonga. She must get it from somewhere. Maybe all the Gods are watching over you Nikos.'

Hunting went well the next day as it did every day. The fish catch was large and he handed the fish over to the women who would share them out as best they could. On his walk back to his house to put Artemis on her perch he saw Manoussos walking towards him.

'Nikos, I was at Dante's gate waiting for the boatman. We have a response.' In the priest's hands was a package, it was the book of the chants required through Holy Week. Manoussos and Nikos went inside the house so Artemis could be perched. Nikos opened the book and there was the envelope tucked inside its pages. Nikos jumped with a joy he had never known in his life before.

'They are coming. They all got my letters and they are coming.'

'Oh!' He spun around like a young woman in love. 'Thank God.'

'Which God are you thanking, the one you believed abandoned you?'

'It was a natural instinct.'

'I wonder why?'

'We need to form a council Manoussos and I invite you to join me on it.'

'I accept.'

'We need the best thinkers we have to get together and make our list of requirements so when our visitors come we are fully prepared to hand over our exact needs. I think we should have twelve members.'

'That is a good number.'

'And as our population seems to be evenly split between men and women we should have six men and six women, like the gods of Olympus.'

'Perfect example.'

Nikos thought of the twelve Olympians and of how each deity represented different aspects of life, just as ministries operated today. It occurred to them both that the domain of each god was similar to a ministerial department. There was education, health, foreign affairs, defense, agriculture, and communication, everything any well run state required, for each one the Greeks had an allocated deity.

'Well I like the idea of a supreme council made equally of men and women, it is a shame that doesn't happen in our government departments today.'

He called a meeting of every resident and announced his plans to establish domains, the leaders of which would be selected by vote.

Pavlos wanted to be the chief of War and for a brief moment Nikos gave it consideration. The man was a natural fighter maybe he could use his street smarts on how to maintain order within the other patients but then the moment passed. Pavlos was berserk enough without giving him official permission to impose his monstrous ways. He would leave it to the democratic process and could only hope it would work.

When all adjourned for the evening to consider their choices for their votes the next day for the first time, every single resident of Spinalonga looked forward to tomorrow. Life now had a purpose.

'Welcome all to the first meeting of the Brotherhood of Spinalonga. I first give thanks to the golden hands of Eva and Aliki who took some of our own fabrics and have fashioned a fine flag for us. The two women held up their creation proudly, it was white for purity and cleanliness but edged with a black meandric key pattern to show their association with their Hellenism and the black for the lives they lost, as a mourning cloth would be. In the center was a capital S in the brilliant blue of the Greek waters. S for Sophia, wisdom, and S for Spinalonga.

The voting took place, it was quick and it was wise. Nikos was voted president and Manoussos was spiritual counsel, the others elected were all the appropriate people for each domain. Pavlos received one vote, his own.

Manoussos stood before them holding a Bible. 'I call for all the newly elected domain leaders to step forward to take the oath.' Nikos had decided they needed an oath and there was no finer one than the one from Homer's Iliad.

The twelve newly elected members of the supreme council of Spinalonga stood in a semi circle before the others and with Father Manoussos holding the Bible in his right hand all repeated the Homeric oath of the warrior, slightly altered by Nikos to suit.

'I do swear that I will lead my domain *'Ever to excel, to do better than others, and to bring glory to our forebears, who indeed were very great ... This is my ancestry this is the blood I am proud to inherit'* and this binds me to the sacred mysteries of the Almighty to uphold my sacred inheritance.'

The formality of the ritual and all its symbolism rested well on the shoulders of all, like a warm cloak after an icy wind. Order was coming and it made them think the most beautiful of thoughts such as none they had ever had before. Many of the patients had never lived an orderly life, their internal thoughts of how life would be in an orderly state were intuitively correct. Order brought cleanliness, which brings beauty, which brings peace, which brings happiness.

The only person not choked up with emotion or shedding a quiet and much yearned for tear of hope, was Pavlos.

'You are all dreaming. There is no point to any of this. We are nothing. Dogs wouldn't eat us when we die so stop trying to believe you are capable of being as great as our ancestors. And what ancestors? Who knows where some of us come from? We could be Turks or Bulgarians for all we know.'

Voices of dissent shouted from the crowd.

'Speak for yourself. I am not Turkish or Bulgarian. I am Greek.'

'Who cares if we are from China? We need rules and laws and we want an orderly state.'

Many of the things required to be done just needed some manual labor. Even that had been difficult before because of the hunger and weakness of the people, fear and low morale as well as having to deal with Pavlos's intent on destroying everything positive. Some of the women stepped forward and looked at Nikos with a look query on their faces.

'Speak up ladies, what would you like to say?'

Aliki spoke first.

'Have you ever heard of the term Syssitia?' Nikos smiled with joy.

'Well of course I have. It is the way many of the warriors were fed in the ancient days of Sparta. Everybody sat together in one space and ate a communal meal.'

'Yes as in Sparta, where I am from. We would like to introduce a Syssitia system where you give us the daily catches of your wonderful Artemis and we prepare big communal meals so all can eat well and together.'

'It is done.'

Eva stepped forward to speak too.

'If the domain leader of the waters can provide it we can organise volunteers with a roster to make sure all here have clean clothes. And we would like to be able to sit properly to eat. There are some timbers lying around all the other old houses. Perhaps the domain leaders of the trades can use the few tools we do have to fashion them into some sort of benches or tables?'

'Yes indeed we can,' said the men.

'Very well fellow members of the Brotherhood of Spinalonga, we all have work to do.'

Ikaros and his team set to work as did the teams of Aliki and Eva. Soon the aromas of good peasant cooking were wafting across the island and the sounds of peaceful industry, the clanging hammer and the sawing of wood became a foot tapping harmony.

By the time the first Syssitia meal of Spinalonga was ready so were the benches. There was enough wood for a table, but only one for the time being. They were set up in the square with the sickest and lamest carried there by the strongest. The first meal was served and though it was a humble meal it was hot, tasty and nutritious. The community spirit was one of elation. Father Manoussos gave a blessing and Nikos quoted Aristotle.

'Man is happiest when he is in a good relationship with his city.'

The meal was fish soup, followed by baked salmon with potatoes, olives and bread. As a special treat for dessert there were *loukoumathes*. It could have been Christmas. Afterwards came all the happy talk that happens out of togetherness and a sated belly. Everyone offered their thoughts on what to ask for when the visitors arrived. Discussions were going on all around. Nikos overhead one on bees.

'Let's find a way to have a beehive. The loukoumathes were good but with some honey they would have been crazy good.'

'Oh we would need two hives. It is warm weather most of time here, the bees would be very productive.'

'You are both sleeping standing up. We have no pollen producing plants here on Spinalonga.'

'The bees can fly can't they? Let them go fly and find pollen.'

On another bench people were discussing ways of making other dishes such as the ones from their villages. Aliki was listening and acted wisely.

'That sounds marvelous come and see me after dinner to discuss giving a cooking class so we can all learn it too.'

'Oh I would love to.'

'These rocky crags are good for goats, can't we sweet talk the boatman to bring us a couple of goats. We could have cheese and every so often we could roast a kid. Poor Artemis needs a bit of a rest.'

The Syssitia meals were an instant success. The sickest of the patients who could barely eat were spoon fed their soup by healthier people would dunk some bread into it for them. Teams of patients took turns in doing the serving and the cleaning up and even Pavlos would come to eat without disturbing anyone. Nikos and Manoussos were overjoyed with the civil atmosphere.

A few days after the first meeting of the brotherhood of Spinalonga Nikos opened the letter from the Department of Health and re-read it with Manoussos.

'They are coming on the twenty fifth of this month.'

'What is the date today?'

'The twenty fourth.'

Chapter 14. The Minister's Visit

Angela was thirty five years old and had served in war zones and in a sanatorium before she was sent to the Department of Health for respite. Everyone thought she was being very heroic when she declared she wanted to be part of the medical staff of Spinalonga. She even declared she would not bother waiting for the infirmary to be built. There were houses on the island already and she could live in one of them while the infirmary underwent construction, after all the residents had suffered long enough. They needed immediate medical attention.

The boat carrying the Minister and his entourage, including Thanos and Angela, landed at Dante's gate. It was the Minister's idea to do so. He wanted to see what the lepers experienced. The sight of the forbidding sign above Dante's gate made them all fall silent.

The guests disembarked quietly as they took in the sight of all the lepers all lined up along the shore at Nikos's request, even Pavlos was there who was instantly captivated by the sight of Angela. The sea provided fresh breezes but the rank of festering wounds was obvious. One of the entourage addressed Father Manoussos who was standing closest to the boat,

'Are you aware the Minister has gone to a lot of trouble to be here today?'

'Are you aware a man died here recently trying to catch a fish?' The *kakomiris* was so weak from starvation he couldn't fight the waves and got smashed onto the rocks.' Kontos stepped forward, this was not the way he imagined things to start off.

'I am Andonis Kontos, the minister for Health.'

'Welcome and not well come. This is the traditional Spinalonga greeting Sir.'

Andonis Kontos had been experiencing deep emotional turmoil all along the journey to Spinalonga. He had kept the horrific death of his father a secret. If he had spoken out about the inhumanity he would never have risen to the career height he had achieved. His mother had spent the rest of her life indoors, never daring to venture out and speak to people again. His father had been given his funeral service through the doors of their barn and when the man shriveled to death after days of unimaginable terror the villagers waited for forty days before going in to retrieve his body to make sure his soul had finished roaming and would not carry out any ghostly reprisals. Andonis had buried his pain as deeply as the villagers had buried Socrates Kontos.

Andonis and his mother never returned to their village and never spoke of Socrates unless asked and even then they said he died of pneumonia after a heavy winter. The enforced silence of shame had killed his mother before her time and had made him an old man by the age of thirty. Andonis Kontos lifted his head in gratitude of being finally able to do something to honor the memory of his father and asked,

'Where is Nikos Lambrakis, the man who wrote me the letter?'

'Here!' Out of the shadows stepped forward a gaunt tall figure. His thick black hair was combed back, his clean white shirt collar loose at his neck. He walked towards him and stopped to position himself directly opposite him, a mere metre separating them but it was close enough to stare straight at him with his black eyes that were showing no gleam of warmth.

'I am Nikos Lambrakis. I am the one who invited you here to witness how the great Hellenic race deals with its sick. Here you will see for yourself how we the people descendent from the creators of logic, democracy, science and medicine treat the most unfortunate? I have studied our ancestor's great writings and nowhere could I find any instruction to torture and starve an unfortunate person in addition to his misfortunes, so what gives you the right to do so?' Nikos was struggling to control his temper. He regained his composure by straightening up even further and clenching his fists. Kontos noticed.

'Nothing Nikos, nothing gives anyone any right to mistreat anyone. I am here to help. What would you like to tell me?'

'I stand before you to represent every leper resident on this island, each one of them is a member of the Brotherhood of Spinalonga. My words to you are their words also.' Minister Kontos looked at all the gathered patients to show his understanding that Nikos was speaking for them then looked back at Nikos and nodded at him to continue.

'I took responsibility for your health and well being and that of your family.' The minister was visibly startled by Nikos's comments. Before he could question its meaning Nikos continued.

'I took responsibility by removing myself from the outside world so you and your family could live a healthy life. I took responsibility by allowing my life as I knew it to be terminated so you and your children could live yours. Ill fated souls like me respected your health and your life and so I live a half life but every life, even a half life such as the one I am living, must be a life of dignity. Minister, I took responsibility for you. Now you must take responsibility for me.'

Nikos never even blinked throughout his talk, his full focus was on minister Kontos who reached for his handkerchief to wipe away the tears he was grateful to be finally able to shed in public.

Maria stepped forward.

'All we ask for is enough to eat.'

Ikaros stepped forward.

'All we ask for is a place to sleep.'

Others spoke up too.

'All we ask for is for somewhere to sit.'

'All we ask for are some medicines and bandages so our wounds don't stink.'

'All we ask for is to be able to read a book.'

'We would like to hear some music.'

'A movie would be nice.'

'I want to work and feel useful.'

The patients were asking for basics, not luxuries, in exchange for their freedom being terminated. Andonis Kontos put his hands up to signify he wanted the chance to speak,

'Mr Lambrakis, patients of Spinalonga, your words have been heard. Believe me. And I am the right person to hear them because I can and will bring the changes you require and deserve.'

Kontos thought it was time to lighten the atmosphere.

'But Nikos, we each got so involved in our meeting that not all the correct introductions have been made. I have brought along the new junior assistant to the Minister's office as well and he is someone who wanted very much to come here and see you.'

Nikos was taken aback, he was not expecting any surprises, and he was even more taken aback when he saw who it was that emerged from the boat.

'Thanos? Is that you? I can hardly recognize you with that fine suit on.' Thanos went up to Nikos and embraced his friend with no hesitation or fear of touching him. His spontaneous display of affection moved Nikos.

'Thank you Thanos.'

'Nikos, I thank you, I wear it because of you and Father Manoussos and your mother. I work in the ministry now and I was given your letter by Nurse Angela, she was the one to read your letter first.'

Nikos acknowledged Angela with a gentlemanly bow, as he was returning to upright he saw Pavlos and on reflex his gaze hardened. He was hoping Pavlos would behave and gave him a withering look which only made Pavlos sneer. Angela caught the entire visual exchange and leant forward to see at whom was Nikos glaring. She looked over at him too and saw Pavlos looking straight back at her. Pavlos was clearly the troublemaker of the island. She lowered her eyes in a flirty manner and the two kept exchanging glances during the entire visit.

'Thanos brought the letter to me and made sure I read it too,' said Kontos.

'My friends, Mr. Lambrakis, the Ministry of Health asks for your forgiveness. As its head I do promise you that I will bring your queries to the attention of all the relevant ministries and all of your concerns will be met. He tried to keep things light hearted and positive but had to look down so no one could see the pain in his eyes. He wished his village had a Nikos Lambrakis, maybe his father would not have had to suffer such a horrific end. He didn't care if his heartache was mistaken for shame.

'Yes Nikos I do agree with you, the health of our citizens is indeed a political responsibility.' As he was speaking another boat drew up to shore. He waved at those onboard and signaled for them to come over.

'We have already begun to acknowledge our responsibility. These arrivals are the workers. We are going to build you a medical centre, a special hospital for you, an infirmary. You will have full time medical care right here on Spinalonga.'

Eva clapped her hands together with joy and she held her Kimon close to her. The other patients took her lead and gave a round of applause. Those who could not use both their hands tried to cheer but only managed to utter awful moans but the effect was perfect. It gave the visitors a quick insight into how poor the condition of the patients really was. Only Pavlos did not clap or cheer, he just stood there with a look of evil on his grotesque face and kept his arms folded against his monstrous chest.

'Construction begins today. Until it is finished Nurse Angela has very commendably volunteered to stay here on Spinalonga to tend to you.' Nikos could see the minister was truly sympathetic to them otherwise he wouldn't be standing here but Nikos took the opportunity to keep asking for more. He had also hidden Artemis. She was their little secret and he was also afraid that if they saw that they had found a way to source food then they might be less generous with the requests that Nikos had to make of them.

'Thank you minister for bringing to us what are the most basic of human requirements as opposed to what has been happening up until today. The infirmary is a long overdue necessity. We can now feel a little more secure knowing there is some medical care instead of the current situation of being abandoned to die a slow and painful death here alone, but I also informed you of our total lack of power. An infirmary will require power and the staff will require food. I fear we will have a situation where we will have a hospital and staff who will not be aware that just meters away the patients do not have enough to eat.'

The arrogant aide who had addressed Manoussos earlier stepped forward to speak.

'We can't know everything. We have our jobs to do.' Thanos immediately pulled on the man's sleeve to drag him back but the man yanked his arm free and went back onto the boat.

'We are your job!' Nikos called after him in a manner that was both polite and berating but it was his bearing that had them all pinned down. The man found himself unable to give a mouthful of tirade back, which was what he normally would have done in a confrontation. Nikos stood facing them all front on, making no dramatic gestures, his hands were only slightly clenched, his chin was not up in defiance and his eyes were looking straight into theirs. Angela watched him, she worked with bodies and this young man was in complete control of his.

'We are not an inconvenience. We are citizens of Hellas.'

Minister Kontos sat down on a folding chair an aide had provided, another one was brought for Nikos and the minister gestured for Nikos to sit and join him. The minister leaned forward.

'Tell me what you need.'

'We need to feel useful and informed. Here is my plan.' Out of his pocket he pulled out some sketches and meticulous notes on what his vision was for Spinalonga. The minister studied them carefully,

'A cinema! Piped music throughout the streets, working shops and cafes! Nikos you ask too much. Why even Elounda does not have power yet. Why should Spinalonga, this is quite irresponsible thinking?'

Nikos stood up.

'Why? We sit here in permanent misery and ask to be able to see a film, hear some music and have basic stores like a barber, a shoe repair, and somewhere to sit and have a coffee like a civilized person instead of squatting on the ground and crawling around for a lizard or a rat to cross our path so we can catch them to eat. You think this is too much to ask?' Nikos was roaring now but was still in control of his body.

'Do you have a reason why we should be exempt from such basic pastimes?' Nikos was the one doing the talking but the minister had the moans of his dying father ringing in his ears.

'No Nikos, I do not. You are right. Your plan is noble yet simple, sophisticated and organized. Well done.'

'My plan is normal life, which is all we ask.'

Nikos hesitated but only to catch his breath.

'Actually there is one more thing. Money, we do not have any at all even though according to the laws of this land we are entitled to a proper disability pension. The only logic I can find for this barbarianism is that you hope for us all to starve to death so as to save the state money.'

Minister Kontos was genuinely startled by this claim of Nikos.

'No Nikos that is not the case but yes, I am aware your disability pensions are meager to say the least and we have been in communication with the Social Security department who told us you wrote to them too.'

'Yes, not only are our disability pensions so inadequate but many months they do not come at all. I have reason to believe there is a corrupt person in the council of Elounda that is tampering with the pensions. He has left us penniless and hungry and that makes him directly responsible for the deaths of many souls here who starved to death or died trying to find food. A simple discreet investigation should verify my claim.'

Kontos got up and turned to Thanos who was standing close by should he be needed.

'How about you personally head the investigation for that Thanos? I will see to it that you have full cooperation from all departments.'

'It will be my total pleasure Sir.'

The three men stood together in a rich silence. It had been a productive encounter and all sides had experienced a profound life change yet it was all in a day's work, the perfect situation. The loud mouth aide came forward and advised,

'Minister it is your lunch time.'

'Ah, very well.'

'Yes Minister, it is our lunch time too.' Nikos said.

Aides were running around setting up tables and bringing baskets from the boat. Nikos smiled knowingly. He and the Brotherhood too had arranged a lunch. They had made their plans to highlight their lack of food, and the visitors seemed to be conspiring to help his cause.

Nikos went to the women.

'Watch where they set up and then go set up for us. Let's not scare them off, set it up about four meters away but just make sure they can see what we are eating.' The women of Spinalonga went straight to work to set up their eating space right opposite that of the special guests, minus the benches and the food that Artemis now provided of course. Each setting was set up with the standard food that each group of people would eat on an average day in their regular circumstances. The settings told the full story.

The guests had picnic tables spread with clean white cloths, glasses, plates, cutlery and plentiful food. The menu was simple, carafes of wine and water glistened, baskets of bread bloomed all the way down the centre of the table. Plates of succulent lamb with lemon potatoes and bowls of green salad were placed at each setting as well as tempting little side dishes of fried whitebait, olives, tomatoes, cheese, spanakopita and some piquant dips of eggplant and garlic.

The patients had no table, no cloth, no utensils and they sat on the rocks. One of them had gathered wild greens from the hill top and boiled them over the campfire they had built, they each got one slice of bread and a handful of caper berries, a bowl of mushy lentils was the main course. Father Manoussos said Grace and all set to eating. The patients ate from the communal pot of lentils using the bread as spoons.

No one at the guests table could eat as they had the shame of their neglect and ignorance at their feet. The Minister got up an offered his seat to Maria, every else got up too and offered their seats to the other patients. As part of the Brotherhood rules Nikos now insisted every leper resident of the island was now referred to as a patient. The healthy were nourished by watching the sick eat a real meal in comfort for the first time since they arrived on Spinalonga. The moans of appreciation soon gave way to silence and the shores of Spinalonga became a picnic ground as every single patient wolfed down their feast. Everyone except Nikos, he would eat later, plus he had deliberately withheld a large salmon from Artemis's last catch for his own feast the previous night. He never had done such a thing before but he knew he needed to be well sustained so he could be at his peak for this very moment. He had eaten guilt free in the knowledge that he had done a lot of work and still had more to do for the rights of the patients of Spinalonga. One fish in exchange for that was, in his opinion, a fair deal. Right now he needed to negotiate some more demands. He could eat again later.

The Minister looked around him.

'Mr. Lambrakis,'

'Nikos.'

'Thank you Nikos, please show me around the island. Let me see with my own eyes how you live.'

'Gladly.' Nikos was like an efficient tour guide, a voice in the ear guiding the eye towards what must be seen and felt. His voiceover work was delivered with clarity and sangfroid. He said it as he had seen it himself on his first arrival.

'The newcomers always arrive here at Dante's gate. It is a very frightening time in their life because they have already gone through hell after having been diagnosed with the disease. The following shock of the shunning by the community is equally horrific and of course the fact that they have to stand in church and get pronounced dead obliterates any hope. The arrival to Spinalonga and coming face to face with that sign above the gate makes the blood turn cold in your veins. Then we enter the Street of Pain....'

He did not omit any details. He wanted the minister to feel what they felt and had succeeded. The two men talked more as they walked around Spinalonga and Kontos almost collapsed twice when the sight of the more seriously affected patients made him recall his ill fated father's last days.

'I'm sorry Nikos but this is terrible to look at.'

'Try living here.'

After looking through a dozen or so pitiful excuses of bathroomless, kitchenless hovels and a church with half a roof the Minister said,

'Nikos, I have seen more than enough.' They had stopped just before Nikos' house. He was pleased that the timing was so perfect, that way he could keep Artemis a secret - but something made him speak up.

'Actually Minister, there is one more thing I would like you to see. I want to show you the only reason why most of us have not starved to death. Please follow me.'

The Minister followed Nikos into his humble shelter. The first thing he noticed was how clean it was and he inwardly marveled at this extraordinary young man who even in the face of complete rejection and destitution had created an inviting home.

It was bare but it was clean. There was no dust smearing the floor and no cobwebs lacing up the corners. His furniture was books. He used stacks of them to form bases and using planks taken from derelict and empty houses placed across the stacks of books he had made a bench. Another stack of books with smaller planks on it formed his table. More planks and some stones formed a bookcase and before it was a desk made from taller stacks of books and more planks. A final stack of books formed his chair.

On his desk was a little blue enamel cup holding a bunch of blossoms from Athena's lemon tree. It was a little silent tribute that Nikos liked to make to the poor girl and her unknowing contribution to the well being of Spinalonga. It occurred to Minister Kontos as he took in the order of the room that he would be happy to live and work in a room like this.

'Nikos, this space tells me a lot about who you are.'

'This is not what I wanted to show you Minister.'
'Andonis.'

'Thank you, Andonis. Please come out into the courtyard.' He had the shutters and door closed. Usually they were always open so he and Artemis could be as close together as possible. He had closed them today so as to keep her hidden but now he felt it was right to reveal her presence. Kontos stood back for Nikos to open the door and waited for it to swing back to reveal the secret.

He was speechless at the sight of the grand eagle perched on a great branch. It was wearing a strange hood that covered its eyes but it still had the bearing of a judge about to pronounce sentence. His muteness continued as he watched Nikos go up to the eagle and the creature, sensing his presence, leaned in to him as if to give him a kiss.

'Her name is Artemis. I caught her.'

'You caught an eagle! How?'

'It wasn't easy but I did it and I trained her to hunt. She brings us food, some fish, a hare sometimes. A handful of fish between over fifty people is nowhere near enough but that little extra protein makes so much difference. The Brotherhood of Spinalonga has the Syssitia system. All the catch is cooked up as one big meal and we share.'

Nikos decided to stop talking during the time Kontos was taking to study the eagle. He almost told of the time last week when Artemis had come back with a wild piglet. It was the day after Zafiris had his attack of guilt and there was cooking oil and potatoes galore. The women had done vast amounts of sensational fried potato slices and the men had slow cooked the piglet over hot coals. There was only enough pork for a small serve each but the festivity in the air along with buckets of potatoes sustained them. The minister had no need to learn that they had festive times.

Kontos noticed the large barrel in the corner and went and looked in.

'It's her nest.' Nikos informed. The fresh gleam of green in the middle of the sawdust intrigued the Minister.

'There is a sprig of laurel in it.'

'I know. Last week I noticed it. There is no laurel tree on Spinalonga yet when I came back here to rest her after she had been fishing, there it was. I took it out and washed it and gave it to the women to use in the cooking. The next day there was another sprig of laurel in the nest. I did it again, and again the next day there was another sprig of laurel in the nest. She seems to insist upon it, and it is always a sprig of laurel, nothing else.

Kontos now had his hand over his mouth as if trying to hold in some sort of exclamation of disbelief. He stood back and watched as Nikos pulled an unusual red embroidered bag out from under his desk, from it he brought out a long leather glove. He put it on and went over to Artemis and she leapt onto his arm as lightly as a butterfly. Kontos was awestruck by the sight of this man, barely out of boyhood, who in different circumstances might have ended up running the country but now stood modestly before him, in a hovel he had made into an elegant library and with one metre of eagle perched on his arm.

'Nikos, the eagle is the symbol of the gods. It was eagles that discovered Delphi and there at the sanctuary sacred to Apollo is a laurel tree. The god of light too deemed it to be sacred. Those who wanted to make an offering to the god would offer laurel.'

'I know. What can I tell you, my goddess seems to need to have a sprig of laurel with her at all times.'

Kontos could only shake his head in disbelief. Even though he was seeing it, he was still having trouble believing the mythical sight before him. Manoussos had found them and was now in the courtyard with them. Kontos had not seen him when he asked of Nikos,

'Who are you Nikos Lambrakis? Are you a God?'

Both Nikos and Kontos turned towards Manoussos when he spoke.

'Nikos once said to me that the only way God would ever come to Spinalonga was if I brought Him myself. But there was no need. He was already here.' Nikos had no idea what an imposing sight he and Artemis together made and he laughed at the comment about God.

'I am just a soul trying to bring light to other souls.' Under his breath Manoussos said,

'That *is* what a God does.'

Thanos came running up to them.

'Minister, it is time to go. The boat is ready.'

Nikos put Artemis back on her perch and the men made their way back to the shore where the boat was waiting, the captain had to return the special guests to Elounda before dark. Thanos got on the boat first.

'Mr Nikos, I am going to enjoy nailing you know who. We all knew he was on the take but to stoop as low as to steal the pensions of the sick, well, like I said, I am going to enjoy the look on his face when he sees he has been nabbed by the former goat herd.'

The minister was the last to board.

'Nikos you have my word I will act fast to bring you all your requirements.'

'Even the cinema?'

'Especially the cinema.' Both men laughed together and waved at each other as the boat left Spinalonga.

Chapter 15. Getting Things Done

The workers got to work taking measurements and marking out the building site and Angela set up a first aid corner and applied antiseptic and fresh bandages to the many patients lined up for treatment. Angela was a veteran battle field nurse but what she saw on Spinalonga moved her to tears. For many of the patients it was the first time their wounds had ever been treated.

They moaned in painful ecstasy when the fresh but sharp antiseptic came in contact with their skin and writhed in bliss when the soft, clean bandages were being wrapped around their exhausted limbs. Before they refused to even look at their wounds now the patients could not take their eyes off their clean bandages. They walked around showing each other their newly treated wounds as if they were comparing Christmas presents.

Angela had instantly befriended Maria and Eva.

'We will take your things and get a nice room ready for you. It won't be much but we will see to it that it is clean.' Angela smiled her thanks and kept working.

The workmen had done all their preparations and were boarding their boat. One of them came over to see Angela.

'We cannot do anymore today. We will be back tomorrow with building materials and get the place built for you as soon as possible. You sure you want to stay here? There is room on the boat. How can you stay here with these people? It will take some time before we can have a room ready for you.'

'Thank you but no, I will stay. And you are not building the infirmary for me. You are building it for the patients. These people need me. You just hurry up and build the infirmary so we can all get to work and do what must be done.'

Angela took special interest in poor Athena who was still trapped in her silent world after the attack from Pavlos. Nikos had been visiting Athena too and always gave her extra generous portions of fish or whatever else Artemis brought in as acknowledgement of the role her puppy played in training her. He would sometimes just look at her for she was very lovely. There were other times he just sat there with her and read his books. Sometimes he read out loud so she could hear and he would discuss what he had just read as if she were participating in the conversation. He would chat to her about what was happening on the island and often wondered if he should tell her that her puppy was part of the reason she now eats fish and wild game every day? He balked. He would have liked to get to know her better and to help her more but he had a very demanding diva of an eagle to look after. It would have to wait for another time.

If he had only looked into her eyes he would have seen the warmth and intelligence that he always wanted in a woman. In Athena's case they were just lying dormant. Staying silent was the best therapy for her right now. The change in her life had been too big and by stilling herself completely she was slowly making the adaptations she knew were needed to make but at her own pace. So she stayed silent.

Nikos, like so many men before him and after, overlooked the pleasure of the company of a good woman because it seemed to be too much effort. For Athena he was making an effort but he didn't know why. No, Nikos was not a God, he was just a man.

The workers came every day and worked hard. They were respectful and kept their distance. To acknowledge the patients they would doff their caps at them and the patients would wave back. The workers were cheerful and energetic and would hold up baskets for all to see, then place the baskets on rocks and walk away. The patients understood the contents were for them and would howl thanks when they saw whatever little treat each man had brought. There were varied delights such as almonds, chocolate, apples and the occasional bottle of wine.

Within a couple of weeks walls began to sprout out of the rocks of Spinalonga. One day one of the engineers came and showed Nikos the plan of the new infirmary as well as drawings of what it would look like when finished. All Nikos saw was a basic rectangular building with bars on the windows.

'These bars on the windows, why do you make the hospital look like a prison?'

'I'm not sure. It was requested of me. Maybe they think if we don't do that all the inmates will break in and steal food and blankets and all sorts of things.'

'It doesn't occur to you why a man steals food or a blanket? If a man has enough to eat he does not steal food. If a man is warm he does not steal a blanket. You are supposed to be the educated people? There are people here on the island who have lost their eyes yet you are the ones who are blind.' His entire rebuke was delivered without him raising his voice and without his hands moving from his sides, his absolute stillness of body and direct speech added weight to his every word. The engineer could only shrug and agree with him.

Angela admired Nikos more every minute she got to know him. Life on Spinalonga was a trial in every way. Even now with more goods arriving life was still uncomfortable yet Nikos kept the morale of the whole island buoyant. He never complained about his fate and he treated every soul as if they were family.

It was a wonderful thing to Angela that she became a nurse and looked after the wounded soldiers. She loved her chosen vocation. Others were quick to remind her that she was already thirty five and unmarried, her luck might just have passed her by. An unmarried woman of over thirty in 1936 in provincial Greece was invisible, unmarriageable, at least that was how some of the peasants thought. Maybe some elderly widower might accept her so she could wash his clothes and spoon feed him his soup because he had no daughters to care for him. Many a spinster did such a thing just to know the feeling of having had a wedding day and of being able to say the words, *my husband*.

Angela didn't care, she would not settle for what amounted to little better than slavery and if she was going to be nursing anyone, then she would be paid for it. Here on Spinalonga she was not pitied, she was adored. Everyone needed her yet nobody infringed on her privacy. She was exactly where she wanted to be.

Thanos and Kontos kept their word. They acted fast on everything. Thanos was lucky enough to catch Christos the council clerk in the act of opening up the pension envelopes and removing the money. He had become so blasé about it that he was doing it at a table in the taverna. It was a corner table and it was a quiet day so he just propped a book up as cover to hide the stack of envelopes he had with him. He plucked eighty drachmas from the one hundred drachmas that each of the envelopes contained, leaving the recipient barely enough money for bread and coffee. He was so engrossed in his work and so confident no one was even noticing him anymore that he did not see that he was being watched.

Thanos had two policemen with him courtesy of the Minister and they looked on in open mouthed incredulity.

'He really has become a law unto himself hasn't he? I will go up to him first.'

'Okay, we will stay here, he will probably try to make a run for it but we will see to it he goes nowhere.'

Thanos walked up to Christos.

'What are you doing here Christos?' The fat clerk was so startled he dropped his work. Money and envelopes fell all around him.

'Oh here, let me help you with that.' Thanos sat opposite him and picked up some of the fallen items. He looked at them before passing them back over.

'What is going on here Christos? These are pension packets with money for the patients of Spinalonga.'

'Patients! Come on Thanos, we put you into a suit and you get a job and suddenly you are referring to filthy lepers as patients.' Thanos kept cool, too cool, and Christos smelled trouble.

'No Christos, the filthiest people I know are not on that island.'

Christos looked sideways at the young man.

'Ah I see, I tell you what boy, I don't have time for this sort of thing so to save us all a lot of talking I will give you a cut. How is twenty percent? Will that buy your silence? That is what this is all about isn't it?'

Thanos stood up and the police took their cue. Christos was arrested and jailed and this time the department of Social Security did not send the pensions first to the local authorities for distribution but the new pensions of four hundred drachmas a month were sent

195

directly to the new infirmary of Spinalonga along with the monthly medical supplies.

The building of the infirmary was one of the fastest constructions anyone had ever seen. It was not a case of supreme craftsmanship or high efficiency. It was merely a case of it needed to be completed in a hurry so the medical team could get in and start work. The result was an ugly red brick box but it belonged to the patients of Spinalonga and it was full of medical supplies so at least the stench of rotting flesh which had partially disappeared once Nurse Angela had joined them now had totally disappeared.

Angela settled herself in nicely. The upper level had residential rooms for staff and she had chosen the light corner room with views of Elounda. Within a week of the completion of the infirmary she was joined by a junior nurse and doctors arrived on a roster. Pavlos was not able to stay away from her.

'So Nurse Angela would you like to take a look at where it hurts?'

She didn't waver for an instant.

'Certainly, that is what I do best. Why don't you lie down here and let me take a good look at you.' Pavlos, for the first time in his hideous life, found himself struggling to be crude. He was not accustomed to confident women and her directness unnerved him. He always brought out reactions of fear and loathing which brought out the monster in him. Angela was a conundrum. He always thought *he* was the conundrum. He had heard the word once and thought it sounded interesting. Pavlos was no conundrum. Pavlos was a monster losing his power.

His vitality was leaving him more and more every day. The women of Spinalonga thought the nights were quieter because Pavlos was no longer prowling due to the extra food and the jealousy that his authority was being sapped away by Nikos and his more politesse way of doing things. His quieter behavior was because he hadn't had an erection for several weeks, not even the morning rise to attention. His disease was damaging the one place no man wants to be damaged. He would have gladly given up an arm, a leg or an eye, but not that.

'No, I have changed my mind, I don't need an examination.' He scrambled away revealing his underlying cowardice that he kept camouflaged by being a bombastic beast. Angela knew men, and she knew that Pavlos was a man who no longer functioned sexually. She'd had experience with such men before. Anyway, he would soon be back to become the very first formal admission to the infirmary. It was all because of his encounter with Artemis.

The sight of a great eagle on the arm of a great man makes an unforgettable impression and when Nikos walked around Spinalonga with Artemis perched imperiously on his wrist Pavlos could barely contain his jealousy. He pretended to be inconvenienced when Nikos was coming through one of the alleys and had to make way for them.

'Watch your back city boy. I just might make a roast out of her tonight.'

Nikos laughed.

'I'd like to see you try.'

Nikos went into his home and leashed Artemis to her perch.

'There you go my sweet girl. And to thank you for all the lovely fish you brought us today here is a nice piece of goat for you.' Nikos remembered to keep the fur on the pieces of meat to provide her with the natural roughage an eagle needs. Artemis tucked into her meal.

'Good girl, you eat up. I am off to see a movie, we are screening Charlie Chaplin tonight.'

Pavlos had hidden in one of the old houses as he watched Nikos leave. He waited until Nikos was out of sight then snuck into his house and found the eagle calmly balanced on her perch.

'Well, Miss Artemis, time for you to have a new master. Hey, you and Pavlos will make a mighty fine couple.' The response from Artemis was to strike out. She scratched him with her razor claws leaving a deep gash in his arm. Pavlos screeched in agony and sent a punch at Artemis. She screeched back at the cowering man then she savagely attacked his face, forced her beak into his eye socket, wrenched out his left eye and gobbled it down daintily.

A bloodied and screaming Pavlos lurched out into the streets. He looked as if he had been in a war. Blood was streaming down his face making him fully blinded and he bumped into walls leaving bloody smudges everywhere. Ikaros and his friends saw him stumbling out of Nikos's dwelling and instantly worked out what had happened.

'It looks like Artemis taught the *malaka* who is the boss.'

'Serves him right.'

'Come on let's get him to this new infirmary we now have.' Ikaros and his friends bundled him over there, pushed him through the door then left.

'We should have let the pig bleed to death.'

'I almost did but after all the work that has taken place around here I didn't want it all messed up with his filthy blood.'

The men considered telling Nikos right away but they checked on Artemis and she looked calm and proud as ever. They went to join Nikos and the others in the cinema and saw everyone was having a wonderful time. They would tell Nikos after the movie was over so they sat to watch Charlie Chaplin and felt free to laugh at someone else at last.

The generator had arrived and had been installed the previous week. Spinalonga now had light! The patients were happy to stay out of sight while technicians came and wired up the town for street lamps and laid wiring for every house to have power outlets. The coup that Nikos had scored was enormous. Elounda still didn't have power but Spinalonga now did.

While the workers were there they also laid a speaker system. Nikos had already known the influence music had on the psyche. The minister had kindly sent over a diverse collection of music. When they were working on the rebuild they played lively Mozart. At night it was the peaceful strains of Bach.

All the patients with trade skills were provided with the tools they needed to carry out their work again. The blacksmith got his anvil and tongs. The dressmakers and tailors got sewing machines and fabrics. Overnight almost the ragged clothes disappeared and the lepers had good clothes again. Nikos spent every moment when not supervising the changes, reading Plato, Thales and Solon too, for timeless and relevant guidance on the running of a city state. His was sitting in his study reading up n such matters when he was interrupted by a couple of the female patients who requested to see him.

'Eh Mr. Nikos, we want to talk to you.'

'How can I help you ladies?'

'Mr. Nikos we want to make a suggestion to you. We want to operate a business too as we use to in our old lives when we were in health.' The two women looked at each other when Nikos raised an eyebrow in question. They exhaled sharply and continued.

'We offer services to men in exchange for money.'

'We can do it in secret or we can do it in the manner of the ancients that you are so intent in replicating. In those cultures it was understood that physical love was a very normal part of life, we even had a goddess devoted to it. Maybe you have forgotten but before you came here the men were lawless. They would attack the women. Because all hope was abandoned any pleasure was sought after, they would jump on us in the streets and rut like animals. Providing pleasure for one's body should always be done in dignity and in private and if there is no willing partner then we will provide one, for a fee.'

'We request from you one of the houses that are being restored to become a house of Aphrodite so we can make a living and the men of Spinalonga get the release they need.'

'If you allow us to do so we will show our gratitude by offering our services to you at any time, free of charge.'

'But just for you, don't go telling anyone.'

Nikos was twenty one when he was diagnosed and for four years before that he had been consumed by study. He had never even had a steady girlfriend. All his time on Spinalonga had been spent lobbying for the rights and conditions of his fellow sufferers. He was also stung with the painful reminder that the sweet Athena lay in some sort of catatonia ever since Pavlos carried out his terrible abuse. Maybe it wouldn't have happened if he had regular sexual release.

'The world's oldest profession, here on Spinalonga?' His fellow students at university had often gone to visit the brothels for some release after exams but he never had the money to spare so would always pretend to be busy when he was asked to join them. Now he was just struck dumb. He found himself incapable of the logical, studied conversation with which he was associated. The two whores picked it up right away. They were the ones now in control of this exchange and they zoomed in to close the deal.

'You are still handsome Nikos, your mouth is still good. Do you think we still look good?'

Nikos looked at the two women, the whores, Stella and Susan. They were hideous. Stella was fat and Susan was ugly and fat. The whore Susan, who was ugly and had a rump as big as wheelbarrow causing her to have a rolling walk, went behind him to cradle him in her arms while Stella straddled him.

'You look very good.' He mumbled, horrified that he had even said it but he was not interested in their unattractive faces and forms but in the fact they were letting him use them. He was becoming hard and was powerless to control it. Stella felt the movement and nestled herself onto him as she unbuttoned her shirt to expose her cleavage, it was not as full and luscious as it once was but there was still plenty of flesh there for a man to play with. She leant forward till her breasts were right in his sight. The other whore took his hands in hers and brought them up to cup her breasts and fondle them.

Stella smiled at him.

'Yes squeeze them Nikos, I love that. Go on, have a taste, give them a little kiss.'

His mouth was already open with wanting and the whore behind him took his head between her hands and guided his mouth so he could suckle on them but Stella was a very experienced whore, she knew a first timer when she saw one.

'Eh Nikos, do you need a little bit of assistance?' She put her hand down his trousers, her warm touch made him spring from firm to hard.

'Oh no you don't.' She pushed him back down onto his bed.

'Now Nikos, let us introduce you to some of the services we will be offering at our establishment and you tell me whether or not you think it would be a good thing for the men of Spinalonga.' She couldn't talk any more, she had her mouth full of Nikos. Susan joined her and Nikos looked down to watch the two women at work with their mouths till they felt him ready to burst, Stella the fat whore lay down and Susan the ugly whore guided Nikos into Stella for him to finish his first experience.

For Nikos it was like medicine, a therapy that gave benefit to his every cell. He released all his pent up passions into the two whores and they enjoyed seeing their skills appreciated by a young man with a fine mind and a still good body. The trouble was they were both so dog ugly Nikos had to keep his eyes shut the entire time the sluts were anywhere near him. They on the other hand were glowing like new brides.

Nikos granted them permission to have a house for their enterprise to be carried out without harassment and the girls showed their gratitude to him over and over and over again, but in the dark.

Chapter 16. Lyras and his Horse

In a village high over Chania there was a young man named Telemachus who liked playing the lyre more than he liked talking to people. He would stare out over the sea and wished he would find a peaceful place where he would be able to sit and play his lyre all day without interruption. He loved living on an island. Island life was very beautiful. But Crete was too big. He wished he had his own island where the sea was even closer all around him.

The sea breezes would keep his fingers on the strings and he never got tired of playing. There was majesty in the sea, no wonder it deserved to have its very own god and its very own saint. Often he would go to the church of Saint Nikolas, the patron saint of sailors to light a candle and then he would dedicate a tune to Poseidon, that way all the divinities would give their blessings for the sweetest of music. His parents were of the very aggressive western islanders who loved to embroil themselves in vendettas. His clan was at odds with another clan and even taking a few melons to market turned out to be an ordeal of dodging bullets.

His life was full of restriction, his sisters had it easier for they got to carry out their chores in the peace of the home. Telemachus had envy for the chores of women. They were meaningful and creative. He would watch his mother spin the wool of their sheep and then as deftly as Zeus threw thunderbolts she would take sticks and click them together and then like magic, from them would grow a garment.

He loved watching his sisters take flour and baptize it then massage the gluggy mass tenderly until it relaxed so much it could be rolled and stretched out into silky sheets so thin he could see the pattern of the tablecloth through them. From those stretched silken sheets his sisters would make the lightest, most delicious pastries in all of Crete. Women were the miracle makers of the world no doubt. Staying in the cool peace of the courtyard while he played his lyre and helped his mother and sisters create their little daily miracles was how Telemachus wanted to spend all his days. His father and two brothers seemed to want to spend all of theirs riding around looking for opposing clan members to shoot.

The way Telemachus saw things men were the destroyers of the world and women were the creators. He also noted that when a man goes out looking for trouble he always finds it, whereas a woman will go out looking for how to make something beautiful either for her home, her family or herself. He wouldn't even join the men at the local *kafenio*, there were no women there.

Telemachus was never taught how to create the types of daily miracles the women of his clan made but he did have something of his own he could create. He could make music. Telemachus could play the lyre like an angel. If he wasn't sitting watching the women he was playing his lyre, he played it so much it that people stopped calling him Telemachus and would call him the lyre player and eventually they just called him by the name of the instrument, Lyras.

He had learnt quickly how music affected the moods of people. When he played with aggressive intention the men would jump up and stamp out the most powerful martial dance of all, the *pentozali*. He sometimes would deliberately do that to get their blood boiling and have them mount their horses and ride to other towns to make trouble, just so he could have the house to himself.

At other times he would play the slower more peaceful tunes that would cause all to stand and do a slumberous *syrto*, the dragging dances which caused the overly macho men of his clan to step themselves into sedation. But his brothers and his father would taunt him.

'Eh Lyras, we need to find you a woman, you are married to that thing.'

Lyras had a dream that one day he would be able to do nothing but sit with the winds and play his music all day. Once in the day of his Pappou there had been a dispute about which sheep belonged to which clan. Both sides made accusations and shots were fired leaving one person from each clan dead. Logic and civility did not reign instead the madness of the vendetta became law. There was never any peace. Even his beloved sisters and mother would tell him he must be more active in his hatred of the other clans.

'I don't want to be active in hatred, I want to make music. I want to feel happy.' Telemachus' father was devastated that a son of his would not want to kill a man. It was his birthright to slaughter offenders.

'But they haven't offended me, or you. They might have said something to a Pappou one hundred years ago. It is not our family honor we defend. You defend someone else's honor, not that of our family.'

'What is that you say?' All his family took one step toward him.

'I read the books in school. I studied our histories, we have the best history why do we adopt the history of others?'

His father looked at him as if he was confused,

'Have you been in the sun too long again, didn't I always tell you to stay in the shade in the heat of the day.'

'No, I am speaking from facts.' He sighed.

'You are simply carrying on a cruel tradition picked up from a foreign occupying force that our ancestors found to be powerful and intimidating and, due to their lack of education, chose to emulate that style in the misguided hope that it would make them too appear formidable but all it did was explode into a pointless chain of murders. You may choose to continue to live a brutal life dedicated to reprisals in the style of the Venetian overlords, I will not.'

'What did he say?' asked one brother.

'I think he said we are uneducated,' said another brother, and yet another one said,

'I think he just called us Italians.' His father stepped forward.

'The only reason you are still breathing is because you are my son. You are speaking soft, like an easterner, maybe you belong there.'

'That is the most logical thing I have ever heard you say. You are right, maybe I belong there.'

Already Lyras had spoken more words to them today than he had in his entire life and he did not want to say any more. He could no longer stay within this stifling and destructive environment. He mounted his other love, his buckskin stallion, Xanthus, hung his lyre

208

over his shoulder and rode east, as east as one could go on Crete, to Elounda.

The poetic looking man riding a blonde horse and wearing the full black garb of the Western Cretan drew a lot of attention at the taverna. Lyras dismounted and sat to order a coffee and the owner asked,

'What brings you here? Running from some vendetta?'

'No not from one vendetta, from all of them. I seek peace and a place to play my lyre.'

The locals admired his powerful horse and gave Lyras work carrying goods up to the smaller villages higher up in the mountains. He made more than enough to live on and was able to spend every spare moment playing his haunting tunes. The locals liked his music, but they only wanted to hear it when it suited them such as weddings or name days. They got upset if he played during siesta or when there was a backgammon game going on in the taverna.

Lyras chose to stop speaking, he let his music speak for him but having his times of when to play music restricted made him very unhappy. One of the locals sitting at the taverna noticed.

'Eh Lyras why is your face on the floor, Eh? Why don't you go to Spinalonga, the lepers could use some sweet music, you will have all the peace you want there.' The man said it as the typical wisecrack but Lyras was already on his way to the dock to worry about answering him. He was done with talking anyway. He'd done enough for one lifetime. But he did have a few more words to say, to the boatman.

'Can you take my horse and me to Spinalonga?' He handed over 200 drachmas.

'My friend, for 200 drachmas I will carry you over on my back if you want.'

The boatman took the wad of notes to count them out, nodded his satisfaction and pulled out the ramp so Xanthus could be led on board. Lyras sat and played to keep his horse calm and the boatman knew to take them around to the other entrance, not to Dante's gate.

'Here you go my friend, enjoy your island holiday.' The boatman pulled out the ramp again and Lyras led Xanthus off and looked around him. He felt the sea air caress his hair in thanks for bringing music to Spinalonga.

That morning Maria was lying on the quilt on the floor of her room. Sometimes she was sure she could feel the life oozing out of her. She had a small mirror but she never looked in it. She wondered if she still looked like a woman or if her hair still shone like satin as it once did. She wanted to feel like a woman again, she started to think to herself but stopped when she was struck by the reality that she had never really lived as a woman. She came to Spinalonga as a girl and within months was now an old crone.

She needed some air. She wrapped her shawl around her shoulders and went out to stroll along the shores of Spinalonga and let herself think of things she had tried to not think about. As tended to be the usual pattern her thoughts went not to the things she had done in her life, but to things she had not done and now never would.

First she let the pain of the obvious omissions pierce her heart as she often now did. She welcomed the sharp pangs of helpless lament. It caused an anger that invigorated her. Why was she chosen by God to never know the embrace of a husband or the sweet pain of childbirth that the women of the town often spoke off. The pain that makes you feel your body is being torn in two and then never truly heals so whenever your child is away from you it feels as if a part of you is missing.

Maria released those thoughts, such was her fate but when her thoughts turned to the limitations placed upon her by the unwritten laws of society that was when true rage rose within her.

She would have liked to have known what love was like. Not romantic love but true passionate, physical love. She would have liked to have gone hunting with the men. She had once asked to join them but was slapped hard by an uncle who yelled at her that ladies belonged within the courtyard. She recalled watching the men ride off to hunt and feeling a slight envy, and she had always wanted to ride a horse. She had always wanted to ride a horse with the men but was told the only women who sit astride horses were gypsies and loose women. She had to remain content with being permitted to sit sideways on the pack donkey once.

She wanted to feel a man's arms around her, she wanted to feel her breasts swell with milk and feel her child suckle from her. She wanted to leave something behind in this world. She wanted to know she offered something and that her life had not been a waste.

She remembered one time when she was out strolling in her old neighborhood. She had looked into the window of one of the houses as one does when out walking. It was human nature to look at other people and into their windows. Maria had known this and always made sure that their own windows, when open, framed a bowl of flowers or a beautiful object so that when someone looked in they would smile because they had seen beauty. She had looked into the neighbor's window one time, at afternoon siesta. The window was curtained but the breeze caused the lacy wings to billow in and Maria caught a glimpse of what was happening inside. They were naked on the bed. The woman was straddling her husband as one would ride a horse and was looking down at him with a haughty desire. The husband was looking up at her in sheer rapture.

Maria looked away quickly moved on but the image of the lovers never left her. She had wanted to be naked with a man and now she never would. Her short life had been devoted to carrying out the will of others, all for nothing. How lovely it would have been to be with a man and have his baby, and to have ridden a horse.

She had wandered long enough, it was time to head back. She turned around before she walked back into the town to take another look at the mainland to transmit her love for her mother across the water. Maria had to look again, in case her weakening eyes were mocking her, and saw a horse standing on the waves.

Maria kept watching as she saw the boat come into view. It moored briefly for the horse to clamber up the boat ramp. A man followed who looked like he belonged in one of the paintings by El Greco that

Nikos had shown her pictures of in his books. He had a lyre hanging from his shoulder. He steadied his horse, grabbed the bridle and took a slow survey of the area.

Maria caught her breath. He had seen her. He stared straight at her and walked towards her. She couldn't move. She panicked. She couldn't even lift her hand to straighten her hair. How must she look? It was too late he was now standing a metre from her and the horse was right behind him nuzzling into his shoulder.

'Welcome and not welcome,' was all she could get out.

Lyras could see that the woman before him was a young and lovely in spite of her dry skin and mouth already beginning to turn down on one side. Lyras looked at her face and saw the generations of wounded women before her. Only women could carry wounds well, men did not know how to manage pain other than to either drown it in drink or drown it out with noise. Women embraced their pain and made it part of them. Maria knew she looked wounded so she did not have to keep any pain in her heart.

She reached over and patted Xanthus.

'I am not sure but I think I love horses. I have never been on one but have always had a secret dream to ride one. But then I was sent here and all dreams have stopped.' She spoke without sorrow, no self pity, just of things as they were.

Lyras stepped right up to her, placed his hands on her waist and pulled her in close to him and she, in instinctive response, placed her hands on his shoulders. He lifted her easily and sat her on the horse. She steadied herself and marveled at how everything looked better when viewed up higher. The next thing he did would make Maria remember all those times she had stood on the upper walls of the old fort with the intent of jumping off. She had reckoned that if the fall wouldn't kill her, the sea would. She did not know how to swim but she hoped that with the grace of God that would mean she would drown quickly. Now she knew why she was still alive.

He swung himself up onto the horse to sit behind her. He leant forward to take the reins encircling her body with his arms to do so. He pressed his chest into her back causing a wave of sensation to course through her like warm honey.

She could never understand why she hadn't let herself fall from the walls. She had always thought it was because Nikos needed her help with all the changes he was fighting to make on Spinalonga but now she knew it was for this. God had remembered her. He must have heard all those prayers she had made. Now she could die knowing what is was like to feel a man's arms around her. She leant back into the body of her man, for he was now her man, and used him as a comfortable armchair. She lifted her head up to let the sun kiss her face, the back of her head nestled perfectly into the curve of his neck and then he stroked her hair.

They rode to the highest point on the island. Somehow she had willed her weak and tiny body to make the walk up there many times before but always alone. Each experience made her feel insignificant and caused her isolation to be magnified to such an extent it overwhelmed her and she would have to close her eyes and dream of a sweeter memory so as not to find herself looking over the fort walls again.

It was different for her now on the back of this great horse with the arms of a man around her. Spinalonga was now her haven, their world. Less than hour ago she had been looking at the boat wondering how to get her legs entangled in the anchor's rope to drag her to the depths so she could leave this island for ever but now it was her personal paradise.

There were a few palms on the island, planted by the Ottomans to ensure their supply of dates. Lyras got down first and lay his jacket on the ground at the base of one large palm then lifted Maria down and placed her on it. He took a bag from the saddle and made a picnic for them. It was cheese pie and fresh figs. If she knew what ambrosia, the food of the gods, tasted like she was sure it would be like this.

Lyras took his lyre and played a tune for her that was a lullaby. As she drifted off to sleep under the date palm she prayed another prayer that when she died it would be in this exact way with food in her belly and a man by her side playing sweet music. The wind carried the tones of Lyras across the island. It whistled through the cracked windows of the patients houses and slid under the doors of the infirmary. The sombre silence of the island was stirred.

Nikos and Manoussos were having a discussion about doing more repairs to the church and the houses. Nikos was pleased with the progress that had been made but he wanted more. They all deserved more. It was possible now they had more income and power. But the truth was it was difficult to get workers to come to Spinalonga.

'We could do so much on our own but we need some sort of pack animal to really get some work done.'

'Yes, we could use a good donkey or a sturdy horse.' Both men stopped talking and the hair on the back of Nikos's neck stood on end.

'Where is that music coming from?'

'I know you have already had installed the piped music you were talking about but that sounds like a lyre not a record ?'

'Yes.'

They set out to try to find the source of the tune but were in no hurry. The lyre was a favorite instrument. Nikos had spent many happy hours in tavernas with friends listening and dancing to its strains. A skilled lyre player could make a good living anywhere in Greece, anywhere there were Greeks.

The older patients hadn't heard such music in over a decade. Three of them were slumped in their corner. They were weeping like babies for they thought Death had finally come for them and they were now in Heaven hearing angels. Angela was standing on the doorstep of the infirmary looking around too, her face appeared softer, lighter, and somehow prettier. The new doctor had come out of the lab to check if he really was hearing things.

Even Pavlos stopped his terrorizing and stood still and turned his monstrous Cyclopean head towards the sound. Nikos and Manoussos left them all in their trance to track the source of the music. Then it suddenly stopped. Nikos and Manoussos looked at each other and shrugged. All went back to what they were doing and imagined they had been hearing things.

Lyras stopped playing when Maria said she had to go.

'I will meet you here later to share bread if you like?' I have carrots too. I will bring some for Xanthus. Lyras went off to the old houses at the edge of the town where Maria had told him earlier there was also room to stable Xanthus. She skipped away giggling and chatting to herself all the way back to the infirmary for her scheduled blood tests. Later Maria hummed as she kneaded the bread. She was no longer a silent servant, dutifully hunched over. She almost looked like the Maria she once was. The aroma of the baked bread energized her like coal to a steam train as she ran back to the palm tree to find Lyras.

He was there, already sitting. Laid out on a cloth in front of him were some olives, some cheese, tomatoes and some fruit, a feast. She ran to him and she pulled apart the steaming bread. They laughed over it together and made the most delicious sandwiches they had ever eaten by squishing together ripe tomatoes and soft cheese between the still warm slices. They talked about everything as they ate and salted their food with the plump olives and sat and ate slowly to enjoy every bite.

He spoke to Maria. She would be the only one he would speak too, only she deserved his words. Their first conversation had been to exchange their names.

'Lyras!' Maria shook her head.

'That is not a real name. No priest would have baptised you with that name. My name is Maria. I have my grandmother's name of course as is the custom. I would have loved to have had a daughter and given her my mother's name of Theodora. It means 'gift of God' you know, Theodora. And in my case it really would be wouldn't it? I mean I am a leper living on a rock, what chance do I have of things such as love and a child? Oh anyway I didn't mean to talk such sadness.' He laughed and tore into a chunk of bread.

'I promise you Maria, if we ever have a daughter, we will name her Theodora.' He expressed it so naturally, as if they had been betrothed for years. Maria's soul quivered within her at the elation of being reunited with its mate.

'Why did you come here? Do you not fear the leprosy?' Lyras shook his head. He had never wanted to speak again, he didn't think he would need to but this pure girl made him open his heart and mouth. They sat together and he told her his story and she hers. Then he opened his arms for her to lie in as he fed her grapes.

'I spend a lot of time in the infirmary. I have a lot of tests because I am very sick they tell me but I also do a lot of helping out. I hear the doctors talking in the lab. They say they think that much of the population is immune to the disease. Wouldn't you know my brother and I are in the percentage that are not?'

'I don't care Maria. I am here to stay, I might get the illness and I might not but I feel more alive here with you than I have ever felt in my life.' He took her hand in his and kissed it. Maria wanted to cry but couldn't, her tear ducts no longer worked. She took the hand of Lyras and held it against her cheek for a moment before she kissed it. The two of the sat in happy silence, holding hands until Lyras took his hand away. He guided Maria to sit next to him and lean on his shoulder while he played his music. After a while she got up.

'I have to go.'

'No, stay with me.' They were the four sweetest words she had ever heard.

'I promised the women I would help them prepare their outfits for tomorrow. We are going to church for the first time, all of us. We are all going to see if Father Manoussos will drink the wine.'

Lyras looked lost so Maria explained, 'You see he was given a choice to make. None of the patients wanted to attend church, we felt it was hypocritical. The church disowned us, yet Manoussos asked us to attend. He was told if he drank all the wine out of the communion cup after the service then all those who can will help him rebuild the church.

The government has helped us a lot, thanks to Nikos, but the church still needs much work, that is the domain of the Archdiocese and as yet they haven't sent any money to help out so we should get a start on it. There is much work to do. To be honest I would like to help but I am still a little weak and I don't want to walk too much yet but I might drop by after the service to see how it all went.' Lyras kissed her hand again.

'It sounds as if they need the sort of help only Xanthus can give.'

'Yes they do. I know they do, Nikos and Manoussos were discussing it when they visited me. They need a strong pack animal.' Lyras read into the pleading look in her eyes.

'Xanthus and I will be at your door to escort you to church tomorrow at whatever time you wish to be there.'

Chapter 17. Holy Communion

Father Manoussos rang the bells of Saint Panteleimon himself for the first call to service at seven thirty am. He had yet to have any volunteers for bell ringer. He then went into the sanctuary and put on the celebratory robes of the Paschal service for he felt the occasion called for it. Today would see the resurrection of his church. He knew a priest in full robes was a commanding sight. He looked taller and carried all the glory of Byzantium.

He had spent all the previous three days preparing for this day through fasting and praying for the will of God to be done. When he stepped out to stand before the Royal gate and begin the service he saw his church was full. They had come. He commenced with gusto and his voice was strong. Nikos, as promised, was chanter. He had no experience in Byzantine chanting but did the best he could. Nikos made a mental note to get Manoussos to ask for a book on the chants to be sent to them. He knew they depended on the correct intonation of eight tones and Nikos was struggling so much that people were snickering at his feeble warbling.

The service had reached the time for the Nicene Creed to be taken, as customary, by the entire congregation. Only Nikos spoke, he had the text in front of him and read it out. A few of the women joined in towards the end but in general it was a solo performance by Nikos. Manoussos did not as much as blink in disappointment but entered the sanctuary to prepare the offering of the blood of Christ. He commenced the preparation of the sacrifice of Communion, *the Anaphora*, and went through all the rituals and prayers until he reached the *Epiclesis*, the invocation of the Holy Spirit to enter the sacramental wine and bread.

He took the bread which he had baked himself and had placed the sacred seal on it to make the special patterns. With his knife he cut out the central pattern of the NIKA then the two triangular patterns on each side of it, one for the Panayia and the other for the saints and angels. He broke the lumps of bread up into crumbs and placed it onto the golden communion chalice into which he had poured sweet wine. This meant that with each spoonful of wine there would be a piece of the bread so everyone partaking of communion would get both the body and the blood of Christ.

He said the complex set of prayers in the traditional low tone and when the time came to kiss the holy Gifts and say,

'I love You, Lord, my strength. The Lord is my rock, and my fortress, and my deliverer,' he said them with a greater depth of meaning than ever before.

He stood in the Royal Gate and held the ornate gold cup up high and pronounced,

'Take, eat, this is my Body which is broken for you for the forgiveness of sins.' Every single patient on Spinalonga had lined up to take communion and the first in line was Pavlos. Manoussos beckoned them forward and Pavlos took his communion with a sickening slurp. The others were more sedate.

Naturally Manoussos was a man of faith who believed in prayer but he also took some more mortal precautions. He had been well trained by his hierarchs in the ministering of the Eucharist. He knew the pure gold of the spoon and cup which were always used did not harbor microbes. He knew the correct technique for offering communion was to tip the spoon so its sacred contents would pour out into the recipient's mouth rather than the using their lips to receive them. He also knew that the high alcohol content of the sweet wine destroyed most bacteria and he took extra care to add an extra shot of the almost pure alcohol of *tsikoudia* which had been given to him as a farewell gift. But none of the patients of Spinalonga, who now numbered over one hundred people, knew this when they all leaned forward to look into the sanctuary after communion was over.

They only saw Manoussos standing tall and proud and holding the cup high in acknowledgment to God. He brought the cup to his lips to gulp down nothing. The patients also did not know there was not a drop left over after they had taken communion. He held the cup to his lips and tilted his head so the patients could witness his throat undulating as he presumably was gulping down the wine.

'He did it and he did it with a smile on his face,' were the sorts of comments from the patients after church service was over. No one was in a hurry to leave. They were behaving as a regular congregation would after a church service. Chatting and catching up with people was going on and invitations for coffee were being given and accepted. They felt elated in the freedom to feel normal again which brought a sense of celebration into the air. Everybody was happy, especially Manoussos who had won the respect of the patients and now had himself a workforce.

Immediately after the service Ikaros began to study the condition of the walls. The priest and Nikos walked around with him as he analysed what needed to be done first.

'We are going to need to bring in extra stones from other buildings. It will be difficult for we have no donkey, no cart here. We could form a human chain but there are few of us strong enough to lift the larger stones.'

'God will find a way my son but you need your strength go and rest. I will pray tonight for enlightenment on how we are going to find a way to bring the stones to the church without breaking our backs. If we had a pack animal it would be different but we do not have that luxury.'

'Father anything can happen. Did you ever think we would have a hospital and a cinema? Besides, if Nikos Lambrakis can catch an eagle then we can find a way to carry stones. Back when I was in the living world I was a craftsman, a stonemason. Look at the village Nikos. The only true ruins in it are us. The people before us are long gone but when we go the stones will still be here. I didn't get to make a family of my own but I made homes for families to enjoy and their families will after them. That makes me very happy Nikos. My life and what I did with it did matter. I can make it matter here on Spinalonga too.'

Nikos had been looking straight into Ikaros' eyes and noticed how they changed when he spoke of the joy his architectural creations brought people. The eyes of a leper have no light. There is an unwritten law somewhere that they must stop shining upon diagnosis, as hope is extinguished so is any sparkle. He looked at Ikaros and saw his light had been switched on again and he hadn't been the one to do it. Serving others by doing what he loved was making Ikaros beam like a lighthouse.

Nikos wanted to see that gleam in his own eyes again before he no longer could use them and he knew that time was coming soon. The doctor at the infirmary had told him the optic nerves were being destroyed at a faster rate than what they considered normal.

'Ikaros you are a saint. I will pray for you to be canonized at the same time I pray for a way for us to move the stones we need for building.' Nikos could not help but smile at Father Manoussos.

'You are crazy you old priest.' In response Manoussos embraced him and kissed him on each cheek.

'I owe you that.' Nikos got to thinking of how the lives of people can change in an instant.

'Wasn't it was wonderful to see Thanos. Thank you again Father for getting this boy into school. He has done so well.'

'Again your first thoughts are for others Nikos. You are the one who made this happen not me. You are the one who saw the potential in Thanos, not me. You are the one who gave up precious time to sit with the boy and teach him how to read and you are the one who told me to send him off to school. Then God took over and put Thanos in the right place at the right time.'

Nikos mused over the words.

'The right place at the right time. Yes, I guess that is how things work out sometimes.' They heard Maria's voice call out to them.

'*Kali mera.*' she was coming towards them with a ghostly looking man and she was on a horse, a big blonde horse.

Angela had attended church too, as an observer. Angela was always watching Pavlos. The patients and staff at the infirmary believed she was in love with him. She sat by his side while he was recovering from losing his eye to Artemis and every time he was brought in for testing and medications she was right there by his side, checking on him, smiling at him even offering to do little chores for him and giving him sweet treats. Now here she was keeping an eye on him at church as well.

She was the one to break the stunned silence.

'You must be the one they call Lyras. The boatman told me he had delivered a healthy man and a horse. I thought he was joking.' Nikos stammered,

'Welcome and not well come,' out of habit, for the man was not a patient. When he remembered it he added,

'That is a fine animal you have there.'

Lyras gently helped Maria dismount and all witnessed the tender glances between the two of them. Lyras and Maria also noticed the eager looks that Nikos and Ikaros were giving Xanthus. Maria snuggled into the crook of Lyras' arm.

'I have told Lyras all about the building program you would like to carry out here and Lyras has kindly agreed for you to have the use of Xanthus to help with the heavy work.'

Nikos shook the man's hand with enthusiasm.

227

'Our deepest thanks to you Lyras.' He spotted the lyre slung over his shoulder.

'That was you playing the music? I thought I was dreaming. It was magnificent.' Lyras smiled at Nikos as thanks for his kind words. They all laughed when Ikaros stuck his head into the conversation.

'I thought I was dead and was hearing heavenly music.' He laughed with them.

'I wish to thank you too, for the use of your fine animal. It will be such a big help to us.'

Maria was relishing her new status as intermediary between them and someone of such importance and firmly advised them of the terms.

'Lyras and Xanthus will work with you every day, for five hours a day until the work is done. Let us know which hours you need. We have to go back to the top of the island now. Lyras needs to play his music.' All the others stood open mouthed as Lyras lifted Maria onto Xanthus and then swung himself onto the horse to be behind her and then canter away to leave as mysteriously as they had arrived.

Manoussos eventually spoke.

'That was a definite example of the right place at the time.'

No one ever heard Lyras say a word, no one except Maria. Every evening she sat with him while he played his lyre. Maria didn't think she could be any happier. She sat against the tree and looked up into the heavens to thank everyone possible, she began with Aphrodite, occasionally she had watched the waves break against the rocks of the shores of Spinalonga and she prayed love would be born the way from it Aphrodite was born out of the foam of the sea. Then she prayed to the *Panayia*, the mother of God, to grant her the strength to accept she would never bear a child.

She would talk to Lyras about her thoughts and the life she once led. They had been meeting every night for days but this time when Maria started to get up to go back to her rooms he put his hand on her arm to stop her. He slid over to be by her side, drew her into his arms and swayed gently with her as if in tune to a melody that only they could hear. He helped her to her feet and before she turned to go he bent and kissed her on the forehead. The next day when she met him under the tree she told him what was in her heart.

'I no longer fear death.' He was startled at her comment. She continued.

'I can die happy Lyras, truly I tell you. My secret dream was to feel the arms of a man around me and you made that dream come true for me.'

She spoke directly, without guile or shyness. Lyras saw more than her purity of heart he saw the bloom of womanhood, he had noticed the deep curve of her waist to her hip, he took in the swell of her bosom. He traced their outline with his finger and watched the way her body reacted to his touch. He did not see a leper, and never had, he saw a woman.

Lyras held her tighter and she leant into him to enjoy the presence of his masculinity. Lyras bent to kiss her but this time he did not bend to kiss her forehead, he cupped her face with his hands so she was looking at him and he brought his mouth down onto hers. He moved his hands down to find hers and guided them up to encircle his neck as he wrapped his arms around her and drew her closer to him, never taking his mouth of hers the entire time.

He scooped her up in his arms and took quick powerful strides to his hut where he laid her on his blanket and stood over her while he unbuttoned his shirt, then dropped to his knees and slowly removed her clothing one piece at a time, kissing each part of her body as it was revealed. Lyras whispered tender words into her ear as he nuzzled her throat and caressed her body. He kissed her with hunger and slowly slid his hand down to between her legs and smiled as her breathing became faster.

'I'm going to kiss you Maria.'

'You already are kissing me.'

'I want to kiss you everywhere.' And he did, he kissed her from her toes to her forehead and then down again, paying extra attention to her womanly folds until she was yelping with utter delight as she felt her body become overpowered by sweet spasms and released a flood of warm wetness. Lyras plunged himself into her at the peak of her moistness and the sharp sting of his entry was absorbed by her juices. He held still as she bit into his shoulder and until he felt her relax against him as the initial shock subsided. He moved back into her and almost instantly she was moving with him faster and faster until his own explosion made him collapse against her and he whispered tender words into her ear. He would whisper tender words into ear every night for the rest of her life.

Maria was due for her regular visit to the infirmary for her medications and monthly check up. The doctor immediately noticed she looked almost beautiful. An instinct told him to do a further examination.

'Maria I want to look at your body please remove your shirt so I can examine your chest.' She had never had that swollen bosom before.

'What is it doctor?'

'I'm not sure but there are slight changes in your body and if I didn't know it was impossible I would almost say you were with child.'

Maria buttoned herself up.

'With child?' she said wondrously.

'I am sorry I shocked you. I know it is impossible and of course you are a moral young woman and would never find yourself in such a situation.' Maria's silence made the doctor question her.

'Maria, could such a thing be possible?'

'It's possible doctor.' He had never had such a situation before, a pregnant leper. He had to consult his colleagues.

Maria ran to find Lyras and there he was leading Xanthus to the church ready for a day's work. She rushed up to him and threw her arms around him,

'I went to see the doctors but I am not sick, I carry our baby.' Lyras spoke. Even Maria was surprised for he never spoke above a whisper and only when they were alone.

'Baby? Maria, you angel. An angel is the mother of my child.' He kissed her, picked her up and twirled her around then kissed her again and they giggled like school children. Lyras lifted her onto Xanthus sidesaddle and took them straight to Saint Panteleimon.

Father Manoussos was standing outside mixing lime-wash for the outside of the church to be painted white. He had seen many things in his time of being a priest and he knew what he was looking at right now.

'Greetings children you both seem very happy today. Is there something I can do for you?'

'Yes Father we wish to be crowned,' said a glowing Maria.

'It is God's will. The church will be looking its best within a few weeks I will advise you when the nuptials can take place.'

'We do not wish to wait Father, we cannot wait.'

'Have you fallen into error, my child? Is there a shame that must be put right?'

'If you have asked me that a year ago Father I would have said yes but we feel no shame and there is no error. What has happened to us is a miracle, a joyous miracle. We just think it is proper to have the wedding ceremony before the baptism.'

Nikos arrived after a hunting session with Artemis, she was perched on his arm and he was carrying the day's bounty, three ducks and four large salmon.

'Sister, what is happening here? You look very happy.'

'I have never been happier brother. I am going to become a bride and a mother.'

'Maria! How can this be?'

'Don't be shocked Nikos, be happy. The gift of life is within me. It's a miracle.'

'Oh I am happy sister and yes it is a miracle but I fear for your health. Can you carry this child?'

'Brother, I feel as if can do anything.' Maria looked at Lyras lovingly. Manoussos patted Nikos on the shoulder.

'One thing I learned in all my years as a priest is that there are two types of people who can make anything happen, a woman who is about to become a bride and woman who is about to become a mother and Maria is about to become both.'

'Do you care if you are showing at the time of your wedding Maria?' asked her brother.

'Not at all dear brother, not at all. I have Lyras and I have a life within me, I have everything I have ever wanted.'

'Well then if you let me get to work I will have your house ready, your church ready and all of Spinalonga looking like a jewel by your wedding day.'

Nikos called a Brotherhood meeting and announced the upcoming wedding of Maria and Lyras. Their romantic meeting and the miracle of a baby coming to Spinalonga caused euphoria to spread among all the patients. All the domain leaders brought their crews and announced what they could contribute to the city state of Spinalonga and to the wedding.

There were now one hundred and forty three patients, souls who'd had every dream stripped away from them and as the sign over Dante's gate declared, all hope abandoned. Now all their lives had purpose again.

'I am a very privileged priest Nikos.' Nikos looked at him and waited to hear why.

'I have given many funeral services. None are ever easy, even of the old and the sick. Today is something else. Today I have the privilege of witnessing one hundred and forty three resurrections. Men stepped forward and declared which skill they were best at such as carpentry, masonry, and painting. From the women there were seamstresses, knitters, lace makers, bakers, decorators, every woman present could do many things.

233

They seemed to be more useful than the men. Lyras stood to the side and watched the proceedings. The findings did not surprise him but only confirmed his adoration of womankind. Men were very good at doing one thing well, women could do many things very well.

Pavlos did not stand to declare his skills. He had tried to intimidate several people into not attending the meeting but he could see he was outnumbered. He stood to one side and watched, sneering occasionally but got quieter as the evening went on. He could not compete when he saw the personal pride the others were taking at being able to feel of value.

One man spoke up,

'I am not a *mastora* of anything but I am good general hand and will help in anyway. I learn fast and volunteer to go where help is most needed. Many more stood up and said similar. Those who did not think they had anything to offer in the way of any special skills offered their willingness to learn one. Everybody at the meeting had stepped forward and offered to help in some way. Everybody except Pavlos, who was now walking around jeering at his gang members for being weak. Nikos noticed him,

'Pavlos come tell us about what you can offer?'

Pavlos slunk out without answering.

In the morning they saw what it was Pavlos could do. Written across the walls of the newly white-washed church in bright red paint were the words, *'Home to whores and mutes.'*

'You like my contribution guys?' Pavlos said to his cronies when they gathered around him.

'Who says I can't offer something too huh?'

'Pavlos we painted the church ourselves, you ruined our work.'

'We liked doing it, the church looks like new and we felt good about making something look nice for everybody to enjoy.'

'Then you can all view my contribution offer to our noble community, as Lambrakis now likes to call us, as incentive to work harder."

'No Pavlos. Nikos has brought us a good life, we can be proud again. No one has anything to fear anymore and we don't fear you.'

Pavlos loped off in fury and at first looked for something to smash into oblivion but Ikaros and Makis were following him to ensure the beast that Pavlos was did no harm. He found himself walking towards the one person who always had showed him understanding.

Chapter 18. Angela

Angela was sitting at her desk looking at photographs, she put them quickly away when she saw him come in.

'Pavlos, good evening. Why do you look so upset?'

Pavlos smacked his ugly hand on the table.

'That is why I like you Angela. You always understand how I feel.'

Angela smiled a discreet smile.

'You like me Pavlos?'

'What's not to like?' he said as he stared suggestively at her, scanning her like an x-ray. He liked to unsettle people, especially women. Except this time, Angela was scanning him right back.

'So why are you upset Pavlos, who has not cooperated with you?'

'Yes, that's right. They are not doing what I want. There is happiness on the island, when people are happy they fear nothing, they get strong. Such happiness is a tragedy. I think I shall have to put a stop to all this.'

'How will you do that Pavlos?'

He got cocky as men with the spotlight on them tend to do, he leaned against the wall.

'Well I could have just taken the bride but the groom got in early and now they are going to breed another little leprous mute. So maybe the groom might just have to disappear. He and that horse of his have made life a little too good, too easy. They need to remember Pavlos is in charge.' He knew Lyras liked to sit on top of the island and play his lyre. He would be easy to find.

And as for Nikos, he had to get him when he wasn't with that eagle. He could not afford to lose another eye. Nikos often sat on the edge of the walls to wait for her to return to him with her catch. It would be quite easy to have him slip off the rocks. Dealing with Lyras would be more difficult, he was bigger and healthier and would put up a fight.

Angela would give him anything he wanted, all he had to do was say nice things to her. At her age she would believe anything. Women have it in their blood to be needed, women think love is everything, make a woman feel loved and she will do anything for you, then start withholding the love and they will turn somersaults to have you show it to them again. But Pavlos didn't know he was dealing with a woman who did not need to be needed. Angela knew that romantic love was merely a sweet, short term trap that often turned bitter.

'Angela, why didn't someone smart claim you a long time ago? If only I wasn't the way I am I would make you happy in the special Pavlos way.' Angela blushed and giggled.

'You are still very handsome Pavlos and I enjoy doing things to help you.' Pavlos swaggered across the room and rasped into her ear.

'You are lucky I am a thoughtful man, even for a leper, I could make you moan like a whore but I wouldn't put you at risk.'

'I am sure you have made many women cry out with emotion.' She kept her eyes downcast as she spoke. But Angela knew the severity of his condition and that his manhood would have been withered by his disease. He would have nothing better than a couple of moldy figs and a withered sardine between his legs.

Angela understood how such a thing could affect a man from her experiences with soldiers wounded on the battlefield. The ones who lost their ability to perform as a man either lost the will to live or became very aggressive and full of scorn, like Pavlos. Then there was the third type, the givers as she had liked to call them. These glorious men were the ones who decided that they would now derive their pleasure from giving the woman they were with all the pleasure she could handle.

It was a wonderful way for a young nurse to remain virginal but still have all the intense pleasure of intimate loving. She shifted in her chair as she summoned moist memories of the oral ministrations of her grateful male patients when she had visited them in their tents late at night. She remembered the first time and how effortlessly it had happened.

'Let me show you how grateful I am for what you have done for me,' a handsome young one had once said. She offered him words of comfort.

'Lie still and rest and you will be fine.'

'Let me put my mouth on your soft angel lips.'

He is handsome, it is dark and he may be dying, what would it hurt? She reasoned with herself as she bent down to brush her mouth against his.

'Lovely, just lovely, now just do as I ask and I will show you what I really meant,' he whispered into her ear.

'Go close the flap of the tent them come close to me so I can touch you.' She did as he asked and returned to him.

'Here I am.' She extended out her hand to stroke his shoulder.

'Undo your blouse so I can see your breasts.'

Angela looked right at the young man who had the will to live but the Fates had decided otherwise. She looked at him and smiled a knowing smile that told him she was going to be very cooperative. She undid her blouse slowly. She knew her body and she knew it was at button three that her cleavage looked its best so she slowed down and bent over him to tend to his sheets. She continued but did not take the blouse off. She just moved it apart enough to frame her breasts so they were presented like luscious petit fours on a tray. She bent over him and pushed her breasts together and leaned down lower until they were right over his mouth and placed a plump pink nipple into his mouth for him to suck on like a cool life giving ice.

He placed one of his hands on the other breast to caress it and slid his other hand up her skirts. He moaned in surprise when his explorations revealed she was not wearing any underwear. It was not intentional but a happy coincidence due to her big bloomers still drying in her tent.

'You still want to kiss my lips?'

'Bring them to me doll.' Angela stood up straight so she could hitch up her skirts, straddled the narrow camp bed and lowered herself onto her young lover's face so he could continue his long, languid kissing.

When his gratitude had brought Angela to her peak she screamed so loud the guards thought a woman was being attacked. She'd had to lie that a man had squealed in pain when she went to re-bandage him. The hospital tent guards accepted her answer without concern, especially the one who had seen her in silhouette grinding down on the soldiers face while he lapped at her till she shuddered into collapse. He showed his gratitude with those sweet kisses for three days until his wounds won the battle and he died. Angela did a little involuntary shudder at the memory of her many mutilated heroes. She had loved them and they had loved her for bringing them the taste of a woman.

She looked over at Pavlos' grotesque face and slobbery tongue and shuddered again, for a different reason.

'You know Pavlos, life is difficult for me, I have no family, I am getting too old to become a mother and all the doctors here are married or only on short term contracts.' Actually that wasn't quite true there was Doctor Lukas, a widower of forty. He had admired Angela from the moment he arrived and had often sat next to her at mealtimes. True love could blossom there if she permitted it but for now she had her duty to attend to, it was far more important.

Pavlos watched her perfectly rounded rump as she walked to and fro fetching papers and filing them away. He had to remember his duty too, he had a wedding to ruin and a leper to deal with. He needed to show he was strong in other ways so he gave in to the demands of his ego, which needed an audience.

'Hey Angela, guess what I am going to do?'

She leaned forward to hear his plans.

'I am going to put a stop to the wedding or at least ruin it so their happiness will be broken.'

'Why would you do that Pavlos?'

'They have changed things around here too much. Lyras plays music and they all feel soothed, Maria walks around shining like a little sun, it's not right. And Nikos is real trouble. Ever since he caught that eagle everybody thinks he is some sort of magician. He is doing everything possible to make life better for the lepers but when their life improves my life worsens.'

'Why Pavlos? Nikos mastered Nature to catch an eagle for you to have food, then he secured you bigger pensions for you to have more money, you have us and the infirmary now and power and many good things. Life is better for you all. It makes good sense to me.'

'That eagle took my eye!'

'I know, I treated you remember. Everybody said you were trying to steal her but I know you would never do a thing like that.' Pavlos turned his face so his one eye looked away from her and changed the subject.

'We all get given more money now. Do you know what that means? No one will want anything from me, my power will be gone. No one will fear me. Everyone will have full bellies to fight me back!'

'I understand you Pavlos. You should be respected and it annoys me too the way they come in here and use our paper to write those letters to all the ministers asking for this and for that. It is an obstacle to me doing my job. I ask you, am I a nurse or a secretary?' She lowered her voice.

'If you want to do anything the others might not like I would help you. I like things better when people are under tight control. It gives me less to do.'

'Ah Angela, what a team we would have made. I am going to get rid of the horse and of Lyras first.

Without the horse the heavy work cannot continue and without the groom there can be no wedding.'

'How are you going to get rid of a horse Pavlos?'

'I can get it to fall off the cliff high on the island.'

'How are you going to get it there?'

'I still have to work out all the details but you will see Angela, my time will come.'

Angela wanted to be as close to him as possible. No one could understand her connection to him. The residents would try to explain it by saying things like,

'It is a terrible when a woman is so lonely that she would follow a man like him just for the hope of hearing a kind word.'

In the small testing room behind Angela's desk a patient lay resting after her regular blood tests. It was good news, a negative result. Three negative results in a row meant release. The result gave Athena the jolt she needed to begin to re-enter the living world again.

In the days before Nikos had come to Spinalonga and brought law and order with him things were a lot different. When a patient tried to escape and was caught, he was glued to a rock and left there to die as a deterrent to others who wanted to put others at risk. Now at least there were the regular tests that gave the occasional negative result and a patient was given hope of leaving the island in a much safer manner. Athena had the milder self healing form of leprosy. Angela entered the room.

'Are you okay? Did you hear everything he said? We need to stop him. But I can't tell anyone else yet. We will have to keep a watch on him ourselves.' The patient nodded in agreement.

'Good, you get some more rest. You are getting better every day. Sleep now and I will bring you some food later.'

Pavlos enjoyed the position of power and prestige that Angela gave him through her absolute trust that he told her everything. He even let her come along with him sometimes to meet the boat and pick up goods. The boatman only ever came to Dante's Gate when he had a new patient to deliver, all other deliveries were made to the other side of the island at ten in the morning, twice a week. On delivery days at around ten in the morning someone would go to Dante's gate to see if there were any newcomers to meet.

Yesterday when the boatman had delivered a load of food for the infirmary kitchen he had told Angela that he would not be doing any deliveries the next due day because he had to do some maintenance on the boat. She kept the news to herself.

'Pavlos I have not been to Dante's Gate since I arrived here, I think I will go there today to greet the boat. I might ask Nikos to come with me.' She said it with the exact note of casualness.

'What's the matter *koukla*, don't you want your Pavlos today?' She blushed.

'Well I would much rather prefer your company of course, I just wasn't sure how to ask you.' She looked at her feet as she spoke.

'Eh I know, the women go crazy for me, come on who needs that city boy. Let's go see if anyone is to be told Welcome today.' She chatted easily to him as they walked down to the Street of Pain and entered the tunnel.

'No boat,' stated Pavlos in surprise.

'Ah well that is a good thing isn't it? Let's chat for a while and enjoy the view.' She took his arm and walked with him to the end of the jetty. Her easy chatting had relaxed him as he stood at the very end of the jetty looking out over the waters to the mainland.

'What do you think about when you look out there Pavlos? Do you ever remember places you've gone and people you've met?'

'No, no I don't I don't think about anything anymore except how to stay in control of Spinalonga.'

'Don't you ever think of the Venetis family?'

She had said it so easily he had begun to answer.

'They got in my way...hey! What are you asking that for, what do you know about that?' She looked up at him and placed one of her hands on his chest, she spoke softly, soothingly.

'I just wonder if you ever felt bad about what you did to that innocent family.'

She drew her other hand out from under her apron.

'Because really even a pig like you should feel something.' She had said it so sweetly and evenly. He faced her, the expression on his face showed he was perplexed at why she was talking like that. He didn't even see the long scalpel she used to efficiently pierce his right lung. He gasped and stepped back and bent low. He tried to speak but the air whistling out of his lungs was the only sound he could make. He leaned against her and she spoke, still sweetly, still calm.

'Don't struggle Pavlos, just fall to your knees as your body wants you to do. I knew exactly where to strike. You see I want you to feel what my brother and his family felt as you took their lives. I want you to have the same shock I did when I arrived to celebrate his name day but instead had to arrange four funerals. Is the breath trickling out of your body like my poor niece when you strangled her after you violated her tender body?' Her voice was as steady as a surgeon's hand. He leaned further into her and she stepped back slowly to allow him to slip to the ground till he was kneeling.

She deftly withdrew the scalpel and tipped the kneeling man over so she could reach his crotch. She hacked at his tattered clothes till his genitalia were exposed and sliced them off like a dry wart, as the blood began gushing from the wound she stuffed the mushy package into his gaping mouth, still releasing air like a slowly deflating balloon. From out of her pocket she drew a long thin needle.

'Did you know you pierced my brother's heart? I am not going to do the same to you, death would be too quick, too easy,' she said evenly as she skewered him in the left kidney. His body arched up in agonising speechlessness. Angela was as calm as if she was administering medication. She had played this scene over and over in her mind ever since she requested her transfer to Spinalonga. Her entire remaining family had been wiped out by one man. Everything her brother had was now hers but she could not live in any peace knowing they were all gone but their killer lived free. Leper or not, he was free to breathe and eat and sleep while they never would again.

Her precious little nephew who had his head crushed against the stone walls of the house was in her thoughts as she walked up to the edge of the jetty where Pavlos was gushing blood and hissing like a snake. Here she knew was where she needed to use all her strength.

She kicked him in the back and he rolled a little but not enough.

In his fury he was able to stick out his hand and grab her ankle bringing her down to the ground with him. He was gurgling something that was not discernable but she knew he would be saying something along the lines of, *If I am going, I am taking you with me.* But she was ready for him. She had been ready since the day she buried her family.

She reached over the edge of the jetty and easily found the large stick she had put on the little stone lower ledge the day before when she knew the boatman was not coming. She brought it down on Pavlos' hands making him let go of her ankle. She got up quickly and swung it like a baseball bat to hit him square in the face but he got up in one last super human effort and whacked it out of her hands leaving her vulnerable and weaponless. She knew he was fatally wounded but in the time it would take him to die he might kill her too. He tried to lurch at her but she poked him in his one remaining eye and then ducked down to regain a striking position and to try to reach out and grab hold of the stick.

She saw her fallen stick get lifted up. It swung up and struck him on the chin knocking him right back to overbalance. He arched backwards and swung his arms violently to try to keep his balance but he was too far over, he crashed onto the rocks at the base of the pier smashing his head open before he sank into the water. Angela looked up to see who had struck him and saw Athena, his rape victim.

'You left the infirmary? I told you to stay there so he wouldn't hurt you again. Go back quickly so I can finish up here.'

'That was for my puppy.' Athena embraced Angela.

'Thank you.' Athena left quietly to return to her room at the infirmary, but with a smile on her face. She was definitely getting better and her recovery would be even speedier now. Angela sighed in satisfaction as she tilted her head up to feel the sea breeze applaud her actions.

Behind her, high on the fortified walls of Spinalonga stood Ikaros the stonemason who had walked to find a few extra stones to even up a wall he was completing.

Angela did not brush off her clothes or fix her hair, it was more convenient to her to appear disheveled. She had grazed her face and arms when she fell. She slipped the scalpel and skewer back into her pockets beneath her nurse's apron. No one would search her and she would have ample time to sterilize them and put them back into their places. No one would miss them anyway, she did all the stocktaking and ordering. The shock of what she had done began to overwhelm her. She knew it would, it was a natural reaction and anyone else would assume it was the shock of the attack.

Ikaros came running down to see her and met her when she emerged from the tunnel.

'Miss Angela let me help you.' Others had seen Ikaros running and followed him to see what was wrong. Her distressed and disheveled condition was obvious as they formed a protective circle around her.

'Did anyone see what happened?' asked one of the women. She had her story all ready but Ikaros spoke first.

'I saw the whole thing. Poor Miss Athena must have been out wandering. Pavlos got to her and began to attack her. Before I could start my way down I saw Nurse Angela come looking for Miss Athena, she tried to stop Pavlos. He went for her with a scalpel he must have stolen from the infirmary. You put up one hell of a fight Miss Angela. Pavlos was so violent and then tried to force himself on her, she fought back, he lost his footing and fell onto the rocks smashing his head before falling into the sea, I know he could not swim and the currents are strong today.'

Angela stared at Ikaros as he spoke. He never once looked at her to suggest he had something over her. He held his chin high and he spoke convincingly and asked nothing of her. That told her much. He was as glad as she was that Pavlos the monster was gone. After all the suffering that fiend inflicted upon women Ikaros thought it was sweet justice that the person who finished him off was a woman.

Nobody questioned a thing. No reports had to be written and no authorities had to be informed. He was already dead and buried. It was over.

Angela fell into a small depression afterwards. Her major purpose for living had been carried out. With Pavlos dead so was her family. Up until then they had lived within her, now they were laid to rest and all she had was the bitterness of everyday routine.

Doctor Lukas thought it was the after effects of the shock. He had always found her to be an efficient worker and very well organised.

'I will be having a coffee break shortly Angela, please join me.'

'Thank you doctor, I will.'

'Call me Lukas, please. You know Angela, I do not know hardly anything about you, where you are from or if you have a family, or a husband.'

'I am from Athens, and I have no family, no husband. I was sent to work early to send money back to support my younger brother so he could get his technical training. Our parents were killed in the Smyrna genocides so I took the responsibility for his education. He became a very good rail engineer but he died suddenly. I never got married because I was either working or mourning.'

He was much moved.

'Angela the refugees from Smyrna suffered unimaginable loss. I am sorry you faced such hardships. I was married, quite happily. We were expecting a child, things were going quite well and there were no signs of any problems but the birth came early and it was a very difficult one apparently. I was away on duty because I thought there was enough time. There was no one there to get her the medical help she needed, I lost her and our baby daughter on the same day.' He rested his hand on her arm in a gesture of comfort.

'Sometimes Angela a traumatic past is what it takes to make a person work hard to have a peaceful future.'

Angela did not believe that. In her past she had always been wary of people who confide their past tragic circumstances too quickly into a friendship. It is a sign that they believe by sharing their most painful memories they can form a more lasting bond. She was wary because she did not want to build a friendship on a foundation of tragedy. Friendships that start that way can only grow by being fed more tragedy. Happiness would change it too much until it was no longer what it once was, so it too dies.

Lukas had always been professional and kind so she allowed the friendship to continue. They spent every coffee break together from then on and soon started dining together. He opened up to her about all aspects of his life and they developed a warm and easy friendship that they had never experienced with a person of the opposite gender before. They became each other's best friend.

'Angela when do you finish your term here? Mine is for another year.'

'Mine too.'

'Then, if we do not choose to renew them, perhaps you would consider working with me in the clinic in Athens, I will need efficient assistance such as yours.'

'Thank you, I will give it consideration Lukas and give you my answer in a few days if you don't mind.'

'Of course, what about Sunday, take until Sunday, we can take the boat to Elounda and make a day of it. We can eat at a taverna and bring some sweets back for the patients.'

Her decision to accept made their Sunday pass happily. To remember the occasion he insisted on buying her a gift. He bought her a necklace of turquoise and a pretty shirt with an embroidered collar. She bought herself a pair of lovely brown suede platform shoes. The celebrations continued into the evening when Angela needed help carrying the goods she had bought up to her room. Lukas put the parcels down while she poured him a glass of her secret supply of cognac. He put down his glass and took hers from her hands and put it down next to his.

'Thank you for a lovely day today and for agreeing to be with me in Athens.'

'I think it will be very enjoyable working for you too.' He stepped in to be closer to her.

'We will work well together. I confess to you Angela it is my wish that we will be doing everything well together, not only work.'

'Lukas...,' she hesitated and almost went to tell about what had happened to Pavlos and why, but she realised it was not a burden she needed to share. There were no feelings of guilt just an inner calm. She would tell him one day and he would love her even more for it but for now she was enjoying being with a man who wanted her by his side in every way.

'Yes Lukas, I want that too.'

He stepped back again remembering his sense of propriety which had been weakened by the closeness of a woman with the green eyes, small waist and slim ankles of Angela Venetis. She knew enough of the male body after almost twenty years of caring for them to know that this man was a fully functioning man. Her satisfying encounters with the soldiers had never caused her any shame or regret. She had found physical pleasure to be the most beautiful thing she had ever felt. And she wanted to feel that good again with Lukas. He seemed to be a lot more puritanical than she was but she needed to see if they had some compatibility in that area. Then she corrected herself.

'Have patience Angela; here is your chance to have a much more normal life.' She was proud of the work that had happened on Spinalonga but she was not a leper and did not want to spend all her days on the island. She had settled her family problem and she was classed a spinster. To be with Lukas was a blessing. It would just be better if she and he had an amorous affinity.

Lukas had been watching her think and he caught sight of what he had been hoping to see. He saw the desire in her eyes.

'I'm glad you want that too Angela and you know what I would like right now?' He smiled and let the desire show in his eyes too.

'What would you like to see right now Lukas?' she said as she held her bedpost and swayed provocatively.

'I have read your medical records and in it next to the section on any identifying marks it says that you have a small brown beauty spot on your inner left thigh.' They both sighed in relief that their thoughts were in accord and they burst out into laughter. Then they looked at each other lovingly before hugging each other and falling onto the bed.

'If you want to take a good look at that beauty spot then you are going to have to help me take these clothes off.'

'Of course, and I will have to spend a lot of time down there taking a very, very good look.'

Spinalonga bloomed like the love of Angela and Lukas and like Maria with the baby of Lyras inside her. With Pavlos gone their wedding had turned Spinalonga into a mini Riviera. Nikos had been the best man and their wedding crowns were made from the lemon blossom from Athena's tree. Maria even had a ring.

When he had heard that there was to be a wedding Ikaros had gone to see Maria. She had always been kind to him and shared her food or cooked fish for him. He loved her like the sister he had left behind.

'You look so happy Maria. I want you to be happier. You need rings.'

'Oh I don't care Ikaros, even we make them out of paper.'

He reached into his pocket and pulled out a little package of rags, he peeled them back to reveal the contents. Maria peeped in and saw there were two gold rings.

'Where did you...?'

'Don't ask, just take them and be happy.' There was no way he was going to tell her that the gold came from the teeth of a dead man. He left quickly before she asked more questions. She didn't need to know that when he help to bury the poor soul who drowned trying to catch a fish to eat he had reached into his mouth and pulled out his gold teeth. The guy had five! He must have been rich in his former life. Ikaros had been saving them to trade them for a gun but changed his mind when Pavlos starting getting more vicious. He would have stolen it and killed everyone.

He was considering buying a little caique for safer fishing but he didn't think he would be permitted to keep in case they thought he was trying to escape and spread the disease. So the gold teeth stayed hidden until Father Manoussos confided in him about the wedding plans as a precaution so he could keep Pavlos preoccupied. They had yet to learn that Pavlos would no longer be a problem.

Ikaros had gone to the blacksmith patient,

'Could you melt these down and fashion them into rings?'

'I need fine tools, we could ask the boatman maybe?'

'No I do not trust him.'

'Well then we will have to improvise. You go to my hut and feed the fire in there, keep it blazing hard, feed it a lot of fuel, dry branches, there are plenty of those here. I will go see what I can find.' The blacksmith went to the infirmary and said to the assistant on duty he needed some medication for sleeping. He went to get something for him and the blacksmith snuck into the lab and found a few tools that he could use to do the job.

'Stop right there! Just what do you think you are doing?' Angela had caught him.

'Speak up, don't just stand there. How dare you steal from us? We are here to help you.'

'Forgive me Nurse Angela, I just wanted to borrow some tools so I could make wedding rings for our engaged couple.' He placed the gold teeth and the tools on her desk. She picked them up and handed them back to him.

'Oh for goodness sake, just ask next time.' So there high over an island leper colony using the teeth of a dead leper, symbols of love were fashioned. Maria and Lyras never found out the origins of their wedding bands but they would have approved.

Chapter19. Theodora

The wedding was glorious. The weather was perfect, the groom was handsome and the bride looked lovely. Nikos was the best man and he and Artemis had hunted for three days to provide all the fish for the wedding feast. Maria, with the extra pension money had ordered a fine bed with pale blue sheets and a sofa. She felt as fulfilled as any new housewife setting up her first home. But she was getting very weak. She was struggling with the demands the life within her was making of her body. Doctor Lukas ordered Maria to full bed rest in the infirmary as her time to deliver drew nearer.

'You may stay with her Lyras, we will organize a bed for you and you can play your music.'

Nikos was a daily visitor too.

'Please Lukas tell me the real situation.' The doctor signaled for Nikos to follow him into his office and gestured for Nikos to sit down. Angela brought them coffee and pie. She left them in private to discuss what she already knew.

'Nikos, even if Maria was not carrying a child her time has almost come. The fact that she is pregnant will actually speed things up. She might not even survive the delivery.' Nikos stared at the floor for several moments before he spoke.

'My eyes might be troubling me but I am not blind. I can see my sister has become very frail. Does Lyras know?'

'Maybe. Maria seems to feel it and she is always telling us to ensure her baby survives.'

Doctor Lukas had other things to discuss too. 'Nikos, the child?'

'The child has me. I know there is Lyras but he will retreat into his music. The child has me. Fear not.'

'I thought as much.'

Maria went into labor on a warm night with a full moon. Lyras was right by her side but as her moans got louder he left the room and started playing his lyre. Angela and Lukas took over. Eva came to help as did Aliki. The birth was taking a long time and at one point Maria had passed out but the contractions woke her up again. At seven in the morning after eighteen hours of labor Maria gave a final push and Theodora was born.

She held her in her arms while Lyras cradled them both. She inhaled the sweet new baby scent of her perfectly healthy daughter. The tests were run immediately and a beaming Doctor Lukas pronounced her to be in full good health. Maria was so tired she could barely see her beautiful girl. Lyras was a blur to her and she couldn't seem to hear what anyone was saying. Through the buzzing she did hear Lyras whisper in her ear.

'I love you.' She saw her beloved brother cradling his baby niece and smiling at her, telling her what an amazing thing she had done. She looked over and saw her beloved father. He was standing within a bright light that looked so warm and inviting that she was overwhelmed with the urge to join him. He spoke without moving his lips. She could hear his words in her soul.

'My child, you have carried out your tasks here in this world. It is time to progress to the next.' He held out his hand to her. Maria looked at the perfect child and at her husband who was now cradling her as tenderly as he held his lyre. She saw her brother gaze on at them in pure paternal love and knew that all was as it should be. She took her father's hand and joined him in the warm light.

She had brought another wonderful Theodora into the world, she had loved and been loved, and there in her full happiness Maria slipped away from this world having fulfilled all her dreams.

Chapter 20. Operation Mercury

On mainland Greece the prime minister of Greece, Ioannis Metaxas was trying to do exactly what Nikos had done on Spinalonga, restore order and dignity to a ravaged country and a people exhausted by much turmoil.

In Germany another man was also trying to rebuild a weakened country and wanted to make it bigger and more powerful than ever, the most powerful country in the world. He was a young soldier so desolate after Germany lost the First World War that he turned to politics and joined the national socialist Workers party known better by its acronym, the Nazi party. His name was Adolf Hitler.

He was poor and he was dull, the result of a sadistic father and a doting mother. He was a lazy dolt at school and failed his medical exams for the army but reapplied for a smaller less demanding unit and got accepted. He had few interests except polemics but he did enjoy painting and for some still unknown reason had built up an obsessive hatred of Jews whose only crime was that many of them were good at commerce and owned lovely homes of the type his family never could afford.

The other natural talent he did not know he had until he joined a political party was the ability to give a stirring speech. With its focus on the well-being of the average German worker along with the bankruptcy of the country and the ensuing massive unemployment of Germans the time for the Nazi party had come. They won the elections and Hitler for the obvious rhetorical reasons had been made its leader, making him the legally voted Chancellor of Germany. An unstable man with a grudge and a big ego became the leader of a country out to build an empire.

Metaxas declared Greece to be a neutral country which desired to be left alone for a while to rebuild itself after finally liberating itself from the crushing Ottoman occupation and the many wars that followed.

Greece was tired. Next door in Italy, Mussolini had other ideas. He had allied himself with Hitler and declared he wanted to use Greece as a thoroughfare for carrying out his plans for empirical expansion. When Metaxas famously advised the response of Greece was a definite NO! Mussolini declared war against Greece.

Hitler was against the idea, telling Italy, his axis partner, that their main goal was Russia not a tired little non-threatening country. He wanted to get in there before the winter took hold. The only people who could handle a Russian winter were Russians. Hitler correctly believed his Axis soldiers would not be able to sustain a fight in such conditions. There was no time to waste.

Mussolini told Hitler the facts as they stood. His country had four times the population and ten times the money of Greece and had not been under long occupation as the Greeks had been. In his opinion these were a weakened people with little to no resources. It would be a walk in the park. On the 28th of October in 1940 Italy invaded Greece.

But in Greece, Metaxas had readied the Greek people by calling them to arms. He knew the enemy would be coming from the North through Albania and had ordered that the northern front be lined with trenches and fortifications and that every available citizen prepare to fight for their country using whatever they had. This front was known as the Metaxas line.

He demanded window boxes and flowerpots be stripped of their blooms and replanted with edibles instead. Everywhere across Greece planters, instead of geraniums and daisies, sprouted beans and spinach, tomatoes and herbs.

The attempted invasion was over in a few weeks. Greece not only crushed the Italians but drove their line so far back they had taken over almost half of Albania and they had done so with archaic weaponry and an army of peasants, elderly and children bearing pitchforks and sticks. It was one of the greatest defeats in military history and a deep humiliation to the Axis.

Hitler had no choice but to deviate from his plan and teach Greece a lesson. Every radio blared, 'The Germans are coming!'

Mainland Greece had put up a fierce resistance, the fiercest civilian resistance the Germans would ever encounter. Hitler had known they would so he had sent advance warning to the Greek people that their formidable reputation as tough fighters would work against them. Every act of resistance would be met with fifty reprisals.

Greece was ravaged as the Germans carried out their promise with relentless savagery. The allied armies of Britain, Australia and New Zealand retreated while Greek people gave up their lives protecting them as they exited Greece leaving the people to continue the battle solo with the Nazi juggernaut. The allies retreated to Crete.

Hermann Göring Commandant of the Luftwaffe adjusted his new uniform before he popped his morphine pill. He liked to look sharp at all times and this new uniform was cut well. He turned sideways to look in the mirror. Yes, his big barrel of a stomach did not look as protuberant as normal. Too bad the mirror only showed from waist up, he would have seen that the beige suit together with his porky legs made him look like a walking strudel.

He popped another morphine pill, the first one had started to induce the haze of happiness he liked to feel. He picked up his jewel encrusted baton and headed off to the important meeting he had requested with the Fuhrer. He wanted to put forward his plan to both punish the Allies and gain a valuable base in the Mediterranean.

'Invade Crete from the air you say?'

'Yes, using my method we could quickly place our men on the ground. Paratroopers Mein Fuhrer. We will fly them in and then parachute down to directly where we want them.'

Hitler eyed Göring up and down. The fat show pony was wearing yet another new uniform and the baton was sheer affectation, but he was a ruthless and meticulous operator which was the exact reason he had chosen him as his successor.

'This is quite an audacious plan. Fortunately I am partial to audacity.'

Hermann Göring breathed a sigh of relief. His proposal had been accepted. After The Battle of Britain had gotten them nowhere and then the cancellation of Operation Sea Lion he and his Luftwaffe had to regain credibility in the eyes of the world and also in the eyes of his Fuhrer. Being the subject of his annoyance was not a position he wanted to be in any longer.

Hitler looked up from his maps.

'I seek your absolute reassurance that this operation, what have you called it?'

'Operation Mercury, Mein Fuhrer.'

'That this Operation Mercury must be rapid and ruthless and it must in no way whatsoever cause any hindrance to Operation Barbarossa.'

'You have my absolute assurance Fuhrer.'

Hitler went back to his maps,

Vorgehen Proceed!'

The allies retreated to Crete because that was where the Royal Navy had its fleet. The many harbors and the strategic position of Crete in the middle of the Mediterranean made it very covetable. The Germans were coming for it and to attack the Royal Navy. All the while on Spinalonga the patients could only sit and listen to the radio to learn what was happening to the world and their country. Their unusual isolation had previously been a source of despair. Now it had become a guilty sanctuary. Unlike so many on the mainland they were fully abreast with the situation.

'It's an eerie feeling knowing our countrymen are suffering and here we are getting government supplies sent over twice a week as if nothing was wrong.' Nikos had a worried frown on his face as the men gathered in the square as they did everyday to listen in on the radio.

'It was a good idea to install a radio system at the same time the cinema was installed Nikos.'

'I was merely being logical at the time. We needed to be able to be in touch with the mainland in case of emergencies. I could never have envisaged that we would be hearing the types of things we are hearing.'

All the men nodded solemnly. Every single one of them secretly wished they were in full health so they too could join the resistance and defend their motherland.

'Who would have thought we would now be needed by Elounda? How life can change eh?'

'Well as long as we are able to receive Greek news and tune into other channels as well, like the BBC, and even intercept the occasional German message as we have it is our duty to pass the messages on to the boatman so he can keep the others informed of what is happening.'

'I know Makis but we need someone who can understand them. I know some English but I don't know German and I don't know anyone who does. If they come down here from the mainland then our supplies might get cut. We have a lot of work to do.' Maki chewed on his cheese pie.

'The Germans are not as smart or thorough as they like the world to believe. They go to the trouble of creating codes but the British break them. If the Germans are going to head down this way, we will learn it in plenty of time.'

'Nikos, are the Germans going to kill us?' Aliki asked him while he was sitting at the cafe.

Old Barba Christos said,

'Let them come and kill us, what do we have to fear.'

'Well my friends, the brotherhood has to prepare itself that is for sure.'

Aliki put her hands on her hips.

'We are playing our part gentlemen. Just so you know we of the domestic domains have been implementing certain measures since we have had more food made available to us. We have been so deeply affected by the hunger we went through in the past that we always order extra food. We keep the storage rooms full at all times. We make pasta and *trahana*. We have so many jars of preserved fruits and vegetables that we need more shelving. We have olives and oil and spices. We have enough stored food to last a winter.'

'Well done Aliki. You could not have given me better news.'

'Don't thank me Nikos. It was the idea of Athena. She is the one you must thank.'

'Oh, oh yes of course. In the meantime do you think you could double your efforts? I fear this war. If our pensions are cut because of infrastructure breakdown or any other reason we will be in big trouble. Keep storing as much food as is possible.' Aliki smiled and saluted him and strode back to the laundry where the women were working. She kept smiling as she walked along and thought to herself, *Nikos Lambrakis you are the most stupid smart man I have ever met. Like most stupid smart men you cannot see the real treasure you have right in front of you.*

Ikaros called out from inside the café next to the cinema where the radio system was housed. 'Our radio has picked up much information. Invading Crete is an ego trip for the Luftwaffe. The British beat them off in a battle and the commanders of the Luftwaffe had put an audacious plan forward to Hitler to allow them to attack Crete. Hitler liked audacity but warned them it must not interfere with Operation Barbarossa.'

'What is that?' whispered Ikaros.

'Why are you whispering, they can't hear us.'

'I've heard that name before, Barbarossa, it is the code word for their plan to invade Russia.'

'On the mainland they have been bombing all the airfields to make it impossible for the allied forces to land planes or to fly out they will try to do the same here.'

It was Nikos' turn to man the radio station, the others took in shifts, and even Father Manoussos would come in to relieve the operators just in case any special news came through.

Since the loss of Maria little was seen of Lyras. He would come to eat, occasionally he would play with little Theodora or take her for a ride on Xanthus. He spent the rest of his time playing his music. His self imposed silence meant that nobody knew he had been sent to study in Germany for over two years. He had always wanted to serve in the diplomatic corps and relished the thought of working alongside a great statesman like Venizelos. His studies in Germany had been terminated when he was recalled to the village. The vendetta had resulted in yet another senseless murder of one of his relatives and he was needed to help with the crops and the animals. But in those two and a half years he had learned more than enough German to reach an adequate level of fluency.

At mealtimes he had overheard what the men were doing with the radio system. It ate at him that he could help them but how could he let them know without sacrificing his music time, and he might even have to speak. At the next mealtime he sat next to Nikos. Little Theodora sat next to her father playing with her pen and pencil and proudly showed him how she could now write her name. Lyras was so moved at the sight of his girl who looked so much like her mother that he picked her up and held her close. She was worth the sacrifice. He pointed to the pencil and paper and held out his hands. She understood and passed them over to him.

Nikos was eating his succulent salmon so elegantly caught by his Artemis when Lyras nudged him. He looked at him in surprise. Lyras had never done that before. He was even more surprised when Lyras handed him a piece of paper. Nikos took it and unfolded it. Written on it were the words, *I can understand German, Lyras.*

Lyras was on temporary relief duty when the message was intercepted. It was clear and sharp. The soldiers would be dropped from the air and ammunitions, weapons and supplies would also be dropped by parachute. The parachutes were to be color coded. Red was for ammunitions, blue for weapons and green for supplies. The paratroopers would use standard white parachutes. Lyras could not leave his post until his replacement came to take over the shift but he had to let the mainland know how that attack would take place.

No one but Maria had heard his voice, he hadn't spoken to anyone else in years. Finally the person to take over the next shift walked in and Lyras ran out to find Nikos. He found him in the taverna. The taverna was full and they all turned to look at him. They had never seen him like this before, he was always passive and engrossed in his music.

'What is it Lyras?'

'They are going to fall out of the sky!'

For the first few seconds they were engrossed in hearing his voice for the first time but once he started talking the information he was giving them was even more engrossing. The patients of Spinalonga relayed the message to Crete and the people prepared for the first day of the Battle of Crete.

The Battle of Crete commenced on a clear May day in 1941. At 8.00am precisely Stukas flew over the northern coastline of Crete and spewed out their contents. The skies filled with white balloons with smatterings of red, green and blue larger ones. It was an almost festive air. The entire civilian population of Crete was out in the united mission to protect their sacred and ancient land. One old man out walking on the hill to watch had a paratrooper land in front of him. The young German saw the old man hobbling towards him with the use of a walking stick and began to disentangle himself from all the ropes of the chute. The old man reached him and the German sneered at him.

'Hey old man,'

'Go to hell.' The old man whacked the soldier on the head in the same way he knocked out goats before he would bleed them out by cutting their throats. The soldier slumped and the old man whacked him again.

'You think you know how to kill do you. I'll show you how.' Within seconds the soldiers head was a mushy pulp. The old Cretan stripped the body of its boots, belt and gun and wiped clean his favorite walking stick on the khaki trousers of the soldier, he let the carrion birds do the rest of the cleaning up.

The men of Crete had developed a clear plan, as soon as the colored parachutes become visible they would break away and get as many of the red, green and blue parachutes as possible to get to the weapons and ammunitions they were carrying. To do that they needed to get backup fighters and the only extra available backup were the women who were more than willing to fight.

Theodora Lambrakis was no different. She led her feminine battalion to the coastline, all of them resolved to the plan they had made.

Mrs. Theodora Lambrakis woke up that day ready to die. There was nothing she wanted more. Her arranged marriage at the age of fifteen was carried out purely for the convenience of her family. But as soon as she was wed her husband was conscripted and sent to fight the Bulgarians in the Balkan War. He served away for two years. All that time she lived with her in-laws and became as dear to them as any daughter. They died elderly and frail but grateful to God their boy had a partner like Theodora who could be what a woman was truly meant to be, the centre of the family and Theodora was a woman who lived for her family.

When her husband had returned from his military service he feared the young girl he had left behind would have turned into a bitter shrew as some women tend to do when their personal desires are not fulfilled and they have not been smart enough to develop positive ways of feeling fulfilled when their fate and their dreams do not match. She appeared in the gateway of the family home.

He had left behind a girl and standing before him now was a beautiful woman in the full blossoming of her beauty. Weaving between her long skirts was a child, their son Nikolas. Her in-laws were wise and decided to leave for Heraklion to visit family giving them the house to themselves for ten days.

Kostas was proud he had such a good and beautiful wife to come home to and he knew in his heart he wouldn't have appreciated her as much if he hadn't been sent away to war. When a man has a wife all he can think about is getting away from her. When a man goes to war all he can think about is going home and holding her in his arms.

Now it was her turn to fight for her country. She and her fellow female warriors stood and watched as man after man hit the water and struggled with the weight of their chutes, the water making them even heavier and the weight on their backs making it difficult to even stand on their feet. The women stood together lining the beachfront, smiling warmly in welcome and beckoning them closer. The soldiers relaxed and stopped worrying and worked on trying to stand up in the water.

'Oh look at them, they are so clean faced.'

Theodora was like a Miltiades at Marathon, studying the lie of the land, using her troops to absolute advantage.

'Come, come.' They beckoned. The men were struggling to swim so the women entered the water without bothering to hitch up their long black skirts or their equally long aprons and outstretched their arms to them. Germans knew about the legendary hospitality of the Greeks, they never really had a chance to experience it because they had taken what they needed without thought to social graces. What were these smiling women saying? Did they want to offer them hospitality in exchange for their lives? It was a natural instinct to swim towards these maternal figures, sweetly smiling *Panayias*.

The women had spread out to form a coastal frontline. Each woman placed herself to be at least a metre apart from the next. Theodora watched the men intently, studying their every movement in wait of the moment the soldiers would be at maximum struggle. They were wet and carried heavy packs and were trying to get out of their parachutes without strangling themselves or each other as well as try to inch forward to the shore. Theodora watched as they reached the spot where they would be about ready to attempt to stand up in the water.

'Now! Strike down these Satans.'

From beneath their long skirts they brought out their scythes and as swiftly as Artemis would draw her bow they moved in unison, bringing their arm back then forward delivering a swoosh of steel through the heads of the soldiers. One soldier had the top of his head sliced off, lobotomizing him.

Theodora saw his eyes lose life as he stumbled, unable to think in any capacity the man slipped down into the water to drown. The men didn't even have time to scream in horror. Weighed down by water and their parachutes and trying to keep their heads above water gave the women clear access to perform the efficient beheadings. The scythes operated as efficiently in lopping down men as they were in cutting through wheat stalks.

The women had spent all of the day before peening them and honing them on whetstones till the curved blades shone like scimitars. They had rubbed the grips to be smooth so as to make it as easy as possible to swing the blades. The scythes skimmed the surface of the water like hovercraft. Theodora had made them do a rehearsal run the day before at sunset so the sun would not reflect off the blades and arouse suspicions.

They kept up their unified front line, slashing and sweeping, lopping off heads, slicing off arms, amputating limbs until not one man was left whole. Theodora had struck two down in one sweep. Some women shouted, 'God forgive me' with each swipe. Some screeched with success and others worked silently focused on their grim reaping as they embraced the role of feminine executioner. And grim the task was, they were knowingly slicing up someone's son. God would forgive them for these demons had come into their land to kill their sons. What did they expect?

When the women stopped to observe their work the water had turned red and German heads were bobbing around like split watermelons. An explosion from within the shoal of soldiers sent a couple of the women off their feet to splash back into the water but the other women helped them get up.

'What was that?'

'I don't know,' Theodora answered but she soon found out when another soldier stood up and was clearly seen to reach over to his belt and unclip his hand grenade and hold it out while he glared at them defiantly. The grenade exploded in his hand and caused another spurt of water, a few of the body parts bobbed around. The soldier who had held the grenade had disappeared into a puff of smoke. Two more Germans did the same thing, preferring to be blown up quickly than hacked to death by peasant women. Frankly the women were happy for the break.

'Couldn't more of them have done the same, my hands were getting blisters.' The women nodded with the same subtle satisfaction as when their olives are pronounced ready. Theodora called her troops together,

'Ok ladies, I commend you on a job well done. Now according to the intelligence we received many of these men will be armed. We activate the second part of our plan.' Part of their information package was the soldiers would be only lightly armed with knives, grenades and pistols. The heavier weaponry would be parachuted down in the containers but a few of them would have machine guns strapped to their bodies.

Her troops splashed around in the red waters to get as many weapons as possible from the remnants of the German paratroopers. They managed to get hundreds before they had to run for cover as another wave of airplanes roared above them. They looked back at their handiwork before they ran.

'We made *Kataifi* out of them.'

Theodora looked out over the sea to Spinalonga where her only family lived. She would gladly swim through the human *chum*. She would gladly embrace the lepers. She would gladly live for the rest of her days on the island eating grass and lizards, as long as she could be with her family.

All over Crete there were similar successes to Theodora and her team. Women at every harbor had led the first onslaught and picked their victims clean of their weapons. Even the priests and the children had played some role. But the men of Crete were not hiding or idle, they were with the allied troops or covering the backs of their loved ones on the frontline who were picking off paratroopers. They were also targeting the parachutes that were not bringing in men but containers.

In particular they were on the lookout for containers attached to triple parachutes. These heavier containers were carrying a new weapon, the Leichtgeschütz 40, a light field gun. The intelligence they had received from the radio station at Spinalonga had told them these long range guns were light and easy to move, perfect for the mountainous regions and easy for the resistance to conceal. Using German weaponry on Germans was something they were looking forward to doing and Nikos had made it possible.

There was not going to be a manned assault on the eastern side, the Germans wanted to only attack the western hard for that was where the Royal navy had its fleet moored. Greek military personnel with the most ancient weaponry were sent to the eastern side. It was no comfort to know that there would not be a major invasion on the eastern side.

'So what does that mean?' asked the people. 'Is there such a thing as a minor invasion?' The information from Spinalonga was precise, the civilians of the eastern side of Crete were not armed or poorly armed at best. Theodora's battalions had fixed that problem.

The people of Crete won the first battle but the Germans kept coming. Crete had no option but to eventually surrender so as to avoid decimation. Punishment was how Germans operated. Their philosophy was that the more people got publicly punished the more those remaining would obey. Theodora knew they would be coming for her. One of the men of the town came to see her.

'Theodora you are a heroine but they will come for you. Come with us to hide in up in the caves.' She was grateful, not for the compliment of being called a heroine, but that they accepted her to be with them instead of shunning her as they had done.

'Thank you my friend but if I am truly a heroine then I have no business running from the enemy's bullets, if they indeed consider that I am worthy of one.' The land was already full of stories of the warped economy of the Nazis such as how the soldiers would get the mothers to hold their babies up in front of them so as to save bullets for the firing squad. That way they could get two with one shot, then the Germans would congratulate each other for their efficiency.

'Theodora you are wrong. A true hero saves himself for the next battle instead of becoming a worthless sacrifice. Come with us.' She took in the man's determined gaze and became solemn. He was right.

'Very well then but first there is something I need to do.' Theodora Lambrakis went looking for the boatman. She had made her way to Elounda and was told by the people there that he was the one who goes to Spinalonga. She watched the harbor from her hiding spot and could see the where the boatman was moored. She stayed concealed until darkness fell. The moonlight was her guide as she made her way to the harbor. He was loading up the goods stacked on the pier for his dawn departure. In her black clothes and headscarf she had blended into the darkness startling him as she suddenly popped out of the black, her face a disembodied visage floating in a sea of night.

'*Panayia mou*, you ripped my soul out sneaking up on me like that. What do you want?'

'Boatman, I face the firing squad so I ask you to take these things to the island. I have two children there, Maria and Nikos Lambrakis. I have nothing left for me, the Germans will find me and kill me but I don't care. I die as happy as it is possible for me to be, I fought for my country, the same country that stole my children from me. Now I give my life too. God decided I should not enjoy the things that so many people take for granted, a man, a home, a family. I was given them for such a short time but it was long enough to know they are the greatest gifts of all along with health. If you have those things you can survive anything. But I have nothing left, except these few things.'

The boatman saw she held in her hands the personal treasures of a family, worthless to others but priceless to them. He saw a man's watch, some photographs, and a gold cross. He stayed silent as he studied her. She was slender, not too tall and had a face he had seen on ancient coins. His silence concerned her.

'I suppose you are waiting for payment.' She sighed as she reached into her bosom and pulled out a couple of crumpled one hundred drachma notes.

'Here, this is all I have in the world, but please take these to my children. I have no need of anything anymore, I am dead anyway.'

The boatman reached out his hand and took the trinkets and the money.

'I will take them. But I have something to suggest to you so listen to me Mrs. Lambrakis.'

'You say you do not fear death?'

'I do not. I fear life without my family. Death is better than watching these Germans rape our land.'

He spat, 'These Germans! I have never seen a people so obsessed with hygiene yet so filthy in everything else they do, as if taking a bath and splashing on cologne washes away all the other sins. Better a man smelly with sweat from hard work and a clean heart than a sweet smelling German so hungry for power he thinks nothing of killing women and children and innocent Jews.' Theodora handed him the items.

'Tell my children I die with them in my heart.'

'Tell them yourself.'

'If only I could.'

'You can.'

'What are you saying?'

'This is the only vessel that never gets inspected. The Germans, so efficient and thorough in checking everything to capture any smugglers, were lax in only one area when it came to detecting contraband, and that was the boat bound for Spinalonga. They are too paranoid about infection. They reason no one would want to go there and if anyone did they would never be leaving and therefore be no threat to them, so no checks take place.

If you do not fear death then I am about to load many sacks of potatoes and onions for Spinalonga along with other supplies the Germans are allowing. They have some sort of international agreement to treat Spinalonga as a hospital zone. Also they are scared shitless the lepers will infiltrate the mainland and give them their disease.'

The boatman looked up at the sky, it was mottled now turning from black of night to grey of dawn. He walked over to get closer to her.

'Quick,' he whispered.

'While it is still dark get into the boat and hide behind the potato sacks, I will take you to Spinalonga. You can be with your children and the Nazis will never find you. You said you do not care about your life without your children didn't you? Well this way you can be with them and your life will be in God's hands. Stay here and you put your life in the hands of the Nazis, you choose who you want in charge of your life.'

Theodora made her choice happily. She scrambled into the boat and crouched down among the hessian bags.

'You okay back there?' The boatman yelled out.

'Yes, yes all good.'

'Do you feel afraid?'

'No, not at all. I have never felt so happy.'

'I am not going to take you to the regular entrance where the supplies are taken. We are going to Dante's Gate the entrance of the lepers. Just in case anyone has been watching they will just think you are another leper.'

'I am happy to hear that. I can see what my children saw when they first went there.' Before too long she felt movement and she knew that meant they were sailing. She closed her eyes and welcomed the arrival of sleep until she was woken by a bump. 'Okay, get up now we are here.'

Her legs had lost their feeling and shaking out the pins and needles had at first occupied her more than taking in the surroundings. The boatman got out of the boat.

'Come closer. Come to the side of the boat.' She stood near the edge and steadied herself by putting her hands on his shoulders. He scooped her up in his arms and swung her out of the boat landing her feet first on the ground.

'Walk through that arch. I am going around to the other entrance. There will be people waiting there to unload the goods.'

'Thank you boatman, be well and have courage.'

'Wait!' He put his hand into his pocket and pulled out her trinkets and the money she had given him and added a thousand drachmas to it.

'Here, you need it more than I do. Give my regards to your children.'

He sailed away and she stood before the gate reading the inscription above it, feeling the dread her children would have felt. She proceeded, not knowing that she was the only person who ever walked through Dante's Gate not abandoning hope but with more of it than she had ever known. She pulled off her headscarf and let the sea air comb out her chestnut colored hair.

The Greeks say they can spot a *xeno* from across the street. He smells different, he walks different, and he doesn't need to open his mouth for them to know Greek will not come out of it. They say it because most foreigners walk around like they do not fit in their body.

Lepers have the same insights. They can spot a healthy person before they get up close, even if the person is dressed in the drabbest of clothes. The healthy walk differently, with a bounce. They take their body for granted. The leper treasures every step. The healthy are not aware of the light in their eyes. Even if the healthy person is troubled their eyes still have light, their gaze may be steely or have become clouded but there is still light.

Theodora looked up at the street sign exactly as her son and daughter had years ago. She was still looking up at it when Father Manoussos saw her.

'Theodora! Oh my dear child have you too been struck down with the disease.'

'Father.' She fell to her knees and kissed his hand.

'How good it is to see you. I have come to be with my children, with my Nikos and Maria.'

Manoussos lowered his head in the painful realization this mother did not know her daughter had been dead for three years.

'Father what is it, are my children alright?'

Aliki and Ikaros had seen the newcomer and walked up to greet her.

'Welcome and not well come. What brings you here woman?' Asked Ikaros.

'Ikaros!' Manoussos was appalled at his abnormal curtness.

'What do you think brings her here?'

'No Father, this woman does not have the disease.'

'He is right Father. I am well, praise God.'

'Theodora, what is going on?'

'I am in health but am willing to risk losing it to be with my children. I prefer a slow death with my loved ones instead of a quick death to an invader's bullet.'

'Good choice. The world has been dragged into hell by these Satans.'

'The children Father?'

'Yes Theodora, come with me.' Manoussos prayed for strength as he walked her towards the house of Nikos and Theodora. He would take her to Maria later.

Theodora had drawn a crowd. The residents of the island could see there was a newcomer walking the street with Manoussos. It was Stella the fat whore who noticed the high wide brow of the stranger and the steady rhythm of her walk was familiar to her. This woman had the brow of Nikos and the bearing of Maria. Stella called out.

'Ay, Welcome and not well come lady. Tell us, would you be the mother of Lambrakis?' The woman stopped and looked at Stella in the same way Nikos stops and looks at people, with a gentle half smile and a direct look in the eye, and all present noticed.

'Eh Nikos, come out. Someone is here to see you,' yelled the fat whore.

'Uncle Nikos, someone is calling you,' said his little niece.

'Yes I heard that Stella yelling again.' In his mind he hoped she wasn't yelling to try to have another session so she could secure some more funding for her house. He was already bored with the two fat ugly whores. Their services meant no more to him than a haircut, just something that could be done as required. Their conversation was shallow and their voices were harsh and horrible to listen to. He had used them just as they had used him, they were whores after all.

'You keep drawing the pretty pictures *koukla mou*. I will be right back.'

He stepped outside and expected to see ugly Susan or fat Stella undoing the top buttons of her shirt in playful seduction. They were there but quickly disappeared out of focus. It was the woman standing next to them who had captured all his attention.

Neither of them could speak. Mother and son sighed together. It was Theodora who stepped forward first. Nikos was still wary, believing he may be seeing things or having a strange dream. His mother was right in from of him now and put her hand to his hair to flick away an unruly lock just as she had done when he was a child, but he still wasn't sure. Theodora placed her hands on each side of his head. Nikos instinctively lowered it for her to press her lips to his forehead.

This woman smelt like his mother. He would bring lavender and lemon blossom for her to add to the water in which she washed her clothes. She would also put them in the cupboards for all the clothes to take on the fragrances. She kept his head in her hands but moved her face back to study his. He couldn't see her at all now, tears fully blinded him as he allowed himself to realize who was in his arms. He could only say one word,

'Mama.'

Within their embrace they swayed in unison as she whispered into his ear, '*Agori mou*, my boy. I have come to be with you and Maria.' He stopped swaying and looked over her shoulder and saw all of Spinalonga packed into the street outside his house. All were weeping with them. Theodora looked around too, still clutching her son.

'So many people here to see us together but no Maria?'

Nikos held her hands in his and took a deep breath.

'No Mama, no Maria.'

She turned around again for any reassurance. No one had dispersed. They were not going anywhere. All wanted to stay there to support Nikos' mother when she would learn about her daughter. It was Manoussos who spoke first.

'Theodora, your Maria has fallen asleep.

'Fallen asleep?' It was the term used by the church to describe the passing from this world to the next.

'Yes Theodora. She fell asleep some three years ago.'

The unspoken words choked in Theodora's throat. They would not come out. She was different now. The old Theodora would have wailed for her loss but the old Theodora had already done that. *Why am I numb?* She asked herself. *Why aren't I wailing? Who have I become to hear news like this and not feel the pain?*

And she answered herself, *'You are different now. You are not the same woman you were then. Your children were lost to you. How can you mourn what has been gone for so long. But you have taken the life of another mother's child as he scrambled in the waters like a child in his bathtub. You hacked him up like a piece of liver. And then you did it again and again. And you enjoyed it. For you it was as easy as plucking eggplant off their vines. You liked it and you cursed their mothers as you did it'.*

She was crying now but not just because of her lost girl, she was crying because she was tired of death. Her life for the past few years had been nothing but the dead and the dying and now their beloved country was under attack by monsters that spread death everywhere they stepped. She yearned for the promise of life, of hope, of a feeling that the future carried purpose not more death.

She felt the comforting arm of Manoussos around her shoulder when she saw her come out and smile at her. Little Maria, her girl was an innocent child again. She smiled at her and waved one of her long plaits at her just as she had done long ago. Theodora took a deep breath to bring herself back to reality and to enjoy the presence of her one remaining child. She opened her eyes again but the child apparition was still there. Little Theodora walked up to Nikos and took him by the hand.

'Uncle Nikos who is this pretty lady?'

'Theodora, this is your *Yiayia*, Theodora.'

'You are my mother's mother? Uncle Nikos talks about you every day. Hello *Yiayia*.' The little girl kissed her on both cheeks as if she had known her all her life, all because of the stories of Nikos.

'Hello my golden one.' The two Theodoras walked off together holding hands.

'You look just like your mama my darling.'

'I know *Yiayia*. Uncle Nikos told me all about her. Father Manoussos explained to me that she is with the angels now. Come on I will show you where I go with *Baba* to send her flowers.'

Nikos marveled at the little girl and the natural way that the dilemma of taking Theodora to her daughter's grave was overcome. The two Theodoras returned after a few minutes. They were smiling and calm. It was the right time for the patients to wish her well and welcome her to Spinalonga.

'Are you okay Mama?'

'My son, I am in a strange place yet feel completely at home. Yes I am very okay.' Nikos followed them into the house and for two days they sat and talked and talked. The other patients brought them food and drink while the little family shared every detail of what they had been through. Lyras came to meet the mother of his love. Theodora knew who he was as soon as he walked in and stood to greet her son in law. He bowed low and kissed her hand and left.

'That was a great honor he just gave you. Lyras bows to no one.'

Theodora blended easily into life on the island. She was devoted to her grandchild and son and even carved up meat for Artemis who showed her acceptance of Theodora by spreading her wings for her. One time Nikos took Theodora up to the heights and let her watch him release Artemis for a hunt. They watched her scan the sea below her for a few seconds then dive in quickly.

'That was quick, she must have spotted a big one.' When they went to the edge to look down and see where Artemis was they saw her struggling on the surface of the sea. Nikos knew his goddess and could see that she had latched onto something that she was not going to release. They ran down to the shore and were astonished at what they saw.

Artemis was swimming. In her beak was the biggest salmon they had ever seen. It had to weigh at least ten kilos. Right before their eyes Artemis flapped her wings so as to hover on the water and raise the fish out with her claws. She twisted her head to get to the fish and with an elegant snip of her beak had cut its spinal cord and the fish hung lip in her beak.

With the fish in her mouth she began to use her enormous wings as oars and rowed herself to shore and with the fish still in her beak delivered it straight into the hands of Nikos. Theodora crossed herself at the miraculous sight. Nikos and little Theodora both fed Artemis plump bits of juicy goat to reward her supreme effort. Artemis was dripping wet so the spectacular exhibition continued. She waddled over to a spot slightly away from them and stretched out her wings. She ruffled her feathers to dry them and kept her wings outstretched. Then Nikos and Theodora witnessed the phenomena of an eagle drying itself. Her feathers began to rotate as if each row was on its own axle. One by one the rows of feathers ruffled and rotated until she was clean and dry. Only then did she leap onto Nikos' arm and sat there obediently as he put the hood on her for the journey home. Theodora looked at her son as if he was a stranger to her.

'Nikos, even the eagles bow to you my son. What kind of man you have become?'

'I have become the man you raised me to be.'

Chapter 21. Operation Cyclops

Nikos called a council of war. He had a plan. Nikos went to the storehouse and for the first time blessed the memory of Pavlos.

'Rest in Peace you leprous soul.' He had said when he picked the large can of red paint Pavlos had once used to humiliate innocents. At the infirmary Nikos had assembled a full work crew led by Makis. They set to work painting the roof. It didn't take too long to dry in the Mediterranean sun. Nikos, Manoussos and Angela watched the progress from the ground. She had gone to see him about painting the infirmary at the same time as he was organizing the painting crew.

'Nikos, I am familiar with war zones, and we are now in one. It is advisable that we follow the International Humanitarian Law protocol and equip our infirmary with the distinctive emblem.' Then she looked over his shoulder and saw Makis and his team with paint pots and ladders.

'Oh, I see you are aware.' Nikos was reflective as the three of them stood together.

'International law was my special interest. It was my dream to serve the less fortunate through the creation and implementation of humanitarian law.'

Manoussos patted Nikos on the shoulder.

'The Lord works in mysterious ways.' Even Angela who had little time for the restrictive thinking of the old ways added,

'Well they do say everything happens for a reason. If you break it down to more simplistic terms Nikos, you are fulfilling your dreams, right here, right now.' Nikos showed his good humor,

'This was not what I had in mind.' Then Nikos became serious again,

'They will want the island. It is a perfect fort. They may want it for storing ammunition or just as a lookout point. They will no doubt send out a reconnaissance mission to take a look so we must be ready for them. We have a secret weapon that will fight them off without us even touching them.

'What is that Nikos?'

'Leprosy.'

Nikos had two objectives, the first one being to ensure the safety and well being of the residents. They would need food and medical supplies. Nikos had spent years establishing an efficient supply system. Now with wartime restrictions and vicious invaders he had to ensure all the residents of Spinalonga were safe. During winters the waters were choppy and in the past it had often taken weeks before a boat would get to them and also mainland supplies dwindled for the same reason.

The Spinalongans had taken easily to the system of squirreling away supplies in the buildings they had allocated as warehouses. Residents had been trained as store men to stack and stock the shelves as required. They had worked like the possessed to build up a basic food and medical supply of one year.

Nikos had also insisted once their new pensions had commenced that every recipient of the pension give ten percent of it towards a special infrastructure fund. He had allowed it to build untouched for the first year, following that, due to its constant replenishment. He was able to offer small bonuses to anyone who volunteered to work in a position that offered benefit to the population of Spinalonga.

Every single resident applied. The bonus was meagre but the significance of it was enormous. Every single resident could now claim they offered value to their state and were in paid employment. The warehouses were now all full and Nikos wanted to ensure they stayed that way whether the Nazis were around or not. They needed continual fresh supplies so Operation Cyclops was devised.

In the German camp, the onslaught of Crete was viewed as a mere technicality. It was to be a quick sweep as part of a bigger strategy. The Germans had been studying the coastline of Crete and became excited about the excellent location of Spinalonga.

Nikos was tuning the radio and heard German, he knew he had intercepted an enemy military communication, but he could not understand what they were saying. Lyras rode by on his horse, on the way to pick up a load of wood for the outdoor oven Ikaros had built.

'Lyras, come here and listen to these German voices. Let us know if something is going on. I am meeting Manoussos at the taverna. If you need me I will be there.' Lyras sat down and put on the headset, tuned in and indeed did heard German voices.

'It does appear to be very well fortified obviously from a previous era.'

'It looks to be the perfect place to set the storage facilities for all the ammunition and supplies as well as for monitoring enemy naval movements.'

'Is it occupied?'

'I believe it is but we can fix that with a quick annihilation of the population.'

'That will be an inconvenience but Operation Mercury would benefit from such a fort.' Lyras ran to the square and burst in to the taverna. Everybody was startled considering the type of news he had brought them the last time he burst in. The look on his face told Nikos what was happening.

'They are coming here aren't they?' Lyras nodded very fast.

'Did they mention a day?' Lyras shook his head very fast.

'Then we need to get to work right away.' Nikos made sure they were prepared. He installed a twenty four hour lookout roster with every single resident of Spinalonga involved, all except the children of which there were now four, the oldest being little Theodora, the women had set up a nursery house and would takes turns in shifts for watching them.

Every adult had a four hour watch and he had three vantage points on the island. They were unarmed of course but they had better weapons than bullets. Radio communication from the partisans on the mainland gave them some warning.

'Boat approaching! It is coming from the North. They have departed from Rhodes. There is a large castle there built by crusaders, the palace of the grand masters.

293

That *malaka* Mussolini was using it as a summer home. *Po po* these Italians have no shame.'

'There are a lot of Greek Jews on Rhodes.'

'There were but not anymore.'

'They took them and they executed them all.'

'Why? What is this madness? Why are they killing Jews? What have the Jews ever done to them?'

'Always hold grave fears whenever one type of people is singled out for punishment. It won't be long before they will have a problem with another nationality too, it won't stop with the Jews.'

It was a small stroke of luck that the Germans were bringing their own boat and crew down from Rhodes. It gave them some more time to prepare. Nikos estimated that if an expedition boat was to come it would come in the morning so all night the Brotherhood of Spinalonga finalized the details of their plan. Nikos was right with his timing. The German expedition boat moored just off the coast of Elounda, a dinghy was lowered into the water and five soldiers climbed in and they rowed over to Spinalonga.

'I thought they told us it was populated,' said one as they all looked around taking in the high stone walls and all internally agreeing this would be an excellent base. They stepped out of the small craft into the thigh high water and began to tow the little boat in behind them to moor it and investigate the island.

'This is a full fort. It will suit us very well.'

From behind the fortifications Nikos observed them and waved his frontline forward to carry out the first volley. Out of the small opening in the wall clambered out what looked to the Germans to be zombies.

'*Mein Got.*'

Nikos had handpicked the residents who were the oldest and with the most advanced stages of leprosy. All the filthy old rags of their life pre Nikos had been burned so they had spent a lot of their preparation time making new old rags.

Old Barba Timos with the one leg and completely blind hobbled towards them guided by the equally wretched Anthea who had no fingers left on one hand and whose face looked like an open can of tomato paste. She was supported by Mitsos whose ancient face was so distorted by his condition that he looked like the wind had frozen his face into an evil grimace. He had lost one eye but his elegant eye patch Nikos had ordered for him especially was now replaced with a tattered head bandage.

Mitsos had lost all the toes on one foot many years ago as well as the use of his tongue which now hung out of the corner of his hideous mouth, dribbling saliva down his chin. His hardened skin had turned deep grey and the saliva glistened like large pearls, catching in the sweet Spinalonga sunshine. Anthea waved her stubby arm at them and with her good hand, well reasonably good hand, it still had two fingers on it, pulled out a wooden stick from her ragged dress. The other two lepers pulled out sticks too.

In any other situation the soldiers would have viewed this as an act of aggression and opened fire without hesitation but they were transfixed by the macabre apparitions before them. It was almost impossible to look at these human ruins but also completely impossible to stop looking at them.

The sticks were flag poles and each unfurled theirs. The two men waved theirs first. The flags were white, a tattered off white. It would not be in keeping with the image Nikos had worked hard to create to wave a pristine pure white cloth. That would signify there was some cleanliness on the island and he didn't want them thinking that.

Anthea then unfurled hers.

The Germans were riveted to their spots, their breath caught in their throats. This flag was pristine, it's crisp folds still visible, as if it had been storage somewhere on site because it was a standard requirement but with no intention of ever being used, unless in war. Squarely in the middle of the white cloth was the Red Cross. All three mutants shuffled forward and tried to speak. The two men could do nothing but expel muffled moans but the woman was clearer. She spoke one Greek word but that word had the same meaning in German.

'Lepra.'

Leprosy! The two junior soldiers had already started to splash back into the dinghy as if the very water they were standing in could infect them.

'Halt!' ordered their captain.

'Do you understand what has just happened?'

All the soldiers sensed movement and turned to look at the wall behind this terrible trio. It began to seethe with life. More wretched ragged creatures appeared, some sticking their repulsive heads over the parapets and others straining out of the narrow openings, all were chanting, 'Lepra, Lepra.'

'This is a nightmare Captain, why are we still here?' The captain had a defeated look on his face. With utter frustration at the situation he informed them,

'We have an obligation under the Geneva Convention to them.'

'We do? Do you care about such things anymore, I mean with the concentration camps and all the other things?'

'That is an entirely different situation.' The captain snapped at him, 'They have surrendered to us and they have displayed the symbol of the Red Cross which means this is a war time hospital zone. We have no invasion rights here.'

'Do we want them?'

The captain held up his hands to show the islanders he was calm. Anthea reveling in her power and loving the full knowledge she was the star of the show, played her role of the all powerful crone to perfection. She crept forward and in a grating, high pitched shriek said, 'Food!'

They understood that word. Her cry for food was accompanied by the international gesture for '*I need to eat*'. A normal person would press their middle and forefinger to their thumb and make movements as if putting food in their mouth but poor Anthea with her two remaining stubs of fingers looked as if she was trying to claw at her face.

'*Ja. Ja*' the captain kept re-assuring. '*Genfer. Genfer.*'

'What does *Genfer* mean?' Nikos whispered to Lyras. 'It means Geneva. They are referring to the Geneva Convention. You did it Nikos. Operation Cyclops worked.'

Spinalonga would be the only part of Greece upon which no German soldier would ever set foot.

Chapter 22. Healing

The war raged around them but on Spinalonga life was virtually normal. The only way they could deal with the guilt was by accepting that just as their disease had kept them from the joys of life it also kept them from some of the horrors. All of them agreed they would rather be healthy and fighting for their country than be on Spinalonga. Their radio kept them informed of the level of suffering of the outside world that seemed endless until finally they heard the one they had been waiting for.

'As a result of pressure being exerted by the Greek freedom fighters, the withdrawal of German forces was continuing with increasing speed.'

The world got down to the business of recovery from the horrific madness inflicted upon it by Nazi Germany. Spinalonga continued to run as the elegant city state Nikos had designed it to be except he was seeing less of it than he would have liked. He had been feeling ill and Doctor Lukas had him confined to the infirmary for a week. His disease was progressing. For a while he felt that maybe there had been some sort of terrible error. He always felt good and he hadn't appeared to have physically changed but he had been deluding himself.

Beneath his shirt sleeves the skin on his arms was full of dry white patches, he could feel the pull of his facial muscles drooping and his eyes were hurting. His left arm had been numb for weeks but he had put it down to carrying the weight of Artemis around on it for too long. When Angela examined him she excused herself. She returned with Doctor Lukas and both doctor and nurse studied him in silence.

'Tell me what is wrong.'

Lukas sighed and sat on the bed while Angela went over to the other side to hold his good hand.

'Oh now I really know something is wrong. Speak up doctor.'

'Nikos, the nerves and muscles in your lower arm are pretty much destroyed. Really the best thing I can recommend is that we amputate.'

'Well hurry up then. Artemis needs to hunt. Can I be back with her by tomorrow? If not send Manoussos to feed her.'

'I give the orders here my friend and we will inform Manoussos to feed your Artemis. Maybe you might be out of here within ten days but not before.' The surgery was performed that afternoon and Nikos was tended to by one of the volunteer helpers. When he woke from the anesthetic, Athena was standing over him wiping his brow.

'You are doing very well Nikos.'

He smiled so much he couldn't stop smiling. He smiled because he was full of gratitude that Spinalonga now had the resources to give life saving operations to its patients, and he smiled because Athena looked so beautiful. She had recovered from her trauma and spent most of her time helping out in the infirmary. She did not seem to be too affected by her disease.

'Athena! How kind of them to send me such a beautiful nurse.' Athena laughed, 'You have such humor Nikos.'

'You know that is the first time I have heard you laugh.'

'I am feeling much better in so many ways. I have had my second blood test and it too came out negative. I have deliberately delayed having the third because if it too is negative then I will be able to leave. Except, I really have nowhere to go and everything I care for is here.'

'Athena, that is very good news about your blood tests. And everyone here cares for you. We would like nothing more than if you stayed here with us.' The two were temporarily trapped in their gazing at each other. They did not hear Angela walk in. She had stopped in her tracks when she saw the two of them stuck in their sweet stare. It was wondrous to see but she took a step back softly so as to give them this moment.

Did they even know they were in love? She coughed, slammed a door and walked heavily for her footsteps to be heard. Nikos and Athena both looked away from other, too afraid to continue looking at each other in case the other wasn't feeling the same thing. Angela made her entrance into the room and checked on Nikos and read all the records Athena had written down. 'This is all looking good but it is back to sleep with you Nikos, you still have a lot of recovering to do. Athena, make sure you are by his side when he wakes. Am I understood?'

Nikos and Athena smiled at each other as she answered.

'Understood.'

That evening Athena spoon fed Nikos chicken soup. He looked directly at her the entire time and she delicately dabbed at his mouth with the napkin. At the final spoonful she used the napkin to disguise the way she used her finger to trace around his full mouth. Nikos did not disguise the sensuous sigh that was the result of her covert caress. She cared for him, fed him, sat with him and spoke with him every day for nine days.

She wasn't there on the last day. Another volunteer was on duty for his room, Aliki. When Aliki entered the room his face fell.

'What did I do to deserve that?'

'Oh sorry, I didn't mean anything. I was just expecting someone else that's all.'

'I know but Athena volunteered to do your washing and housekeeping so you can go back to your house and find everything clean and in place. She is also tending to little Theodora. She has taken a real liking to Athena. Did you know Athena was a kindergarten teacher before she came here?'

'Really?' Nikos smiled in happiness. He knew his mother had everything in immaculate order and there would be little for Athena to do but he liked the thought of Athena in his home, dusting his books, washing his clothes and preparing a meal for him. He had always been proud of his independence and never thought of being with a woman just so she would do his chores for him. He had always wanted a real companion, someone he could talk to about anything, someone he could sit in silence with and not feel awkward and if there were chores to be done, they would do them together.

Little Theodora was with him more than she was with her father. Now with her grandmother present to do the mothering, just as Nikos had predicted, Lyras withdrew into his music. Nikos and Theodora had developed a loving relationship exactly like father and daughter. The thought of Athena, his mother, and Theodora together with him in his house made him feel pure joy. Aliki came to the side of the bed and started to feed him his breakfast eggs.

'No thank you Aliki, I am fine. I can feed myself.'

'Okay, I will just straighten up your bed linens then go.' When Angela came in she could see Nikos was lost in thought.

'What's on your mind?'

'I can't stop thinking about Athena.' Angela smiled at her friend and he smiled back.

'She will be here soon. It is her job to help you pack and to walk you back to your house. You are going home today Nikos.' Angela helped Nikos dress and the two chatted easily, like brother and sister. When Athena arrived Angela made a discreet exit. Nikos was feeling well. His walking was not affected and he could carry his small bag easily with his other arm.

'Nikos please, I'm the one who is supposed to be helping you.'

Nikos looked at Athena and smiled.

'Do you really want to help me?'

'Yes, Nikos I really do.'

'Then let me carry my own bag and take what is left of my other arm and escort me home. They made a handsome couple as they strolled through the streets of Spinalonga, through the square, past the taverna, bakery and café and around the church. Everybody stopped and stared. The two fat, ugly whores Stella and Susan looked at each other in disappointment.

'We won't be seeing him again.' When Nikos and Athena arrived at his house Theodora came out. He opened out his good arm for her to come to him for a hug but she ran to Athena first. Manoussos and the senior Theodora had been watching them too as they walked from church.

'Well Theodora, it looks to me like there is going to be another wedding on Spinalonga.'

Chapter 23. Vincent Barry

Nikos knocked on the doctor's office door at exactly two pm, the time Lukas had requested the appointment, and walked in through the open door. Doctor Lukas usually had the permanently pleasant face of a seasoned professional whose day to day business was death and darkness. Today the doctor looked different, Nikos could tell.

'Doctor you look like you have seen the second coming, what is it?'

The men shook hands.

'Sit down Nikos, I have news.' Nikos sat and arranged himself to be sitting in a way that he could easily stand up again. He was expecting to be told that he and Angela were to be wed.

'I want to share it with you first before we tell all the others.'

'Well from the look on your face I believe it must be very good news. Are congratulations in order?'

'Oh!' The doctor blushed.

'You are referring to my friendship with Nurse Venetis? No it is not about that but thank you for your good feelings in that matter, things are indeed very good in that regard. No Nikos that is not the good news I have today. My news is far better than that.'

'Something has happened?'

'Yes. Something has happened.' Doctor Lukas poured a glass of water for Nikos and made sure he was comfortable then began his mini lecture. He knew he had to start with Nikos. He had considered first talking to Father Manoussos who was a wise man but he was by nature a hermit. Nikos was the one who could talk to people better.

'Science is finding out more and more about leprosy every day due to brave men who approach their research with logic and caution. The Danish doctor Gerhardt Hansen made a tremendous discovery when he was able to prove leprosy is caused by a bacterium and is not hereditary. He was able to isolate this bacterium to see it under a microscope and through lab research and he found that most people have a natural immunity to it.'

He stopped there. The words had to sink in, and they did.

'Most people have a natural immunity to it?' Nikos repeated slowly but deliberately.

'So that means that all for these years we have been forced to live away from our loved ones, we were killed off by society, when the reality was that we were less infectious than a man with a sneeze?'

'Well yes and no. The ignorance of the past is something out of the control of either of us. We can now only help to shine a light to the future. The sneeze might have brought influenza or pneumonia at worst. More people would have been infected but the contagion would have been more minor. A leper might only infect one or two people but they too would have been made permanently ill with a terrible and fatal disease.'

'So all these years of not even being able to write letters because of the fear the leprosy might somehow have found its way into the ink, of having to wear a bell so people could hear us coming and run away, all of that was for nothing.'

The doctor could only hang his head out of sympathy for the unnecessary suffering.

'Well thank you doctor for the insight but what now does that mean for us here on Spinalonga?'

'There is more Nikos, there is more. A doctor in the city of Dublin in Ireland has done some excellent research work. His name is Vincent Barry, he and his research team have done wonders.'

'Yes and what have Doctor Vincent Barry and his research team done?'

'Doctor Barry was charged with studying tuberculosis and he found the bacteria of tuberculosis and the bacteria of leprosy are very similar. They are actually of the same strain.'

The words of Doctor Lukas had seared into his brain. His body, tense from the trauma of the memories, slumped into the chair but only briefly, Nikos was now leaning forward. His one good hand gripped the arm of the chair, his disease had made him lose two of the fingers on the other. He looked straight at the doctor so as not to miss a word.

'Similar to tuberculosis? They can cure tuberculosis. Doctor what did this Vincent Barry do?'

'He performed tests. He used the same treatment for tuberculosis on people with leprosy and noticed a difference, an improvement. By the way how are you eyes today Nikos?' For the last few weeks Nikos had been experiencing diminished vision in one eye, when he woke up this morning he could not see from it at all. His other eye had also begun to have a burning sensation some time ago but he had narrowed it now to focus closely on Lukas and take in every word he was saying.

'My eyes are not doing very well, but my ears are open, keep talking.'

'Nikos, Doctor Barry and his research team did many more tests. The breakthrough is enormous. There is now therapy for those with the mild version of leprosy, it takes six months of the treatment. For those with the severe form like you, the treatment takes two years.' Lukas was now sitting in the other chair directly across from Nikos so he could be looking straight at him when he said,

'My dear friend, there is process involved and it takes time but, the cure has come.'

'There is a cure now?' Nikos could barely speak.

The doctor nodded to confirm Nikos' question. Nikos felt his body turn to jelly. He slid off the chair. He sat on the floor curled up like a foetus, all his strength went into trying to contain the great racking sobs that were contorting his lungs. A terrible sound emerged from his throat like a confusion of joy, anger and frustration that came out like the fearful howl of a wolf at full moon. The doctor fell to his knees too and embraced Nikos as tightly as he could. He wanted at that moment to be everything to him, protective father, brother, team mate, close friend. He held him tight as Nikos bayed out the terror of the past years and battled with the rage that even with the cure his body was too far damaged to ever be normal again.

Angela had burst into the room when she heard the cries of pain and took in the sight of her beloved and her dear friend on the floor weeping together and gently backed out of the room to allow them the privacy that men need when expressing emotion. She wept for Nikos too, but quietly and alone.

Educated men do not like to give in to their emotions believing it is a sign of irrationality, of weakness. They believe reason should rule but often neglect the equally important fact that a little venting is a very good thing. So when Nikos and the doctor composed themselves for a few moments they could not, and would not, look at each other. It was the doctor who broke the silence.

'Yes Nikos it is indeed a very big step but there are still many to be taken. The therapy is long and painful, it will require injections over several months and experiments are ongoing.'

'The leprosy can now be controlled but the sad truth is the damage that has already been done to people like you cannot be undone.'

Nikos sighed.

'I didn't expect that. But this must mean we can leave Spinalonga?'

'Eventually, yes. But first we must receive the medicines and places for you must be prepared. There is still much work to be done. For the more severe cases like you there will be transfers arranged to Athens. This news will change the life of everyone here. I told you first so you can decide when to let the others know.'

'I understand you doctor. You do not want to cause any heartache, any yearning, but your news will give us something we have not had in years. Hope. I will not deprive them of that. We have gone through so much together I cannot keep this from them for one more minute.'

'I understand Nikos. Would you like me to make an announcement on the speaker system to assemble here at the infirmary for a meeting?'

Nikos thought for a moment about what would be the best way to handle sharing the news. He was weaker now, walking around was still something he did everyday with relative ease but it wore him out a lot more quickly.

'I have a better idea. How about we make the announcement together, tomorrow at my wedding?'

'As your *koumbaro* it would be my honor.'

'Good, now what about you and the staff of the infirmary?'

'Angela and I will stay here until we know where every single one of you will go. Some are still in the early stages of the disease so it might be possible they be cured completely, without significant damage to their nervous systems. Some like you are more damaged and although you will be cured of the disease you will still require ongoing care because of the damage to your body. I'm sorry.'

'I am not alone anymore Doctor, I have a family now. I will be just fine. I am still in communication with Thanos and Minister Kontos. In every letter he tells me that if I ever was to leave Spinalonga he would have me on his team. Let's see if he really means it.'

'Something tells me he does. There is a very good infectious diseases hospital in Athens, Saint Barbara. I have had talks with them. They are the ones giving me all this information and when the medicines do become available they will be sent to us from there. When the time comes for you to leave that is where you will be taken first, all of you.'

They were interrupted by the ring of the telephone. Angela came in.

'Lukas, it's Saint Barbara's hospital for you.' Within a couple of minutes Lukas returned.

'They have them Nikos. The medicines have arrived and they are on the way.'

Nikos's voice trembled slightly.

'Do you think that when I get to Athens I could be taken to visit Plato's academy and Delphi?' The doctor wiped away his tears as he walked up to Nikos and put his hand on his shoulder.

'My friend, I promise you I will take you there myself.'

Nikos was not aware he was also in tears.

'I must see Delphi, for Artemis, and in spite of living in Athens I was always too busy studying to ever really go anywhere. I kept promising myself I would visit The Academy. To be off Spinalonga and walking in the footsteps of Plato, two dreams come true.' Nikos returned home and told his family what happened during his meeting with Doctor Lukas.

'My Nikos, tomorrow my dream comes true too. I get to see you go to church as a bridegroom.' Theodora and Athena beamed at each other. Athena had become as close to her as any daughter. They had spent the last week finalizing all the wedding preparations. Theodora had made her a beautiful gown and little Theodora had her bridesmaid's dress hanging up ready for the big day.

All of Spinalonga were present to see their own eagle wed his true love.

'Congratulations to Nikos and Athena,' cheered the crowd. Ikaros called out.

'Hey Nikos how is it we only dream of goddesses yet you get to have two?' Even Artemis was present at the wedding feast. She sat like a haughty mother of the bride on a temporary perch built just for the occasion, a large white tulle bow decorated her leash. At Nikos's insistence Theodora even got out of her traditional black garb and wore a flattering suit in a rich chestnut color the same as her hair. Doctor Lukas proposed the toast.

'To our very own eagle, but ours is an eagle without wings. To the eagle of Spinalonga.'

'The eagle of Spinalonga,' repeated all present. Nikos leaned in close to his new bride and whispered into her ear. 'My glorious goddess, here is to our new life together. I hope you are pleased with your choice. Eagles mate for life.'

Chapter 24. The Departure

'The ship will be here tomorrow, I can barely believe it. Manoussos, all the packing up is done but you and I still have one more job to do. You were with me when we caught Artemis you must be with me when we set her free.'

'A noble sentiment Nikos but I am not going with you.'

'What are you saying Manoussos? You can't stay here alone.'

'I can and I will. I cannot go. I cannot leave the souls here unattended.'

'But everyone is leaving. There are no souls to attend to anymore.'

'Yes there are, the ones that died here. I must stay and carry out the traditions and rituals of the memorial services for each of them. The Church requires they be done every year for five years. We only buried Stella yesterday. She died from choking on a chicken bone. The disease took her friend a week earlier.'

'You know tomorrow is the one year memorial of Lyras.'

'I know. What a sweet death he had to die in his sleep next to Maria's grave. The doctor says he had a bad heart, that's why he was always so pale. At least he is with Maria.'

'As I was saying, when the last memorial is done is five years time. I will leave then.' Nikos knew there was to be no dissuading him.

'Then you will need some company. I was going to release Artemis today but kept holding off for some reason, now I know why. We do have one big advantage. Artemis already knows you.'

'It will be an honor to take over the as the eagle hunter of Spinalonga.'

'You are an eagle too Manoussos. Some people are born to soar and you are one of them. Just make sure you always give her the best and juiciest pieces of meat.'

Theodora came to sit with them and all three of them watched Athena and little Theodora playing catch with a ball in the middle of the square.

'How do you feel my child about leaving Maria here?'

Theodora gave a heavy sigh.

'I was hoping nobody would ask. I feel terrible of course, but the truth is this is where she belongs. She fell in love here, and the man she loved lies next to her. She wed here. Her baby was born here. She and Lyras and Xanthus are together on the place where they found true happiness. I now belong with her child.

How do I feel Father? The bitter things life fed me make the sweet things even sweeter. I feel blessed to be alive and with what remains of my family.'

Athena joined them while little Theodora played on.

'I need to sit down, I feel quite dizzy, Nikos, please pass me your glass of water.'

'Of course, have you developed something?'

'I certainly hope so,' she said as she patted her belly.

Manoussos led the congratulatory toast.

'To that grand and mysterious wonder, the cycle of life.

1962 – Five Years Later

The boatman moored at Dante's Gate and for the very first time, walked through it. He entered the tunnel, the famous tunnel, the infamous tunnel, that so many had walked through and not known how they could face another day of life. He shuddered for them. He found his way to the church where he found Father Manoussos standing there, his bags all packed and a magnificent eagle perched on his wrist.

'I have a canary myself.'

'Very funny.'

'You ready to go now or have you gone crazy after five years here on your own, just you and the eagle?'

'*Kapetan*, this is Artemis. She has helped to feed many people over the last few years. Nikos caught her.' The boatman was suitably impressed.

'Nikos caught her! Why I am not surprised? Eagles belong with eagles.'

After everything was loaded on board they took off, with Artemis still on the wrist of Manoussos. He looked up at the sky, his favorite phenomena was taking place. The sky was full of sunburst rays. God's fingers Nikos used to call them. Manoussos held his arm up high and whispered goodbye to Artemis. He took off her hood for the last time and with a subtle flick of his wrist Artemis extended her colossal wings and flew up higher and higher until she disappeared into the place from where she had come, the hand of God.

10658782R00186

Printed in Great Britain
by Amazon.co.uk, Ltd.,
Marston Gate.